CATCH MY FALL

JESSICA SCOTT

CATCH MY FALL
The Falling Series

Former Army Sergeant Deacon Hunter is trapped.

Trapped in the friend zone. Longing for the woman who captured his heart when they were deployed in Iraq.

Former Army Sergeant Kelsey Ryder has scars, the kind of scars she hopes that no one ever sees. Working around the guys at the Pint, she's reminded of everything she lost when she left the Army behind.

But some scars refuse to stay hidden.

One fateful night changes everything and neither of them know if their relationship will ever be the same.

All Deacon knows is that he'll be there to catch her when she finally falls.

THE FALLING SERIES
Before I Fall: Noah & Beth
Break My Fall: Abby & Josh
After I Fall: Parker & Eli
Catch My Fall: Deacon & Kelsey
Until We Fall (2018): Caleb & Nalini
When We Fall (forthcoming)
After We Fall (forthcoming)

Note – these books are fiction. Any resemblance to real people or events is purely coincidence

Learn More At...
http://www.jessicascott.net
Follow Jessica on Twitter
Like Jessica on Facebook
Sign up for Jessica's Newsletter

To Lauren
For being an inspiration, a mentor and most importantly, a friend.

Printed in the United States of America

First Printing 2017

Author photo courtesy of Buzz Covington Photography

Cover Photo courtesy of iStockphoto

Cover design by Jessica Scott

For more information please see www.jessicascott.net

CATCH MY FALL

JESSICA SCOTT

CATCH MY FALL

a falling novel

PROLOGUE

Durham, NC
Six Months Ago

Deacon

"CAN I TOUCH IT?"

Sweet baby Jesus, the things I do for my job.

The woman leaning across the bar is about one deep breath away from bursting out of her top, and I'd bet every red-blooded man in The Pint is hoping for just that.

The bar is busy tonight, filled with a very unusual mix of customers, even for a place that's known for its unusual mix of customers.

And by unusual, I mean veterans mixing with college students. Almost all of us who work here are vets or, as I like to call us, refugees from civilian life.

My very friendly friend leaning across the counter is not a vet. Otherwise, she wouldn't be nearly as enthralled with the branches of the tree tattooed into my skin as she is.

And I wouldn't be nearly as drawn to the distraction of her touch. A certain part of my anatomy is fervently hoping her fingers will linger a little longer. Maybe drift a little lower.

He's been feeling neglected lately and, well, she might be just the one to help me pass the night away with some smooth body rocking.

She leans over a little further and runs her finger over the edge of the tree tattooed into my bicep. A pair of dog tags is nestled in a little silver line of tiny silver balls threaded among the branches, pieced together to represent the real chain I no longer wear.

The dog tag tattoo was the first one I got when I joined the Army, the stuff that NCOs laugh at privates for doing. I damn sure laughed at my joes when they did stupid shit like I did way back when. The tree came later, along with the crow that she can't see.

If she did see it, she might ask me about it. And I'll play its significance off, saying it was a gothic phase I went through years ago.

She doesn't need to know the story behind it.

The girl leaning across the bar smells like oranges and sunshine, and maybe a little too much Patrón. I lean closer, in part to do my service to mankind and to keep her from actually falling out of the top she's dangerously close to abandoning.

Eli, our boss and de facto commander even if he doesn't want to be, tends to frown on public nudity. The cops don't really like getting called for those kinds of things, either.

The cops like bar fights even less, and naked chicks tend to spark the caveman in even the most civilized of hipster college dudes. And well, The Pint has a reputation to uphold as an upscale establishment. It's just that every so often, when we get the ratio of veterans to college students a little too high, we collectively give in to mankind's baser needs: whiskey and sex.

All that being said, it's part of my duty description to help Ms. Patrón keep her clothes on and keep her hands on my body.

Her finger is soft and smooth against my skin, and she traces the small chain over the inside of my biceps until it disappears into the white T-shirt I've worn to work tonight.

The slide of her finger over my skin should be arousing but tonight...it's not nearly as compelling as I want it to be. I want to lean closer to let her press her lips to my skin and see what else she'd like to do with that perfectly painted mouth.

It should be no sacrifice to stand perfectly still while she touches me. Her touch is a connection, linking me from my alcohol-induced haze to the world of sensual sensation.

It's a fantasy. One that doesn't exist for me, hasn't existed in several weeks if I'm being honest with myself. Christ, I need to get fucking laid.

But my friend across the bar with the barely contained breasts is not going to be the one to break that streak.

It's not an easy thing to break the contact but I do. Because what I need will not be satisfied in a simple connection. At least not hers.

Christ my dick is picky these days. Miserable fucker.

"Another drink?"

Ms. Patrón leans back and traces the same finger over her bottom lip. "I'm trying to behave," she whispers. "But yeah, I think another shot would be just the thing."

"You misbehave often?" Because I can't quite help myself. Maybe if I flirt, I can summon the energy to ask her to come home with me. To strip off her clothing and see if she's willing to do a little service for her nation.

I really need to stop drinking. That sounded fucked up, even to me.

"A little too often, to be honest."

"Why do you sound like that's a bad thing? Everyone's allowed to misbehave. Isn't that the fun of being an adult?"

She knocks back the shot and smiles at me, licking her lip. "I'm trying to pretend I'm not an adult tonight."

Danger, Will Robinson. Abort! Nope. No way in hell I'm keeping this conversation going.

"Well, I'm not into daddy fetishes." I grin and wink at her, trying to take the sting of rejection out of my words. She wants to keep drinking, she can, but I have to see to other customers.

Eli steps out of the cellar, kicking the door shut behind him and sets two bottles of whiskey on the counter that, between them, are worth over three hundred dollars. "So, any takers on how long before we have our first fight tonight?"

I glance over at him, then out at the highly unusual crowd at an already unusual bar in a town known for unusual bars. The Pint is in one of the old tobacco brick buildings in downtown Durham and it would be unremarkable except for Eli and the space he's created here.

He's somehow managed to become the center of gravity for the small veteran community here in a hipster college town. I can't really tell you how I stumbled into a job here. It wasn't on purpose.

And yet, here I am, serving expensive ass whiskey to a bunch of college kids who are looking at the crowd up from Fort Bragg for a night on the town like they are from another country.

Which, to be fair, is an accurate statement. Fort Bragg is a long way from Durham as cultures go.

It doesn't help that somehow, tonight became an unofficial Ranger Panty Night. I'm not sure if it was a dare on social media or what, but there's about two dozen people in the bar wearing the ultra-short running shorts made famous by, well, the Rangers.

One half of the population I mentioned before is wearing Vineyard Vines and Sperrys. The other half is literally wearing combat boots and Ranger panties. There is some mixing between them, but for the most part the military folks are on one side of the bar, laughing and getting tanked, and the college crowd looks like it's doing an ethnography of military bar stories, watching warily from a distance, like they're afraid one of the vets is going to snap and shoot the place up.

This is fine, I'm sure. Like, what could possibly go wrong?

I'm not sure how I feel about half the bar population running around in those shorts.

'Course, half the population in the bar includes a lot of the women wearing them, too, which makes it really fucking hard to concentrate every time someone decides to bend over.

Dear God in heaven, thank you for the women who decided tonight was laundry night, too.

"It should be okay. So long as Caleb doesn't show up tonight," I tell Eli.

"Cut him some slack, will you?"

I breathe out through my nose. "I have no idea why you continue to support him. He's ended up in the hospital after trying to kill his liver one too many times, he's an obnoxious drunk, and quite frankly, his latent ammo-sexuality is fucking annoying." I toss back a shot of Patrón at the thought of my least favorite regular customer.

"I'm trying to get him into CrossFit or something to see if it can help him quit drinking," Eli says. I ignore the fact that he doesn't comment on my opinion.

"That's all we need. Mr. Shoot 'Em in the Face wearing TapOut gear and getting a fucking Jeep Wrangler."

Eli glances over at me as he shakes a drink, then strains it into the glasses. And knowing Eli like I do, I wisely change the subject.

"Ranger Panty Night seems to be a success," he says, sliding the drinks across the bar to the waiting frat brother. "It's definitely brought in a different crowd."

"Hard to argue," I say mildly, playing along with the impersonal conversation because it's better than the alternative. "Ranger Panty Night is practically printing money. How the hell did you come up with this?" Receipts are way up tonight. Especially since it's a Thursday, and the Fort Bragg crowd most likely has to be at PT early tomorrow morning. They've got at least a two-hour drive home.

"It was completely by accident. Caleb sent me a link to the Amazon reviews for Ranger panties. I laughed my ass off then posted it on social media. Somehow, I ended up offering a free drink to anyone who showed up in Ranger panties and, well, the rest is history."

I lift my glass to him in mock salute. "As long as no one calls someone else a fucking moron, we should have a real productive night."

And hopefully not *too* productive, because it's just me and him running the bar these days. We really need to hire some additional staff, especially if we continue growing like we have been.

But it's a bar. And despite our efforts, there is a schism down the middle of our space, one that I'm not sure how to heal. I love the brick walls and the low-hanging lights. The black and white pictures of soldiers mixed with photos of Durham's history.

Technically, it's not my job to heal anything. That's Eli, everyone's favorite Boy Scout who looks like a Hell's Angel.

Unlike me—I look like an angel but raise holy hell whenever I get the urge.

Except that lately, I haven't felt like raising hell.

I wish I knew what the problem was because I fucking hate feeling like this.

A shorter dude in Ranger panties changes the music from something pulsing and intense to a smooth country song. And of course, that's when the shit show begins because clearly, the Sperry's crowd wants more unknown alternative remixes.

In the middle of the beginnings of a bar fight about what music should be played, a sleek woman wearing jeans and a black tank top slides into the space between the opposing sides and starts to dance.

And I mean really *dance*.

Her hips sway to the music, her eyes close. Her lips part just a little.

One of the Sperry-wearing trust fund babies moves in behind her, his hand sliding down her hip, his body moving in sync with hers, like they've done this before. Her movements make her tank slide higher, revealing the ink that spreads out around her waist.

It's enthralling, watching her move. Watching her lose herself in the feel of someone else's body against hers, the smooth slide of his hands down her flesh, drawing her closer.

I'm not the only one captured by the sight of the erotic duo. As the smooth, slow, country music continues the tension in the bar is replaced by a sensual energy, from people daring to cross the gap and make that most elemental human connection.

She turns and the light hits her face just right. Her eyes are closed, her lips parted.

I'd recognize her anywhere.

And suddenly, I'm no longer enthralled by watching her dance.

This is how our night ends, ladies and gentlemen. With me standing there, fighting the urge to drag that guy's fucking hands off a woman I haven't seen in three years. A woman who could fuck my brains out and still be up and ready to go on patrol in Iraq the next morning.

Kelsey. Fucking. Ryder.

Watching her move, watching his hands slide over her body, I am hit with a violent longing.

I am suddenly, starkly, alone.

Just like always.

Kelsey

I NEEDED a whole lot of space and yoga to find my center again today. But today was going to be the day I broke through barriers. I was going to stop feeling sorry for myself. I was going to get a job and get my transfer paperwork filled out at school. When I walked into The Pint, I was trying to pretend tonight was a normal night. But it's not. The loneliness that slammed into me full force after walking through campus today hasn't gone away, hasn't let me go.

All of those lofty goals changed the minute I walked into The Pint, prepared to fill out an employment form to ask the owner for a job, and instead saw Deacon Hunter standing behind the bar.

Three years since I'd seen him.

Three years since I'd run away from the shit show my life was becoming with him.

And now there he is.

I could have left before he saw me. I could have walked away and pretended I never saw him. Maybe I'd forget that punch in the gut feeling of heat and warmth and arousal when I saw him.

But it would take a while.

So I did what I always do when things are getting overwhelming. I seek connection. Touch.

I need to feel. To be reminded of why it is that I'm here. I close my eyes and let the body moving in sync with mine surround me.

It would be far too easy to pretend these are Deacon's hands on my body. Deacon touching me, holding me, reminding me of all the good we had before things went to hell.

But they're not.

My dance partner's hands aren't rough like my memories call

for, but smooth. Still, he's strong and—most important—confident as he moves behind me.

I focus on what I notice about him. His cologne is nice. Not overpowering.

Even when overpowering is what I want. What I need. I need someone to take the emptiness and block it out with sensation. Something that will blind me to the memories and the bullshit that chase me in my sleep and haunt my waking hours.

I want to forget. I want to forget the ache in my heart, the emptiness inside me.

I crave this: connection. Touch. Being part of a whole.

He rubs close against me, close enough that I don't have to guess what he's packing. It would be good, so good, to take him outside and let him do what I want him to do.

I glance over at Deacon, glaring at the iPad they apparently use for a register. He's chewing on a drink straw like he's going to snap it in half. I should tell him he might choke but somehow, I don't think he'd appreciate the warning.

At least not without a hello first.

"What's your name?" My dance partner's voice is rough in my ear.

"What do you want it to be?"

His laugh vibrates down my spine. "I've seen that movie a thousand times."

I spin then, and study him with narrow eyes. "You've seen *Pretty Woman* a thousand times?"

He presses in, rubbing his thigh between mine, trying to coax me back into the rhythm.

The moment is gone, now that I'm reasonably certain we're playing for the same team. I pat his cheek. "You should try to hook up somewhere else. I'd hate for you to be alone tonight because you got cock blocked by the bartender." I point to a broad-shouldered guy wearing a green T-shirt and Ranger panties. "He looks cute. And single."

Hands lifts one eyebrow but doesn't even blink at being called out. "Thanks."

And just like that, I'm alone again. Time to make my way to the bar and try to find the owner.

Deacon still looks like he wants to stab something when I slide up to the bar where he's loading the glasses into the dishwasher. He stops and watches me. The silence isn't hostile, not exactly. It's...wary. Tense.

And then he looks up at me and smiles in a way that lights up the dark. As if he wasn't just looking like he was contemplating murder.

"You should get that looked at," I mumble by way of greeting.

"What's that?"

"Your wild mood swings." I hope he takes the joke. I don't want to fight with him tonight.

I can't. Not tonight.

He slides a shot of vodka across the bar toward me. It stirs something warm and fuzzy inside me that he's remembered what I like to drink when I'm drinking.

I toss back the shot of vodka, feeling the burn all the way down to the pit of my stomach. I wish I could feel the slow slide of a buzz spread through my veins but I've been drinking way too long for that to happen anymore. It takes enough alcohol to kill an elephant before I even start to feel the effects.

I've either got a super liver or one that refuses to accept defeat. Either way, sometimes, I just wish I could get drunk.

"So, what brings you into our humble establishment?"

The question is informal, the kind of question you ask to get someone to open up.

"I heard the owner tends to hire veterans. I'm looking for work."

His throat moves as he swallows and it's hard not to notice everything that's changed about him. He's thicker now, his shoulders wider. His skin is darker than I remember, the color of a deep smoky whiskey. It might be the shadows or from the low lighting.

But it's his mouth that captures my attention, just like always. The way his lips curl at one side still drives me wild. And his too-full bottom lip is perfect for nibbling on. I remember that all too well.

"He's in the back." He leans on the bar, slinging his bar towel over one shoulder. "What are you drinking tonight?"

I grin. I know this game. And tonight, I'm willing to pretend we're just two strangers at a bar instead of two people with a fucked-up history that we both ran from, in our own fucked-up ways.

It's a comfortable game. Far easier than the alternative, where I ask him what he's been up to the last three years.

I lean forward against the bar, offering a half-smile. "You buying?"

His eyes are dark and cast in shadows, his mouth set in that cocky half-grin I used to love. If I close my eyes, I can imagine the bite of lemon and whiskey on his lips. "If you're drinking, I'm buying."

"Make it a seven and seven."

"On the rocks?"

I lean closer. "Yeah, that sounds good."

This is a game I've played all too often from the other side of the bar. Tonight, with Deacon, it's a safe one. One that will end with me alone and him most likely pissed off at me again, but for now I'll play along. It's a nice distraction from the looming silence of my apartment that I don't want to face.

He pours the Seagram's Seven and splashes the Seven-Up into the glass, then slides it over to me.

"What are you drinking?" I ask.

"Same as you."

I lift my glass in a mock salute. "Bottoms up."

It's just me and Deacon and a whole lot of memories.

He clinks his drink against mine.

The Seven and Seven is smooth against my lips, sparkling a good time down my throat. He's made it strong. "This is really good."

"If you're going to do something, do it well." He takes a sip and my eyes are drawn to the movement of the muscles of his arms. I don't want to remember the way it felt to press my lips against that dead tree tattooed on his skin.

Not all of our memories are bad. But the good ones...the good ones are too fucking good. Too filled with temptation.

And I know where temptation leads.

I've been to that hell before. But I need a goddamned job and I feel in my bones that this is the place I'm supposed to be.

In spite of or because of Deacon, I have no idea.

"You used to say that a lot."

"Lots of things I used to say."

If I close my eyes, I can see him, younger. Less cynical. Less hair.

He's grown his hair out since he left the Army. I don't wear my hair up much anymore. I've gotten used to wearing it down.

Except I still can't wear it down when I work out. It feels weird running and having it sweep along my neck. I twist it into a bun for doing yoga.

He slips the glass from my hand and takes a sip from it, then gives it back. "So how far we going tonight?"

"How far do you want to go?" My voice is thick, laced with need and something else. Something I don't have the name for.

He looks hard at me, his expression shifting to something akin to stone. "I gave up playing games with you a long time ago, Kels."

I suck in a sharp breath. No one has called me Kels since the last time I saw him.

Some nights, it's easier to pretend we don't share a past coated in blood.

"Then I guess we've found our line."

I managed not to argue with him.

This is a good sign. A fresh start.

I wonder how long it will last.

Probably until I do something else to screw up with the one guy who knows everything about how fucked up I am, and all the reasons why I will never be able to leave the war behind.

1

Present

Kelsey

THERE ARE times I miss the Army.

And other times, I hate with everything that I am what it did to me.

Most of the time, though, I try to just get through the soul-crushing days at school without stabbing someone.

Which is why I do yoga. Lots of it.

And doing yoga is after I count to one hundred, do some deep *ujjayi* breathing, and remind myself that I am working on non-violence these days.

Today might be a breaking point, though.

"You're serious?" I'm breathing. I promise I'm breathing. "What the hell can I teach a bunch of brainiac cadets about being an officer? I was enlisted, remember?"

Professor Blake leans back behind her wide mahogany desk

and steeples her hands in front of her. There is something serene about this woman that drew me to her the first day we met.

Granted, I was in full-blown crisis mode that day, trying to get all my paperwork sorted out so I could start classes and not have to mortgage my firstborn child as payment. Still.

She's one of those people who are just naturally calming, polished and poised in a way I will never be. I've been surrounding myself with those people these days. Trying to chain up the chaos Muppet in my head.

"I think you have a tremendous amount to offer the cadets in our program. After all, NCOs train lieutenants. And this is about more than just the cadets. This is a deliberate effort to span the civil military divide."

I twist my fingers into a calming *mudra* and breathe. Just breathe. "Why me?"

"Nalini King can't do it this semester because she's finalizing a program to get her yoga studio certified by the campus wellness center."

"She'd be perfect for the cadets." Nalini is a West Point grad-turned-yogini businesswoman. I swear she's got to be ADHD with as much shit as she gets done on an everyday basis. She makes us mere mortals look rather mundane.

"She has been. And she recommended you as a replacement for her this semester."

"I'm probably not the best fit for this." I can't get up in front of cadets, all bright-eyed and bushy-tailed, and blow smoke up their asses about how great the Army is.

Even if I miss it every fucking day.

Professor Blake slides a sheet of paper toward me. "You get teaching credit out of it. Which will make your application to grad school that much more competitive."

"I'm not sure I'm the best person for this." I can barely get myself out of bed some days. Don't make me tell the cadets that the Army will do this to them. That it will ask them to give up everything, then cast them aside when it's over. But I say none of those things. "There are a bunch of guys out at The Pint; why don't you hit them up?"

She arches one perfect brow. "What makes you think I haven't?"

That catches my attention. "Who else signed on?" My stomach is tight because I'm willing to bet I already know the answer.

"Deacon Hunter."

I clear my throat. "It's definitely not a good idea for us to work together on this. We have a history together." On a tour to Iraq that marked the beginning of the end of any semblance of normality in my life, but no one needs to see me pick those scabs in public.

She motions toward the sheet of paper that I tried to ignore. "You're already approved by the university. And you get a stipend."

"'Stipend' sounds like beer money," I say, leaning forward. "Visiting Assistant Professor of Military Science? I don't even have a master's degree." It's hard not to be impressed with that fancy-sounding title. I've certainly come a long way from sweeping up spilled diesel in the motor pool.

"Yet," she says. "This is an excellent opportunity for you. The cadets need your experience and they need to hear from women veterans just as much as they need to hear from men. They need to know what they're getting into when they get out into the force." She pauses. "I wish my son had had an opportunity like this."

My throat tightens at her words. Her son Mike died in Iraq a few years ago. His death is part of why she's so active with the student vets on campus.

"Well, when you put it that way," I finally say. I don't want to work with Deacon. We've had a strange truce the last few months since I got here and I'd like to keep it that way. It's only worked because we're so busy at The Pint that he hasn't had time to rip the bandage off the still raw wound between us. "Guess I'm going to have to watch my swearing, huh?"

"Just be yourself. Be the amazing Sergeant Ryder that you've always been." She smiles and it's hard to ignore the quiet pride I see looking back at me from her eyes. I've done nothing to earn it. And if she knew everything, she wouldn't let me within ten feet of the cadets. When I don't argue further, she takes my silence for agreement. "Thank you. I think you're underestimating how valuable what you have to offer them really is."

"Yeah, well, let's hope I don't scar them for life first, okay?" But I could use the money and the teaching experience.

"I'm not worried about that in the least," she says in a way that seems to suggest everything will work out. I head out, a little disjointed from our meeting. I don't know how she can be so damn calm all the time. I've never even seen her do more than lift that one eyebrow in reaction to whatever else is going on around her.

I'm envious of her serenity.

I head out of the old Wilson building and cross the quad toward the library and my own personal lord and savior The Grind, where one can find the strongest coffee on campus. Whoever decided to put a cool, hipster coffee shop in the middle of the main library should get a speed pass to sainthood.

And given that I'm used to some pretty strong stuff, that's saying something. I order my coffee and then weave my way through the tables to take one near the door where I can keep an eye on who is coming and going while I try to wrap my head around the proposed syllabus that Professor Blake sent me.

"Hey you."

I glance up at the familiar voice as Nalini claims the chair across from me. "You don't look very happy."

She was also in the Army once upon a time, and now she's a small business owner who's dedicated her life to yoga and her fellow fucked-up vets like me.

If I believed in reincarnation, I would think that I must have been kind to animals in a previous life to be as fortunate as I am to have her in my current one. It's amazing how having someone around who speaks the same language as you can be so reassuring. It's like a physical reminder that your experience wasn't just a figment of your imagination.

"Nah. I just found out I have to teach your cadets this semester."

"And you're not happy about it because...?"

"Because..." Why? I don't have a reason. It's just that something about it makes me uncomfortable. But I'm not ready to go there. "Because I haven't had enough coffee yet."

Nalini grins and flips open her iPad. "Yeah, well, I can't help you, unfortunately. I'm fighting with the wellness center bureaucracy this semester, otherwise I would." She frowns a little and looks up at me. "Why are you so hesitant to do this?"

I narrow my eyes at my friend's apparent mind-reading skill. I'm reasonably certain she's probing for a specific answer or that she already knows the answer. But I'm not going to call her out. Because I'm working on not being an asshole.

"Because I really don't think my war stories are the ones the cadets need to hear." I sip my coffee. "I think Professor Blake likes doing this. I'm not the only one she's made take on classes that push our boundaries."

Nalini laughs. "Oh yeah, I heard about Josh's incident. He almost got arrested after the Violence and Society class, didn't he?"

"That's the rumor." I stretch my arms over my head. Being around Nalini reminds me I need to go to yoga, seeing how it's her studio that I attend regularly. Haven't been to a session in a couple of days, for no really good reason. "What's going on with the wellness center?"

"Well, they're claiming that I need a certification from a specific yoga certification organization in order for them to allow me to officially teach classes there. Every time I explain to them that the certification they want is the equivalent of a diploma mill, they send me to another person. It's rather frustrating. This is taking up an extraordinary amount of time."

"Why do you get to do the fun stuff?"

She beams and I am jealous of her smooth, amber skin. "Because I'm not a student, I just work here. Trust me, it is more than enough to keep me up at night."

"Completely not fair." I wouldn't mind taking that class. Teaching the cadets... I'm sure I'll figure out in about thirty minutes what's bothering me about it but until I actually set foot inside that classroom, all I can do is quietly panic.

"Yeah, well, life's not fair. And speaking of not fair, here comes a tall drink of water with your name on it. Someday you're going to tell me the rest of the story about why you avoid Deacon Hunter so completely." Her lips twitch. "Otherwise, I might start thinking it's a case of 'the lady doth protest' and all that."

She motions with her head toward the archway that leads into the library but I've already seen him.

Deacon Hunter is walking up.

Not really walking, though.

Strolling, his eyes always searching, looking as if he's scanning the horizon.

It's hard not to appreciate how he owns the room as he walks in. He doesn't stand out because of how he's dressed or what he's carrying.

He stands out from the raw power that radiates off him. There's something about the stiffness in his spine, the strength in his shoulders, that draws people to him. It's a quiet power. The kind of power that's confident in its own skin.

It's what drew me to him when we were deployed, even if neither of us had our shit together in any meaningful way back then.

It drew me, once upon a time. But those days are long gone.

No matter how much I've suddenly realized there may be a party starting in my panties, begging him to come over and play.

Yeah, in the library coffee shop. Because who doesn't have illicit fantasies about doing dirty things on the large tables meant for textbooks and study groups, right?

I wish I could duck down and hide.

I don't want to see him. I don't want to talk to him about the cadets.

I can't.

It's hard enough being around him at The Pint when we have a shift together. When the music is pulsing and the liquor is flowing and I can almost forget all the bad shit that split my life into Before and After.

I'm not sure how to deal with him out in broad daylight when I haven't started drinking for the day yet. Especially since I've been drinking less these days.

And I probably should have figured out how to be around him by now but well, no one is perfect, right?

Unpack one trauma at a time, right?

Nalini waves at him before I can stop her. She must hate me. "What are you doing up this early?" she asks as he walks up.

"I'm teaching a class today, oddly enough. Pretending I'm an adult." I slouch down in my chair as he walks up. His gaze flicks over me briefly. I don't look away from the challenge in his eyes because I refuse to cede the territory to him.

I wish I didn't notice everything about him in the brilliant fall sunlight slashing through the library windows.

He hasn't shaved. There's a line of stubble along his jaw, edging the rim of his bottom lip. Gah, I wish I didn't know how he felt when he touched those lips to my skin.

He looks back at Nalini, but the heat from his dark blue gaze has settled over my skin like heat from a fire. Making me wish for things I cannot have.

Things I should not still want.

"Coffee. Pep talk," my traitorous friend says, then nods in my direction. "Then work."

"Pep talk? Why?"

"Oh, you're about to find out," she says and stands to go.

I stand, too, letting my far-too-perky-to-have-ever-been-in-the-Army friend know that her attempt to leave me alone with Deacon has failed. I scoop up my notebook and coffee. "Got to head out."

I go to pass him but he doesn't move. Standing there, he's a brick wall, immovable.

I sigh and slip by him, saying nothing. My chest brushes against his upper arm, my entire body tightening in response to the briefest contact.

"Coward," he whispers as I slip past, leaving Nalini and Deacon standing together.

I keep walking.

Hating the fact that he's right.

Deacon

I LET HER GO. I probably should stop fucking with her but with Kelsey, everything is complicated. And in the six months that she's been back in my life, it's only gotten more so.

"She's fine, you know," Nalini says softly. Her eyes are always bright and calm. I love Nalini like a sister and I love that she's looking out for Kelsey because I no longer can.

I've known Nalini a while now, ever since I started grad school. She's a magnet to other vets on campus, kind of like Eli is over at The Pint. Between the two of them, they're the sun and the moon. The rest of us are caught in their orbit.

"I know."

She smiles warmly and pats my cheek. "But you're not sure. If you were, you wouldn't watch her like that every time she walks away."

I grin and lean against the broad table behind me. I love that The Grind has broad, wide tables as well as smaller ones and comfy overstuffed chairs. "How much trouble are you causing on campus today?"

"As much as I need to," she says. She folds her arms over her chest. "When are you going to stop pining after her and do something about this awkward standoff you two have going on? I feel like I'm caught in no man's land between the French and the Germans in World War I."

"That is a terrible analogy."

"Yeah, well, you should try being caught between you two once in a while. Take pity on the rest of us who have to deal with your sexual frustration. You can practically touch it."

She follows for a few steps while I laugh and move to the line for coffee. "I don't even know what to say to that." I place my order. "Large latte, extra shot of espresso."

"Well, that'll put hair on your chest," she says dryly.

I shake my head. "What are you poking at, Nalini?" Because she always pokes until she gets around to what she needs to say.

"Nothing much. Just wondering how things are out at The Pint?"

"They're good. I mean, I know you don't drink but you really should come out some time. There's a whole bunch of us out there, even a couple of new guys who came by last week who used to be in First Cav. You could come by and just hang out, swap war stories about Stetsons or whatever you Cav people do."

She grins and glances down at her watch. "I'm good, thanks. Though it's awful tempting. You 82d Airborne guys think you're all that with your raspberry berets."

"Bite your tongue." Damn, sometimes it feels good to walk back over familiar ground, harassing each other because of the units we've both served in. "I chewed the same dirt as you did in First Cav."

"Well, use that common ground to make some damn progress with her, why don't you?"

I sip my coffee and instantly, my blood cells are more awake than they were a moment before. "Does she say anything?" I want to add in *about me*. But I don't.

Because I'm a coward when it comes to Kelsey.

"You wish. And even if she did, I wouldn't break her confidence."

"I hate playing games. You know that, right?"

"No games, Deacon." Nalini turns suddenly serious. "I worry about her. About the things she doesn't talk about."

I glance toward the door that Kelsey disappeared through. "Yeah, me too."

I know the things she doesn't talk about, at least some of them.

I know what things keep her up at night.

I know how good things used to be between us, once upon a war.

And I know exactly the moment things got screwed up.

I can't fix any of those things now, no matter how much I might want to. Kelsey has to want to unpack that stuff herself. In the few months she's been back in my life, she's given me no indication that she wants to go anywhere near our shared memories of sand and dust and war.

Not that I blame her.

I leave Nalini at The Grind and head to the old Wilson building for my graduate seminar. I've got a relatively light load this semester. At some point, I have to stop avoiding my thesis and actually start typing.

I've become a master of procrastination, among other things. Funny how leaving the war and the Army behind makes you find other things to keep you occupied.

My old first sergeant would kick my ass if he knew how much I was avoiding this work. I grin, thinking of him. I should shoot him a note one of these days.

But I won't.

Lately it's been like I'm running some kind of test with myself or something. How long can I stay away from the lure of the familiar? The good memories.

And yeah, even the bad ones are good when you're talking to someone who speaks the same language. There's something comfortable about just talking to someone who's been there. Bullshitting about the stupid shit we or one of our soldiers did.

I'm pretty sure America would have kittens if she knew the kind of shenanigans her soldiers pulled on guard duty in the middle of the desert.

But I won't make the call. I can't. It's like I'm trying to prove to myself that I can cut the cord between me and the Army, that I can truly function out here as a civilian and not constantly be reaching back to the guys I left behind when I left Fort Hood.

Besides, it's not like I don't have enough Army around me with Eli and the rest of the gang at The Pint.

I smile down at my phone, double-checking the room number for the class Professor Blake asked me to assist with. She was pretty vague about who I was going to be teaching with this semester.

I probably should have asked for more details but she's pretty much been my fairy godmother since I decided to go to grad school and get my master's in public administration, so I figure I owe her whatever she needs.

The classroom is just inside of the old Wilson building. You can practically smell the history in this place, along with the chill from the stone walls and ancient windows. There's too much history here for a working class kid like me. I suppose people who are used to this kind of place aren't really awestruck by it like I still am.

I still have no idea how I got accepted here. Or how I haven't managed to be politely asked to leave.

Ah well.

I push open the door to the classroom, tucking my phone into my back pocket, and then stop short. The classroom isn't empty.

"You've got to be shitting me." What's that they say about fiction? It's supposed to be believable, right? You can't make this shit up because no shit, there is Kelsey Ryder sitting in a corner, her back to the wall.

And she looks ready for war.

2

Kelsey

I THOUGHT I was braced for this. For the moment that he walked through the door and saw me.

I still wasn't prepared for the utter devastation of watching the realization hit his eyes that we're going to be working together for the entire semester.

The cadets aren't here yet.

We're not teaching today. Professor Blake wouldn't be that sadistic that she'd drop us both into a classroom with no prep. No, today we're supposed to meet them and pass out the military science syllabus.

Right now, that feels next to impossible. The weight of the room is closing in on me with Deacon standing there.

I was wrong. I was so fucking wrong about being this close without the distraction of the noise and the chaos of The Pint. About being alone with him.

Everything about him draws me closer, makes me crave the feel of his skin against mine.

We probably don't have that much time to get to some kind of equilibrium before they start walking through the door. Just like a commander and first sergeant, we can't let them see us fighting. They'll exploit the weaknesses and play us against each other. It doesn't matter if they're soldiers or cadets; they'll do it.

Because that's what soldiers do.

He stands there for an impossible expanse of time, his eyes dark and blue and intense.

"Well, this is awkward," I finally say when it's clear he's not going to break the silence. "I take it Professor Blake didn't tell you that I was your assistant?"

"Who said anything about assistant?" is what he finally says.

His words catch me off guard. Then again, he's always been good at thinking on his feet.

"What do you mean?"

"You're my peer. We'll co-teach this." His voice is grating and rough, like there is so much more he wants to say but won't. Or can't.

It's better this way. It has to be.

I make a noise. "I've never taught anyone in my life," I admit.

His scowl deepens. "That's not true. You taught soldiers all the time as a sergeant."

And there it is. The elephant in the room that is our shared history of Iraq and Fort Hood.

"This isn't the same thing." I'm working on hiding the unadulterated panic in my voice. I'm losing the battle.

"Sure it is. They're college students. You and I are going to teach them about the Army. We're supposed to get them to ask us questions. To push them on what they think they know. Professor Blake told me that she and the ROTC commander agree the cadets don't get nearly enough exposure to enlisted folks."

"She doesn't need me to do this."

He drops his backpack on the table with enough force that I wince. "Tough shit." His voice is practically a snarl. And no, I've never described anyone as snarling before but Deacon is definitely snarly. "They're going to be here any minute. Figure out how you want to introduce yourself because unless you feel like arguing with Professor Blake, you're here for the rest of the semester and so am I."

I say nothing at the force in his response. I don't know what I'm supposed to read into his reaction but I'm reasonably certain I can't talk without raising my voice. Here at school, they call that yelling. I haven't yelled at anyone since I got here and I'm not going to start now.

I close my eyes, listening to the sounds of Deacon violently pulling his iPad and his notebook from his backpack.

Breathe in. Deep. Slow. Controlled. Breathing into the knot in my chest. Into the violent heat that burns against my heart and sends my thoughts racing through the tangled maze of memories and fear.

Deacon

PROFESSOR BLAKE IS a crafty old fox, I'll give her that. If I'd known she was planning on putting me together with Kelsey, I would have begged her to do it sooner.

Looking at her face right now, it's easy to see how much this is upsetting Kelsey's carefully crafted Avoid Our Past plan.

That's over now. And I have to say I'm pretty fucking grateful at the moment. Except that I have no idea how to even begin a campaign plan to break down the barriers she's erected between us.

And after six months of letting her set conditions, I need to play this right. If I screw it up, I could end up pushing her to get Professor Blake to take her off this assignment. I can't blow this.

"What crawled up your ass?" she asks, leaning back in her chair and crossing her arms over her chest.

This I can handle. "Seeing you still doubt yourself. I thought you finally broke that habit in Iraq."

Her mouth drops open. That's clearly not what she was expecting. Good. Maybe if she's off balance, she'll stop thinking about all the reasons she left and start thinking about the reasons why us working together can work here just like it does at The Pint.

I don't mind keeping her off balance. In fact, I think it will be fun. A totally new challenge in my life.

Getting back into hers.

"What, no sarcastic comeback?"

"I'm not really sure how to respond to that," she says softly.

"Start by agreeing not to downplay what you did over there and we'll get along just fine."

Kelsey

THE DOOR OPENS and the cadets start walking in. One more breath and I open my eyes, watching them silently file past us and take seats.

I'm not sure how I feel about this. I wasn't sure before he walked into the room and I'm less sure now as the cadets start to fill the small space. I have to put it aside. I can't let them see me having an existential crisis. Shit, the Army at least taught me that much.

The classroom is more of a small conference room. With Deacon at the end of the ancient wooden conference table, it feels smaller. More closed in. The windows are at least a hundred years old. It's the fixing of modernity overlaid upon ancient gothic stone and masonry.

Sums up how I feel right now, really. Like I'm trying to paste a new Kelsey on an older, more worn down one. But the cadets don't need to know that.

I shut down the unsettled feelings swirling inside me and watch them filter in.

The first thing that strikes me is that they're so young. I wonder if I ever looked that young, that...innocent.

I lean back in my chair, watching Deacon scroll through his iPad as the cadets settle around us. The small space is tight with them in the room now.

They're clearly picking up on our tension because they settle into their seats silently, their conversations about mundane things falling away.

Our class consists of eleven people, crammed into this smallish conference room. I'm pleasantly surprised to see that they look like they come from every corner of America. They look like the rainbow of faces I used to have in my MP platoon.

I want them to wear freaking name tags so I can learn their names. I try to always remember who everyone is. It's a holdover from my days as a sergeant. Know your soldiers and all that, right?

"Excuse me?"

The speaker is a thin young man with dark, intense eyes and sharp features, all beneath a cap of vibrantly black hair.

I school my expression to look a little less intimidating. I'm pissed, being stuck in this situation, but that doesn't mean I need to take my bad mood out on them. "What's up?"

"I noticed you have om on your wrist. Do you know what that means?"

I glance down at the sacred Sanskrit symbol tattooed below

my watchband, at the edge of my palm. "I do. It represents an incredibly important part of my life."

He tips his head, curious. "Really? How?"

I inhale deeply. "It's a really long story."

Across from me, I can feel Deacon watching the exchange.

The young man standing in front of me finally sets his bag down and offers his hand. "I'm Veerkar Patel."

"Kelsey. It's nice to meet you."

"I'd love to talk more with you about your tattoo some time," he says as he releases my hand and sits.

"Sure." I wonder if he wants to talk about how yoga saved my life. About how the practice of it helped me put everything back together when it shattered into a thousand pieces of detritus.

But I'll listen. Because it's rare that I find anyone who wants to really talk about the practice. Too often I find people want to etch the symbols on their bodies and wear the yoga pants as virtue signaling but not go any deeper than that.

I know about that, too. That was how I started yoga. I'm no better than any of them.

Except that I'm trying to do better.

I'm still putting the pieces of my life back together.

Yoga has been a big part of that.

I look over at Deacon. At the man who represents the fault line between who I was and who I am trying to be.

And I'm not sure that even the deepest practice will help me keep it together this time.

Deacon

"WELCOME to our military science class. I'm Deacon Hunter and across the table is Kelsey Ryder. We'll introduce ourselves in a moment but first, tell us where you're from, what you're studying and what you've branched."

I'm trying to pretend that I'm an adult and that watching Kelsey from the other side of the small conference room isn't visually stalking her.

I'm better than this.

I'm still agitated, seeing her sitting across from me. I wonder if Professor Blake put us together on purpose. It's not like she could have known that we have a complicated history.

Whatever joke the universe is trying to play, I appreciate it.

I tune in to the cadets again, realizing I've managed to jot down seven names and branches without hearing anything.

"I'm Veerkar Patel. You can call me Veer. I've branched armor and I'm hoping to be a Cav Scout like my grandfather. I'm majoring in biochemistry."

He speaks with a quiet confidence that says he knows who he is and where he's going. I envy him the certainty in so many ways.

"The Army is a family tradition then?" I ask.

He nods. "My grandfather enlisted in the Army after he immigrated from India. Served three tours in Vietnam. My father was in Desert Storm and he met my mother in the Army."

I steal a glance at Kelsey. We could have had a happily ever after if I hadn't been a coward. If I'd fought harder to stay by her side instead of chasing a career I later realized I didn't want.

She's deliberately not looking at me. Rather, she's listening intently to each of the cadets as they tell us who they are and where they're heading once they commission.

"I'm Jovi Sinclair. I also branched armor," says a fierce blonde sporting an intense tan and equally intense eyes. She looks like a Valkyrie come to life. A warrior. She glances over at Veer. "I wanted to follow in my mother's footsteps. She died during the initial invasion in Iraq."

I feel sucker-punched, a direct hit right in the gut. It hits me then in that moment that we have soldiers entering into the war that their parents might still be fighting.

Or who have lost a parent in our longest war.

I breathe in deeply, locking eyes with Kelsey. I see the hurt locked in my chest looking back at me. We've both done far too many ramp ceremonies.

I know the loss we share.

I clear my throat and tear my gaze away from hers, looking at Jovi. "Your mother would be very proud of you," I say, hoping my voice doesn't sound as rough to them as it feels to me. "And armor branch? Congratulations."

She doesn't reply, doodling something along the edge of her notebook. I notice Veer watching her intently. I wonder if there's a history there.

I wonder if the link between Kelsey and me is as obvious as the link between Jovi and Veer appears to me.

"Iosefe Savea. I'm from LA. I've branched quartermaster." He's a big man, thick and broad and dark and soft-spoken. I can see the edge of a traditional Samoan tattoo beneath the hem of his T-shirt sleeve.

"Why quartermaster?"

"Because that's what the Army gave me," he says mildly. I think this man is incredibly unflappable.

"Makes sense to me," I offer.

The last cadet slips his cell phone in his pocket as he starts to talk. I wonder if he thinks I didn't notice he was ignoring his peers.

"I'm Ryan. I'm from Falls Church, Virginia. I'm signal but branch detailed into infantry."

I smile. "Oh, you're going to have fun." I resist the urge to tell him to buy some lube for all the ass chewings he's going to get as a signal officer. No one gives a shit about signal until people can't talk. Then all hell breaks loose. But he'll learn that soon enough. No need to kick his puppy.

I set my iPad down. "Welcome again. I'm Deacon Hunter, former military police NCO. I served two tours in Iraq, one with First Cav out of Fort Hood in 2011 and one with the 82d Airborne out of Fort Bragg. I'm finishing up my master's degree in public administration."

Veer raises his hand. "I thought we left Iraq in 2011?"

I try not to wonder how a cadet who is going to be an officer in a few short months does not know we still have boots on the ground in Iraq.

"We've been steadily deploying troops there since the security situation deteriorated after we left," Kelsey says quietly, her voice heavy.

It's a dirty little secret. We officially left Iraq back in '11, but we never really left. We were back at it before the desert sand had even blown over the abandoned bases.

"I'm Kelsey," she says. "I served two tours in Iraq, both with First Cav. I'm also a former MP sergeant. I'm working on a degree in business management."

I frown, wondering why she doesn't say more. Of the two of us, Kelsey has the much more impressive record. Instead, she's told them next to nothing about her service.

I clear my throat. "Kelsey is being modest. She earned a Bronze Star for Valor when our base was attacked on our first deployment, for leading the base defense."

Her eyes flash and I can't read the emotion before she looks down at her own iPad. The cadets all glance over at her, their eyes wide. A bronze star is essentially a thank-you-for-serving award for officers that civilians tend to think is a very big deal. But for a sergeant to have a bronze star with v device is a very big deal. They might not appreciate the distinction but I do.

Kelsey should be proud of what she did that day.

Instead, I get the impression that by talking about her bravery and courage, I've just royally fucked up.

Again.

3

Kelsey

I'M PRACTICALLY VIBRATING with anger as Deacon releases the cadets with instructions to read an article about the fight against ISIS in Syria and the role of the Kurds.

I've been silently meditating since he dropped the bombshell of what happened back in Iraq. He had no right to do that. Now I just have to get away from the classroom.

Away from Deacon.

Except that he's right behind me. I'm pretty sure I cannot be sociable with him right now.

Ripping someone's head off in public is frowned upon these days.

I glance down at the mandala tattoo on my forearm. At the lotus embedded in the shield that runs beneath my skin above the om on my wrist.

I breathe deeply, tightening the back of my throat in *ujjayi* breathing for calm. For peace.

To please help me hold everything together.

I keep walking, hoping that maybe he doesn't see me.

I'm also in the habit of lying to myself these days. I actually just started up again. In the last couple of hours, in fact.

"Will you wait a second?" So much for hoping Deacon hasn't seen me.

"Can't. Have a thing to get to." It's a sad commentary on my mental state that I can't come up with anything more descriptive than "thing."

He grabs my arm. Something inside me snaps and I immediately yank it free, rounding on him.

"Don't." This command is non-negotiable. "You don't get to put your hands on me without my permission. No one does."

"What are you so pissed about? Because I told the cadets about your Bronze Star?"

"Maybe I didn't want them knowing about that. Maybe it's not something I want to talk about. Did that occur to you?"

"Why wouldn't you tell someone about that? Fucking Caleb at The Pint tells everyone about his Bronze Star and he got it for making coffee at the brigade headquarters."

"Because it's not your story to tell," I say finally.

He doesn't like that response. It's written in red in the veins pulsing beneath the skin of his throat. His nostrils flare as he stands here, his fists bunched at his sides. He's trying to look calm. It's not working.

"Look, I have to go. We can talk about the way forward on the whole semester later. Maybe after work tonight or something, when we're closing up."

"Are you actually going to show up or are you going to flake out again and disappear on me and Eli?"

His words are a direct hit. They fucking *hurt*.

He has no idea how fucking hard it is to get up every single fucking day and convince myself that I'm not going to backslide into the train wreck I was after he left.

For him to take a slap at me...it's a low blow.

And one I do not have to take from him or anyone.

"You, sir, may politely go fuck yourself." I walk off, needing to put some serious distance between me and the history looking back at me in his eyes.

He calls my name but I don't stop. I don't look back.

I can't. Not again. Not when seeing him reminds me of all the good in my life that I had before it all ended.

The anger is a defense against the breaking glass inside me. Against the pain and the fear and the chaos threatening to undo everything I've worked so hard to rebuild after everything fell apart in my life.

MY THROAT IS tight as I head across campus. I don't know where I'm going other than *away*. The wooded path I'm on is well worn, with the surrounding trees blowing in the wind overhead, their branches stretching up as if through space and time, reaching for the sun.

I step off the path. I was lying when I said I had to get somewhere. I just needed space, room to breathe.

It's morally acceptable to lie for self-preservation, right?

I have no idea.

I continue through the woods, toward the stream that runs through the eastern side of campus. I finally settle on a massive rock. The mossy stone beneath my seat is cold and damp, ensconced in shade from the trees overhead.

The noise from campus is far away. I focus on the water flowing over the rocks. On the sound of the water bubbling against the shore.

On the flow of it. The constant movement. The ever-present change.

The life contained between the banks, the continued energy.

I breathe deeply, closing my eyes, focusing on the sound. On the feel of my breath. I breathe into the tight knot in my chest. Slowly, trying to release, to let go.

To not let the memories rule my life. To not let my actions be guided by anger and fear.

To release that knot at a cellular level.

It takes a while. It takes drawing my thoughts back in as they race away, back to the scene with Deacon. Bringing them to this moment, to the river, to the sound of my own breathing.

Slowly, the knot starts to break up. Slowly, the anger leaves my skin and my bones and I set it aside. I am able to breathe normally again.

I don't know how long I've sat here.

I eventually stand and head to the library to do some homework.

It's a small victory, getting back to the normalcy of homework and assignments and the smell of old books and new between the stacks.

Every victory isn't as massive as getting sober and avoiding the toxic self-harm that happens when bad memories and alcohol mix. Sometimes, it's the little ones, like getting out of bed and doing a yoga sequence before I start my day.

Sometimes, it's as small as not crying when someone reminds you how much you've lost.

That's what Deacon did with his verbal slap.

It's like he still doesn't know how bad everything got between us. Like he never saw me breaking down, bit by bit, with every alcohol-induced night of fucking that battered my soul.

It's not his fault. But it still hurts that he didn't notice then and he doesn't notice now.

I'm not going back to the soldier I was before. That soldier got me thrown out of the Army for being too stubborn to ask for help. For being too cocky and thinking I could handle everything.

For being cocky enough to think I had everything under control until I didn't and I ended up getting people killed.

I glance at my phone, checking the schedule at Nalini's yoga studio. Two hours before the sutra class I've been taking for the last few months.

I breathe in, then release it, wishing, praying, hoping that I can release the tight knot around my heart.

Until then, I'll keep going.

One breath at a time.

Deacon

I LET HER GO, hating myself for slapping at her like that.

I saw the hurt flash across her face the moment the words were out of my mouth. It's like I lose my fucking common sense when it comes to Kelsey; no matter what I do, I always make shit worse.

Standing in the middle of the quad, surrounded by ancient trees and students that are so young they hurt my heart sometimes, I watch her go.

Again.

Because no matter what I do with her, I always screw it up. Regret sticks in my throat, cutting off air as students swarm around me, heading to their classes with deep and biting concerns about things that I cannot relate to.

I wonder if I was ever as young as they are now.

I adjust my backpack and cross campus, heading to the library, where I'll probably just stare pointlessly at my laptop screen and pray for inspiration. I need something to hit me for my thesis, which is due to be defended at the end of the year.

I've got exactly zero words written. After almost two years in the program, I still don't know what to write about.

But it's still easier to think about my lack of an academic plan than about the shit show I just created with Kelsey.

It's infinitely easier than missing her.

I've been missing her for years. It's only gotten harder these last few months, since she showed up at The Pint looking for work, and Eli asked me if he should hire her.

I could have told him no to make life easier on myself, but I didn't because I'm genuinely not an asshole and I knew she needed the work. The post-9/11 GI Bill is awesome but it doesn't cover everything.

Plus, a part of me wanted —*needed*— to keep an eye on her.

Especially after the alcohol-soaked way things ended between us three years ago.

I sink into a chair tucked in a quiet corner of the library, near one of the archives, where the bookshelves all slide together. They're kind of terrifying. I mean, are they like elevator doors that stop when they sense someone between them? Or are there hundreds of deaths each year that go unreported, a silent conspiracy by librarians to keep us from knowing the dark truth...?

I rest my head back on the chair, closing my eyes. Somehow, I don't think the university librarians would appreciate my thoughts.

After a while, I have to admit to myself that I'm not getting any writing done. It's not going to happen.

At some point, I need to talk to Kelsey about how she wants to run this semester.

I don't think she's going to respond to any emails today. Or tomorrow, for that matter. But she gets a vote on how our class will have to run. She's always had too much courage under fire and not nearly enough when the bullets weren't flying.

Funny how that works.

Is it wrong that I'm fucking proud as hell of her for what she did that day? Some dudes I know would be telling everyone and their brother about it if they'd been recognized for valor.

But not Kelsey. She acted like I'd told the world she had an incurable, deeply stigmatizing disease. Like cooties or something.

The Kelsey I knew in Iraq would laugh at that reference, by the way. Right now, I'm not one hundred percent sure she wouldn't stab me for it.

I grind the heels of my hands into my eye sockets, wishing everything wasn't so completely fucked up. I can be smooth as hell with any woman in the bar when I want to be.

Any woman except the one who matters most.

I never should have moved when the Army put me on orders for Fort Bragg. I should have declined the assignment and let them thank me for my service and send me on my way.

I should have fought to stay with her. To fix things that went horribly wrong after we got home.

I knew she was hurt. I knew she was in pain. And I was selfish enough to ignore it. To think she was fine.

What kind of a fucking asshole spends a month drunk in bed with someone and thinks that everything is fine? Normal people don't do shit like that.

It wasn't fine. And I should have known better.

I can't fix things. Regret isn't going to help either. "Oh, fuck this moping bullshit," I mumble. Finally, I sit up and open up my laptop, finding a note from Professor Blake with several recommended articles for the cadets to read and discuss in addition to what's on the syllabus. All about the complexities of military life or the unrelenting reality of being part of an Army in a state of perpetual war.

I'm both floored and impressed that she's included one from the Duffle Blog, the military's version of *The Onion*, about a lost lieutenant who gets eaten by wolves.

I smile. Not many people understand the dark sense of

humor the military has. I find myself wondering how she started reading that.

Kelsey's email is in the cc line.

I add her to my contacts, wondering if I'm going to find the courage to actually talk to her or just sit here and lament the shape of my life.

I reply to Kelsey alone. *We need to talk about how we want class to go at some point. I'm not doing all the talking. We owe it to the cadets to figure out how to work together.*

I don't expect a response.

Hell hasn't frozen over lately, at least not that I'm aware of.

I close my laptop. Guess I'll head to The Pint to start getting ready for my shift tonight.

A good stiff drink ought to cure what ails me.

And if it doesn't, well, at least I can get drunk enough for it to hurt a little less.

4

Deacon

KELSEY DECIDED NOT to show up to work tonight. Despite my best efforts of staring at the clock and willing her to walk through that front door, midnight comes and goes with no Kelsey.

I pull double duty behind the bar and try to drown my worry in whiskey.

She's done this before. And that offers little comfort by way of hoping I know the end of this story.

It's just that tonight, I know I'm the source of it. And I hate that. I hate knowing that I hurt her again. That I lashed out and slapped at her because I was hurting.

Neither the alcohol nor the questioning looks that Eli keeps shooting in my direction are helping ease the ache in my chest.

Closing time can't come soon enough. By the time I'm wiping down the bar and prepping to close out the register, I'm wound tight enough to snap and not nearly drunk enough.

There won't be any sleep tonight. And as much as I want to lash out and blame her, it's not her fucking fault.

It's mine.

"Want to tell me what's going on?" Eli finally asks.

"I wish I knew." Stacking glasses is suddenly infinitely important.

"Oh, you thought I meant with Kelsey?"

I look over at him sharply. He's standing there, arms folded across his chest, tattoos flexing menacingly in the shadows. "I meant with you looking like you wanted to stab the customers tonight. But since you brought her up, yes, please share what you suspect about our coworker."

I stack the last glass then flip the towel over my shoulder. There are limits to what I'll share with him. Most of what happened between us downrange is...off limits to sharing with anyone. "We're teaching a class on campus this semester. To cadets in the ROTC program."

His mouth curls unexpectedly. "Really? What brought that about? You two barely speak to each other. I can't tell if you need a closed door and some privacy or couples therapy."

"The universe hates me," I mumble under my breath.

"It's been my general experience that the universe tends to put things in our path we can or need to handle."

I toss back a final shot before I slide the glass into the dishwasher. "That's a pretty fucked-up way of looking at things. How are you supposed to tell someone who just got raped, for instance, that, well, 'the universe thinks you can handle this'?"

My words are harsher than they need to be.

"I didn't say that everyone gets what they deserve." Eli holds up one hand. "It's the way I choose to relate to the shit in my life. I would never say that to someone who'd just been through something like that and fuck you for thinking I'm dense enough to do it."

I snatch my phone off the counter and slide it into my back

pocket. "You're right. My bad." The apology is bitter on my tongue. I know what he meant. I just don't care. "Do you have Kelsey's number? Is she okay?"

He looks at me silently for a long moment. "She's having a rough night. I was going to swing by but she told me she wasn't alone. Nalini was with her."

Relief is a tangible thing crawling over my skin. There isn't anyone better. "I've never met anyone with their shit together like Nalini King."

His expression relaxes and just like that, we're back on solid footing. "Yeah, she's a good egg. One of the best. She was my cadet company commander my plebe year."

"Oh yeah?"

"She was terrifying then as a twenty-one-year-old future lieutenant. Now that she's got experience? She's got the city council eating out of her palm."

"Apparently she's got issues with the wellness center on campus." It's so much easier talking about the mundane things like bureaucracy than it is to talk about Kelsey. I know he wants to ask. But Eli is too much of a Boy Scout to pressure me into breaking her confidence.

"I'm sure she'll get it sorted out soon enough." He slips the iPad we use as a register from its dock.

"Why do you do this? Why do you let her just miss work whenever she wants? I mean, don't you have a business to run?"

He looks down at the counter. The silence hangs between us for a long time. "I don't know what it's like to come back from the things Kelsey is dealing with. And I don't know the whole story. I can't fix that for her. The only thing I can do is make sure she has space and time to work on whatever it is that she needs to work on." He pauses. "I could fire her. Any other boss might do exactly that. But I won't. Because we look out for our own. And if all that means is I provide something to anchor her while she's working through whatever she's working through, then that's my role here."

"What's the difference between that and enabling a guy like Caleb?"

Caleb is a sore subject between us. I don't like the guy. Never have.

"His story is not for me to tell. And I worry about him, too, in a different way than I worry about Kelsey. About how much I'm enabling versus supporting." He clears his throat. "Look, whatever is going on between you two, work it out. Don't run her off. Because we can't keep an eye on things if she's gone."

That right there is why I love this man. He cares so fucking much about the people around him. He didn't get that from the Army. No, he brought that with him when he showed up on R-Day at West Point. The Army just helped him refine it. Hone it.

Makes him damn good at giving a shit about people.

About us.

About the fucked-up little tribe he's managed to build here.

"I won't." It's a promise I'm not sure I can keep.

But I'll go to my grave trying.

Kelsey

I LOVE that Nalini curled up on my couch and watched *Deadpool* with me. It felt so good to laugh at the raunchy humor and tell terrible stories of life since we left the Army.

But like all good things, it had to end. She went home and I stayed at my apartment. Alone.

I lie in my bed, one palm over my heart, the other on my belly. Breathing. Trying to let my mind wander enough to fall asleep.

Guilt is tight in my chest after the silence of my apartment wraps around me. It's the silence that gets to me.

I should have gone to work. Should have sought the noise and the chaos and the thumping music. Anything to escape the creeping quiet of the dark.

But I know my patterns. And tonight, I was walking on cracking ice, the fissures spreading out beneath my feet, threatening to shatter and drop me into the cold water of nightmares and memories.

And I know how I would react if that happens again. How I always do.

With too much alcohol. And too many bad decisions.

I'd meant to go to yoga and then go to work.

But the sutra tonight...the sutra had hit a little too close to home. Nalini had spoken about prisoners and the prison guards. About how they were both inside the same structure but the guards saw the walls as an opportunity, whereas the prisoners saw it only as restraint.

Her point was that if we believe we are trapped, then so we are.

And it hit me hard, like a wall of truth crashing over me. That I was trapped, still stuck in the past, letting my fear and my nightmares control my present.

It sounds so easy, so fucking simple. Just change the way you are looking at things and voila! The prison becomes a castle.

I continue to breathe in, out. Making my inhale match my exhale.

After class, I couldn't lift myself from savasana. And Nalini had come and sat by me, talking to me until the tears started flowing down my cheeks and running into my hair.

She stayed.

And she never asked me to talk about it. She just kept talking about the way the body stores our memories and how we release them through asana practice. And I listened as I tried to let go, a little bit at a time.

I don't know if I drift to sleep or not. It doesn't feel like it but before I realize it, the sun is piercing the veil between the curtain and the wall, reminding me that it's time to get up and face the day.

It's so easy to drag my corpse out of bed and to yoga. I don't even have to argue with myself about whether or not I'm going. It's the one thing in my life that's simple. Even when it isn't.

I can't point to the moment I decided to commit to making a yoga practice a part of my daily life. It just kind of happened. I walk into Arjuna Yoga, inhaling the warm scent of sandalwood and patchouli and fruity teas. It's a light scent that wraps around me, helping my mind shake off the sleepless night.

Every day is a struggle to find balance. To try to let go of the things I can't control. To not hold on to the past.

To try and stop blaming myself for everything that went wrong, no matter how good my intentions had been.

It's more difficult these days because every day, I'm around the person that represents everything I ran from when my life in the Army ended.

Deacon.

Being around him is a subtle type of self-harm. How close to the vein can I get? How hard can I push up against the flesh before I bleed again? Can I inhale the scent of him as he walks by and not beg him to touch me? Can I brush against his arm and not remember how it felt to feel it wrapped around my stomach, holding me close as he pushed into me, fast and hard, the way I wanted him then.

The way I want him still.

But the flip side of the harm is the rush, the endorphins of surviving another encounter. Another moment of proving to myself that I'm still alive. That the pain and the fear and the alcohol-drenched return home are only a memory.

That my past is not my future.

My mind is fuzzy, despite sweating on the mat in class as Cricket, one of the new instructors, calls out chair pose.

Sometimes that happens. Sometimes, I'm able to disappear into the space and simply be in the poses and the movement. Other times, I can't connect, can't release and lose myself in the flow.

It's not the end of the world. I've had days like this before and I will have days like this again.

But it's weird that today when things go sideways, I have a text from Deacon asking if we can meet for coffee to discuss class with the cadets.

I suppose I have to say yes. If cadets are anything like privates, they can figure out when the platoon sergeant and platoon leader don't like each other. And all sorts of shenanigans can ensue from that.

I know. I took plenty of advantage of those situations when I was a junior enlisted soldier.

We agree to meet downtown, a block or so away from The Pint. I love the downtown Durham area, especially the old tobacco district that has been converted and is now chic and trendy and new mixed in with the historic brick and ancient paver stones. Maybe I'm supposed to be too cool for all that but I love the way the old brick buildings make me feel *connected*.

This town is a lot like me, I guess. Trying to wrestle with its own past while trying not to lose its present in a violent shit show. I guess maybe that's why this fits so much better than central Texas for me. Texas was more Army, more old Kelsey. This is more...civilian Kelsey. Like Durham, I guess I'm still working on figuring out who that is.

The Pint is nestled between several restaurants. Around the corner is a coffee shop that's been converted from an old garage called Espresso and Fizz. I have no idea how they decided on the name of the place but I love the espresso chocolate blend they offer. I'm skeptical of Deacon's choosing this as the place to meet because it's almost always packed.

Today, though, he's waiting in a corner, having snagged a large couch and wide flat table. He's got two cups of coffee in front of him.

"Nalini told me you like the chocolate one. Hope I got it right," he says, handing it to me as he slides over and makes room on the couch.

The moment hangs between us.

I've never done well with guilt. Since I walked into the bar six months ago, I've kept him at arm's length. I've deliberately been standoffish and distant.

It hurts. It hurts me every time I turn away from the concern in his eyes.

It hurts every time I see him flirting with someone else.

It hurts because I know that if I dare to take what he's offering, even if only for a night, I risk backsliding into every bad habit I'm trying to unlearn.

"I'm only offering coffee. Not marriage," he says when I hesitate. His words are lighter than I think he meant. They crash into me, though—a wave of simplicity captured in those simple sentences.

I take the coffee and sit next to him on the couch. "Thank you. This is perfect." The coffee here is never burnt. Never scalded.

"Glad I got the right one." His body is angled toward me, his elbow resting on the back of the couch.

The world falls away. His eyes are warm, a physical caress as I sit, surrounded by his energy and the warmth of simply being near him. He's close. Closer than he's been. I think it's the stillness. Behind the bar, we're both always moving, always crashing into each other and moving quickly away, like waves being drawn back into the ocean after slamming into the rocky beach.

Now, I'm still. Warm. Drawn closer to the heat, to the promise of his touch.

It's such a human thing to want to be touched. To be loved.

We had that.

And then it ended.

Because neither of us was capable of handling it.

Me most of all.

Deacon

IT'S TEMPTING to lean closer, to see if she will let me penetrate the boundaries she's erected.

But I can't do that. Not if I want to win the war.

I have to be strategic. Deliberate.

At least, that's what I think I have to do. I'm pretty much winging this.

No matter how much I want to stay, I move away, giving her space.

It's a small thing but the flash of awareness in her eyes tells me I'm not doing too shabbily right now.

"The required discussions are pretty straightforward." It's easy to talk shop, to talk about the cadets and the classroom.

"I didn't really get a chance to do too much digging into it." She turns toward the paper copy of the syllabus I have spread across the table. "I get the impression Professor Blake wants us to do more talking and less focusing on the reading."

"I had the same impression." It's amazing how this neutral territory is so easy to navigate with her. Nothing personal. No real connection.

But no animosity either. She's not actively working on keeping the boundaries up between us.

I suppose that's good, right?

"I guess I'd start with what do we want them to know? When

we think back about our lieutenants, what do we wish they'd done differently?"

She sips her drink, nodding after a moment, before she reaches for her pen. "I think there's so much going on, we need to really push them beyond what they think they're going to be doing."

I smile. "Eli told me when he graduated from West Point, he thought he'd be kicking in doors every day. Turns out he was doing a lot of paperwork and dealing with marital infidelity and soldier pay problems."

"I had a platoon leader that was so bitter that he had women in his platoon," she says with a smile.

"That doesn't seem to be the kind of memory that would make you smile." I'm curious about her reaction. We weren't in the same company downrange, just the same battalion.

"Well, when he tried to trade his female private and me for two dudes, First Sergeant told him to get the fuck out of his office and if he ever tried any stupid shit like that again, he'd make sure the old man relieved him and ended his military career before it started." She takes a sip of her coffee. "I loved working for First Sarn't Sorren."

"It helped that he had a teenage daughter so that kind of attitude didn't play well," I say. "I wonder what he's up to these days?"

"I don't know. I lost touch with him when I left Texas."

I glance down at my phone. "I still have his number. I wonder what he'd say about this teaching-the-cadets thing."

She leans back into the couch. The movement is relaxed and comfortable. Easy.

I could get used to this. Just being around her.

Enjoying her.

Enjoying each other.

Like we used to.

"I think maybe we should tackle some of their stereotypes?

Like maybe we should talk about women in combat and try to get them to talk about all the things they're going to do in their job that doesn't involve shooting people," she says mildly.

"That's a really good idea." It's exactly what I want her to do. Lead this thing. Lead them. I know she's capable of it. I've seen her lead and dear lord in heaven she is phenomenal when she's in front of soldiers. "I imagine he'd want us to be realistic and honest with them. Set their expectations to normal, you know?" I watch her reaction to my words, watching for any sign that I tripped across a line.

She lost some of that downrange. And I didn't notice it was gone until it was far too late.

I look down at my coffee. At the espresso and dark chocolate blend swirling in my cup.

"Why did you get upset the other day when I told the cadets about your bronze star?" I ask quietly. I'm afraid to look, terrified that if I do, I'll see that I've crossed the line once more.

I finally dare to glance up at her. Expecting anger. Defensiveness.

Color me surprised when she's merely swirling her drink in the mug in front of her

But the coffee must have a magical property in it. She's not angry. She's not even pulling away. "Every time the Army comes up, I feel like I'm always trying not to be that guy that's telling everyone how he was such a badass when he was some Power-Point slide-making coffee bitch."

I lift one eyebrow and try really hard not to smile. "You mean like Caleb?"

She smiles sadly. "He's not nearly as bad as some guys I've met." There's a strange sympathy in her voice, one that highlights the lack of compassion in my own when it comes to Caleb.

"He annoys you, doesn't he?" she says after a moment.

I don't deny it. "He brags about things he didn't do. You...you don't even admit to things you *did* do." I swallow. Fear grips my throat, fear that I am dancing too close to the edge. But I have to press on. Have to ask the question. "Why? What are you afraid of?"

She stares into the coffee cup. Her chocolate brown eyes distant and...sad. Finally, she looks up at me. For once there's no anger. No boundaries. Only a field of emotion looking back at me, a thousand emotions I cannot name but feel just the same.

"Breaking."

5

Kelsey

THE CADETS ARE QUIET TODAY. Veer and Jovi are sitting next to each other again. They're cute in the way they think they're being professional in class but their bodies telling on them. I don't know what the deal is with their relationship—whether it's merely a close friendship or something more—but it's compelling the way their bodies reach for each other even if they're not aware of it.

Kind of like mine toward the brooding, grumpy man at the other end of the conference room table.

I release a deep breath, focusing on an intention of releasing the frustration around my heart.

I left our talk the other day at Espresso and Fizz rather quickly. I was quiet at work that night and I haven't had much energy to really engage in much chit chat, about the cadets or otherwise. I know he must think I'm fucking crazy.

I feel like I'm playing games. I'm not; I swear I'm not. But everything...being around him pushes me so off-kilter. It's already a struggle every day to get up, to get going. To pretend like today will be a little bit better than yesterday.

Opening up, even a little means I have to pull back again. To draw into myself. To re-center and balance.

I hope maybe someday I can tell him that without sounding like some psycho new age chic who likes mind fucking the men in her life.

But right now, he's silent and brooding and dark, a pool of energy at the end of the table that's practically vibrating.

I clear my throat, needing to break the silence and get this started. "Let's talk about the news from Syria. The readings for today's class discuss all the arguments why women shouldn't be in ground combat units but the situation in Syria suggests something else entirely. Does anyone want to recap the article for us?"

Jovi raises her hand. "The article is from al Jazeera, which I never realized was a legitimate news source and it's talking about the fight to retake Raqqa from the Islamic State. It's really interesting how the parliament in the semi-autonomous Kurdish region has requirements for an equal number of men and women to serve in their government. And that the women are just as big a part of the fight as the men."

I nod, loving the passion in her response. "Go further with that. Why is that something that caught your eye?"

She leans forward, bracing her elbows on the table. She's calm and passionate and confident as she speaks. Dear lord, I wish I'd had my shit together like she does when I was her age. "Because it means that all this 'women can't' bullshit is just that... it's bullshit. It's culturally shaped and it limits us. These women are fighting for their freedom. They have the same obligation to defend their freedom and their lives as the men. That is such a powerful narrative for little girls *and* little boys to look up to."

Ryan is clicking the cap on his pen violently. Iosefe looks like he might stab him with it if he doesn't stop but Ryan is oblivious.

"I don't understand what we're supposed to take from these readings," Ryan says. "The Kurds have been fighting for their own territory since the breakup of the Ottoman Empire. Why do we suddenly care about them now?"

Deacon leans back in his chair. "You don't think a people fighting for their freedom from religious oppression is worthy of academic discussion?"

Ryan shakes his head, the pen still clicking. "I'm sorry, but aren't we supposed to be members of the global community now? I mean, the American Century wasn't really all that great. Millions died in our proxy wars with the Soviet Union."

Deacon studies him quietly. "Those proxy wars were part of a global strategy of containment. Similar to what we're doing now with ISIS."

"I get that." Ryan lifts his chin, war in his eyes. "But like, how does this end? The US is funding fighters to fight the fighters we created when we invaded Iraq. We made this mess when we screwed up Iraq. And now you want us to read these articles and cheer for these Kurdish women taking up arms in support of their own liberation because we don't want to put boots on the ground again and get our hands dirty fighting the enemy we helped create? Is that how this works?"

I frown because as much as I want his argument to annoy me, he's got a damn good point. But as with anything, it's far more complicated than can be distilled down to a talking point.

I feel for him. For his righteous anger and indignation.

I was him, once upon a time, wishing our leaders would have a moral backbone and just lead us instead of invoking platitudes shaped by focus groups.

"I guess I'm wondering how else it should work," I ask. "ISIS isn't an easily targeted enemy. They have very strict, un-Islamic views on how to treat women. Why wouldn't we support these women and men fighting for their freedom from this? It's practically our own national narrative all over again, except instead of the fight against unjust taxes, they're fighting against slavery and rape."

I can feel the stress in my voice. Deacon looks up at me as I finish. My skin is tight, stretched to the breaking point over my bones.

Ryan glances over at me, his eyes flashing. "We're just not willing to use the kinds of bombs necessary to end it," he says, then adds tightly, "the Russians don't have a Chechnya problem anymore."

Deacon scribbles something on his notebook that he's resting on his bent knee. "So, the solution is to just kill everyone we don't agree with?"

"No, that's not what I'm saying." Ryan's voice takes on a defensive tone. "This article is about the role of women in war, right? Well, maybe ISIS would be already dealt with if the Kurds weren't bogged down with women fighters. Maybe they can't keep up, you know?"

I tip my chin and look over at him. Across the way, Jovi looks ready to jump across the table and strangle Ryan.

"Why do you want to join the Army?" I finally ask Ryan. There's a selection bias in college that few people ever really talk about. College is supposed to make you challenge your assumptions, make you learn and grow. But the vast majority of students take classes they *want*, leaving them with greater cognitive bubbles by letting them skip the classes they *need*.

Maybe this is why Professor Blake has started working with the ROTC program. To challenge people's assumptions *before* they become officers.

"I want to talk about this stuff before I go out to the Army, I want you to prove to me this isn't just PC bullshit." His voice rings with a spark of passion that's mildly off-putting. As if he knows all about the world already and this class is merely a check-the-block exercise to confirm his brilliance.

Deacon says nothing, doodling on his notepad. I'm mildly

irritated with him but then again, I forget where I am. He's not the commander. Neither am I.

"Prove what isn't just PC bullshit?" Deacon asks softly.

I know that tone in his voice. That dangerous edge to his words. He won't yell. I've never heard him yell. At least not recently. But when he gets that tone in his voice, it's a thing to behold. He can rip someone to shreds with that tone and have them begging for forgiveness.

"That women can do this whole war thing. I've been reading the reports about the women Rangers down at Fort Benning. My uncle says this is just social engineering and that we're setting our boys up to get slaughtered in the name of political correctness."

It takes everything that I am not to get out of my chair and strangle his little ass. But this isn't a fight I can win. Because guys like Ryan never listen to someone who's been there. At least not someone who he thinks lacks the proper anatomy—and by that, I mean penis.

"You weren't too hot last year at training when I had to carry your weapon because you were getting ready to fall out from heat exhaustion," Jovi says coolly.

Ryan at least has the decency to flush. "Yeah, well, so sue me if I wasn't ready for a hundred-degree heat with just as much humidity. That's different."

Jovi shakes her head. "No, it's really not."

I finally dare to look up at Deacon. He's watching me, his eyes dark and burning as he tries to explain to Ryan why he's wrong. Why every life on the battlefield must be prepared to fight and do what's necessary to bring their brothers and sisters home.

His eyes are filled with a thousand memories of another life.

But my story—*our* story—is just an anecdote. Not data. People like Ryan don't want to hear stories like mine. He doesn't want to hear that women are even stronger than we believe. That we can fight.

That we *should* fight.

Because it's our duty.

I can't look away from Deacon. From the memories rising up from the desert sands, circling me like mist. Drawing me back to the dark, terrible joy that exists when civilization ends and war begins.

Deacon

"WHY DIDN'T YOU SAY SOMETHING?"

I follow Kelsey from class. She went silent a few minutes after Ryan's rant and said nothing else the rest of the time.

She's practically vibrating with energy as she heads out of the old Wilson building and crosses the quad. The undergrads get out of her way, clearly recognizing that now might not be the right time to bump into her.

I try not to focus on how fucking arousing it is seeing her walking like this. Stalking, filled with her own power and energy. It's like she's fully back to being the Kelsey I knew downrange. That Kelsey was living wide open, unscripted, uncontained. The Kelsey I know now is more tightly controlled. More tense.

More reserved.

I'm not letting her run. Not today. Jovi and Ryan got into a heated debate about political correctness that basically took up the rest of the class, and Kelsey remained silent, never once putting that little smartass in his place by telling him her story.

She is the living embodiment of everything Ryan was arguing against and she said nothing.

"It wouldn't have changed anything," she says, shifting her bag to her outside shoulder.

"It might have." I resist the urge to grab her shoulder when she keeps walking. I learned that lesson well the other day and I won't repeat it. "Will you stop for a second?"

"I have another thing to get to before shift tonight." There's an edge to her voice. Something jagged and sharp.

"Are you going to actually show up tonight? Or leave us worrying that tonight's the night you decide to off yourself?"

She wheels on me, finally pissed off. Good, goddamn it.

"That's the second time you've slapped at me for missing work. Don't do it again." There is an ice-cold warning in her words.

"Why?" I shrug, putting everything I have into pretending I'm out of fucks to give when the opposite is true. I give far too many fucks about this woman. "Don't you think it's inappropriate to disappear for a few days and not tell anyone whether you're okay or not?"

"Since when have I not been?"

I take a step into her space. "I don't know if you've noticed, but people around here tend to worry about each other. It's kind of what we do. And when people drop off the earth, we fucking worry."

She looks away, shaking her head. "What, are you and your dick the royal 'we' or something?"

My laugh surprises me. It is unexpected and bright, shattering the intensity of the moment to something manageable. I pinch my eyes beneath my sunglasses, wiping away the tears. "Jesus, Kelsey, where do you come up with this shit?"

"Dark corners of the Internet," she says mildly.

And just like that, things are defused. Again.

For now.

I'll let them be. Because I don't actually like fighting with her. "*I* fucking worry about you." My voice is quiet, so much so that I'm actually surprised I've spoken the words out loud.

I can't see her eyes behind her sunglasses. Can't see if my

words have hit home or piss her off. She swallows and looks away, her dark hair brushing her neck with the movement.

I'm still getting used to seeing her with her hair down. Even after the months she's been back in my life.

I like it. I like the way it slips over her shoulders, merging with the black and red and blue ink on her shoulders.

Turns out, I have a thing for women with tattoos. Okay, maybe one specific woman. The lotus flowers and roses that twist up her biceps and over her shoulders are a perfect description of the woman who wears them. A beauty who will fucking stab you if you grab her wrong.

"I'm not yours to worry about anymore, Deac," she says softly.

I take a single step closer. Close enough that I can smell the scent of the beach from her skin. Sweet baby Jesus, my body tightens remembering how she always smelled like Coppertone sunscreen in the desert.

"It doesn't work like that."

She tips her chin and looks up at me. She's not that much shorter than me. Her mouth is there, just there, close enough that I'd barely have to dip down if I wanted to kiss her.

That would get me laid out across the quad holding a broken nose before I could blink. I know better than to attempt that.

No matter how badly I want to taste her again, I won't push. Her boundaries are hers.

Maybe what's between us would be different if I didn't know why she had them. If I hadn't been there the night everything broke.

But I know. And I can only push her so hard.

But I'm tired of waiting. And I'm so fucking tired of being afraid for her every time she drops off the net for a few days at a time.

"You're going to have to accept that we're your tribe," I say quietly. "That means we worry about you."

"There you go with the royal 'we' again. Does your dick have his own credit card, too? His own twitter account?"

I fight the urge to laugh. "That would be a gross violation of their terms of service, I think." I curl my fists, fighting the urge to brush her hair out of her face. Reminding myself that I'm not allowed to touch. "Me. Eli. Parker. We're family. We worry."

She sighs heavily but doesn't back up. Doesn't retreat. Her sheer stubbornness and refusal to back down from a fight are two of the things I love most about her.

It's caused more than a few problems over the years.

"I'm not in the Army anymore. I don't have to sign out on pass and request permission to miss work."

God, but she's working my last nerve right now. "It's called not being an asshole. It's not like we don't have a history of folks ending up in the hospital around here."

Our local community of vets has had its share of problems. And no matter how much we might wish for normal lives, we'll never blend in on campus like we want to.

I've spent too many nights at the ER with Eli, waiting on one of our own. Wishing that we'd been taught healthier stress management techniques than we all apparently were.

She shakes her head and starts walking, leaving me standing there on the grass.

She's right. She doesn't have to tell us where she is. But I can see the dark circles she's trying to conceal beneath her eyes. I know what it feels like when the walls are closing in and you can't sleep.

I hope it's something simple, like not being able to sleep.

I hope it's not something worse. I can't shake the worry. The fear that she's treading dangerously close to the edge.

That she's playing tough, too tough to need anyone.

I know that role. I've played it, too. Far too many times.

And I know how it ends.

6

Kelsey

I'VE BEEN TRYING to quit drinking.

The problem is I'm really good at it. That's what I've been doing ever since I joined the Army and what I've been doing ever since I got blown up downrange. I've been trying to cut back on it. To be more healthy and aware and not as dependent on chemical mixtures to put me to sleep.

But when the insomnia hits, the meditation doesn't always cut it.

It's what I'm good at.

So now, it's a challenge to quit drinking *and* share so much space and time with Deacon. Being sober is hard enough. Being around Deacon sober?

I can handle working with him. I'm even getting used to the idea of sharing intellectual space with him. I can handle teasing and being around him and seeing him go home with a hundred other women.

I can't handle him pushing me for something I'm not capable of. Something inside me broke a long time ago and he knows that, goddamn it.

I'm afraid.

Afraid of what happens when I touch him.

To both of us.

I'm edgy and annoyed after a night of not sleeping. It doesn't help that I'm aching to touch him. To break my own rule and drag my fingers over his skin and draw his dark and brooding self toward my body.

I get dressed and get my ass out of my apartment as fast as I can. When I moved, I was hoping a change of venue would help me sleep better.

I was wrong. The new place is worse than the old one. It's too quiet. The silence. The emptiness.

Oddly enough, the cheapest place I've lived in since I moved to North Carolina was the place where I slept the best. The paint had been peeling off the walls and the ceiling had what I hope were water stains leaking through. The walls in that old building had been paper thin. I'd been able to hear everything. The baby from two floors below me. The fights between the old couple on the bottom floor. The creak of the stairs as my neighbors went up and down.

But it was the noise that let me sleep.

I thought I'd wanted away. Something cleaner. Quieter.

Turns out, a nicer apartment wasn't good for my mental health. I've moved twice since that dive burned to the ground due to faulty wiring. Each time, I hope it will be different.

It's not. And now I'm stuck in a six-month lease for an apartment that I really hate. Guess that's what I get for trying to move up in the world.

It's mornings like this that make me wish my shift from the night before never ended. I need the work to keep me busy. That's part of why I'm glad that Professor Blake has me working with the cadets. I don't know what I would fill the space with if I wasn't teaching and working and in class. I don't like to think of the alternatives. I need something to keep my brain going. Something to keep me away from the silent spaces that let the memories creep in.

I head to the library on campus. I need more coffee and to figure out how to get my GI Bill paperwork fixed again so I actually have a little money to...oh, I don't know...pay down some student loans and eat something other than canned tuna?

Waiting in line for coffee, I glance down at my phone, checking for emails.

A chill runs across my skin. Like someone's walked across my grave, as my grandmother used to say. I stare at my phone. At an email from Deacon from several days ago:

We need to talk.

And at a response I apparently typed out last night but never sent:

I don't want to be alone.

I must have been really out of it. I don't remember drinking so much that I blacked out, but everything's kind of fuzzy after I left Deacon and went back to my apartment.

My brain is fucking with me. It has to be. I stare at the message, searching my neural synapses for a trace of the memory of typing this. It's there, dancing at the edge of consciousness. Teasing me with hints of a memory.

Has it really come to this? Me begging him to give me what I need?

Am I that fucked up that I have to keep playing games with him? It's not right, tempting him, tormenting him. Teasing us both while holding him completely at bay.

But the idea of his body against mine. Of him holding me in the dark.

I don't want to be alone. I just want someone in my bed at night. A warm body to press against in the dark. To remind me as

I sleep that I am not alone, walking through the darkness of my nightmares. The cold dark space on the other side of my bed needs a person in it. Then I'll be able to sleep.

I imagine placing a personal ad on Craigslist, with the accompanying dick pics that would likely be sent in response: *Woman seeking man to share a bed. Literally, I just want you to hold me while I sleep. No weirdos.*

The line moves another step closer to my personal lord and savior Caffeine Jesus.

I almost smile to myself, imagining what my old first sarn't would say about placing an ad like that. First Sarn't Sorren would look at me like I had a dick growing out of my forehead and tell me this was how horror movies started.

I'd kind of have to agree with him.

I place my order, praying for the world to move a little faster so I can get some coffee asap. Maybe my brain will tell me what the fuck I was thinking when I wrote that sad little missive.

The latte is pure heaven. Dark and rich, it slides over my tongue and the caffeine wraps itself around my brain with a smooth jolt.

I read my email again, then hit delete.

I need a little excitement in my life but not where Deacon is concerned, no matter how much my subconscious might be trying to tell me otherwise.

I tuck my phone into my bag and head to my class, wondering what Nalini would say if I told her what I'd done.

She'd laugh. This is the woman who couch-surfed her way across Europe. She'd probably print it out and hand-deliver the email to him, doing her part to help my sex life.

I smile at the thought. My life is so damn weird.

7

Deacon

I SLEPT LAST NIGHT, which is always a good start to any morning. The sunlight streaks across my bed, warming my body beneath the LL Bean sheets I found at the Salvation Army for three dollars. They're damn good sheets, too.

And yes, I get how that makes me sound, but you know what? After sleeping in the red dirt at Fort Benning and the spiders and scorpions in the brush at Fort Hood and heaven only knows what in Iraq, I'm secure enough in my manhood to admit that I like comfortable sheets.

They feel smooth against my ass and I've discovered that I like smooth things against my skin. That's usually a woman but today, that role has not been filled, leaving me to enjoy the softness of cotton alone.

I grab my phone and scroll through the news, checking any Google alerts for The Pint. We all keep an eye out for things that could damage our social media presence. It's funny how we all—

me, Eli, Parker, and Kelsey—take ownership of The Pint. No major scandals to start the day; always good.

I need to get up and get to the gym, then drag my ass to campus for a meeting with Professor Blake about my lack of a thesis. She's been amazing since the first day I met her.

I just wish it had been under different circumstances.

I still remember handing her the folded flag that we'd draped over her son Mike's casket. It had taken everything I had not to break down. I choked on the words *on behalf of a grateful nation*.

Funny how life takes the strangest turns. I wouldn't be here if not for that funeral and my friend Noah Warren telling me that he'd finally managed to get his ass cleaned up down here in North Carolina. If Noah can get sober, well, maybe there's hope that any of us can unscrew our lives. It helps that he has Beth now, whipping his ass into shape.

I wasn't sure me and the South were going to get along. But I was pleasantly surprised.

I head to the coffee shop on campus, scrolling through the Internet and wasting time in general. Every so often, I get bored and read Craigslist personal ads. It's a terrible commentary on my hobbies or lack thereof, but they're a nice distraction from how mundane and boring my own life is these days.

A bunch of us started reading them downrange one night when we were bored in the ops center. My commander caught us nearly pissing ourselves laughing, demanded to know what the fuck was so funny at three in the morning. For the rest of the deployment, we had to start each commander's update brief with a new ad.

He made it an official policy, with a letter and everything.

That policy made the deployment go a little bit faster, always a good thing. One of my personal favorites was an ad down at Fort Bragg offering positive pregnancy tests. I still haven't figured out why anyone would need to buy a positive pregnancy test but then again, I'm not known for my imagination.

Part of me hopes I'll run into Kelsey in the bright light of day. I hate that I continue to worry about a woman who is doing her damnedest to keep the barriers between us now that we're both civilians. That doesn't stop me from worrying about her, though, especially on days like this where my own memories are circling.

Unlike Kelsey, I try not to pretend that my past never happened and... Wow, was that statement sanctimonious.

It's hard not to judge her, though. I've got half a mind to steal her cell phone and turn on Find My Friends so I can figure out where the fuck she's living.

I'm probably going to just ask her straight up. And if she refuses to tell me, I'll just follow her home like any good stalker would do.

It's not stalking if you're worried about someone, right?

I continue scrolling through the personal ads while I walk, more out of habit than anything else. Looking for what, I'm not really sure. One reads like a lonely housewife advertising for a pool boy. I'm not exactly sure she's really looking for someone to clean her pool but she definitely sounds like she wants to have something checked out.

It's just not as funny without the guys in the TOC to laugh at the shit with. And Noah doesn't come by The Pint as much anymore, especially now that he's working hard at staying clean. I can't blame him but fuck, I wish life hadn't gotten so fucking boring without him hanging around.

But I keep checking the personal ads anyway because it feels familiar. And the familiar these days is in short supply.

The word "weirdos" catches my eye and I stop scrolling and read the whole listing. *Woman seeking man to share a bed. Literally, I just want you to hold me while I sleep. No weirdos.*

What kind of person puts a personal ad in Craigslist for... cuddling? Shaking my head at the strange and brave people in the world, I lock my phone and order my coffee.

But something about that ad keeps tempting me to read it again.

That can't be real, can it?

"What's so interesting?" Nalini falls into step next to me. It's hard not to like her. She's infectious in her warmth, her joy for life.

I don't know if there's a god or a higher power or what. Meeting someone like Nalini...I don't share her faith but it's nice meeting someone with such a strength of purpose and belief.

I envy her in some ways.

"Nothing. Just a weird Craigslist ad."

She offers a puzzled scowl. "Why are you reading Craigslist?"

"Long story."

She grins. "I bet. Where are you off to?"

"Meeting with my thesis advisor. About my nonexistent thesis."

"Where are you stuck on it?"

"Let's put it this way. It has to be substantive original research and...I've got my name on the top of the first page."

Nalini laughs and shakes her head. "You'll figure it out."

"I hope so."

"What's your area of focus again?"

"Public administration."

She tips her chin. "Write up something on the VA. Lord knows they need all the help they can get."

"I wouldn't even know where to start with that fucking train wreck."

She holds up both palms. "Just offering suggestions. I know a bunch of us have had a hell of a time getting appointments. Might be worthwhile to take a look at the struggles of young veterans."

She heads toward central campus, leaving me with a hell of an idea to chew on.

Kelsey

I SPOT Deacon striding toward me across the library before I can hide. I'm trying to do better these days and not avoid him. They're my issues, not his, and I'm not being fair to him.

I'm working on being less of an asshole these days. At least in theory. That doesn't mean my belly doesn't tighten as I watch him walk over. God but the man moves with such a surety of purpose. I love watching him move.

It's an easy thing to pretend he's moving toward me. That he'll take me into the stacks like they're a secret bunker we used to rendezvous in for a few moments of illicit connection.

The pure, unadulterated need in his touch. The erotic power of knowing he was aroused by touching me. The fierce meeting of our bodies in forbidden moments of pure pleasure.

"So much for my homework," I mutter as he sits. But I relax my expression, taking the sting from my words as much as possible. I lower my feet from the low table between us and sit up a little, at least trying to demonstrate that I'm not opposed to his company. Because I'm not.

But old habits die hard.

"I have a question for you."

The direct approach is a bit unusual for him, and causes me to lower my laptop lid. It's not that he's not usually direct. It's that, well, academic life teaches you to be a bit *less* direct. "You have my attention."

"Have you been seen by the VA?"

I'm not expecting this one. Not by a long shot. I can feel the ache in my bones beating in time with my heartbeat as his question bounces around my brain, trying to find a place to land.

"Now why on earth would I want to suffer through that shit show?"

His lips part, like he's trying to come up with something to say. His glance slides over my body, at the scars he can't see that I've covered in ink. A shield of ink to protect the hurt I'd love to forget. "Because...you haven't?"

He knows I was hurt downrange after the attack on our base.

I've never told him how badly. He redeployed six months after me and I was already well on my way to falling apart before our month-long bender.

I lift both eyebrows. "Have you?"

It's his turn to frown. "No."

"Then why would you expect me to?"

"Because...you got hurt."

The scars are tiny, so small I could forget about them if I wanted to. I told the tattoo artist they were from an emergency C-section. He didn't ask about the nonexistent child and I didn't tell him.

But suddenly they're aching now, burning across my abdomen and up the side of my ribs. I look away. This is the closest we've come to talking about the war since I've been back. And yeah, it's unnerving to even think about unpacking that box right now. On several levels.

"Yeah, well, there's nothing they can do for me." I don't want to talk about the VA. Or the way my service in the Army came to an inglorious end.

"Why not?"

I lift one brow. "Long waits for referrals that take an act of Congress to get? Lack of a penis? I have other things I'd rather use my time for." I slouch back in my seat. "Why is this suddenly so important to you?"

"Because I just ran into Nalini and she suggested I do something on the VA for my thesis."

I smile, shaking my head. "How long does it need to be?"

"That's the real problem, isn't it? Professor Blake said it needs to be 'sufficient.'"

He sounds so disgruntled. I barely resist the urge to laugh at him. I would, except that when it comes to my own research I'm very much in a similar boat. I don't even have the slightest idea where to start.

"I was just sitting here, trying to do the reading that we gave the cadets for class and thinking about how easy our lives are now," I say quietly.

His eyes darken, and he seems to be studying me intently. I remember that intensity from Iraq. How fucking sexy he was in full kit, back from patrol. "First world problems and all that."

"Yeah." I'm captured in the moment, lost in his eyes as the desert sand rises up around us, drawing me back to the not-so-distant past when things were simpler. When I still believed that what we did over there mattered.

I'm not sure anymore. I'm not sure that anything we did mattered. But I won't tell him that. I learned a long time ago that even if I doubted, others around me were entitled to their fiction.

Beliefs, it turns out, are really important. Bad things happen when people's beliefs fail them.

"Things were so simple over there," I say after a moment.

"They really were." He blinks and looks down, rubbing the edge of the table with his thumb. "I think I'd rather be pulling gate guard than trying to research and write this paper."

I make a noise. "I'm not sure what it says about either of us, that neither one of us is too thrilled with our academic futures."

"Or what it says about grad school that I'd rather be back in Iraq."

I tip the lid of my laptop closed. "Speaking of which, what do we do about Ryan? He seems...like he's looking for an argument every single time we sit down with him."

"He's definitely a challenge, isn't he?" Deacon rubs his hand over his mouth. "Man, he's hardheaded."

"Imagine what First Sarn't would do to him if he was one of the lieutenants?"

He laughs and sinks back into his chair. "Oh god. I think he'd strangle him."

"Right? Remember that time LT Woodbridge told him he was in charge at the range?"

He chuckles. "Yeah. The commander had to threaten to court-martial First Sarn't after he choke-slammed his ass."

The memory is something that links us together, the kind of thing that only other soldiers understand. A shared language based on common suffering that only those who have gone through it can understand.

"Well, honestly, Woodbridge needed a beating. Something to take the edge off his arrogance." See what I mean about people not understanding our sense of humor? Here we are, discussing the casual violence against one of our own like it's a joke. And it is. But I can understand why bystanders would be horrified.

"Daddy was a drill sergeant," Deacon says, as though that explains why Woodbridge was such an entitled douchebag.

It's so easy to sit here and pretend that everything is normal. That there's not a thousand bad memories and a nightmare that stands between us, keeping us forever apart. I wish things were different. I wish I could crawl across the table that separates us and slide onto his lap. Bite his lip while his fingers dig into my hips, like they used to when we were sneaking into the bunkers for quickies before he or I headed out on patrols.

It's so easy to remember the things that weren't absolute shit.

When I come out of my thoughts, it looks like he's noticed my thousand-yard stare. His gaze locks with mine, intense and demanding. "What are you thinking about?"

"Just remembering." I don't want to fight with him. But I can't go down that path. Not now. Maybe not ever.

But the more time I spend with him, the more I start to wish *what if I did*? Would I survive it? Would I stay whole and not break?

Could I touch him and not shatter?

Deacon

THERE'S NOT MUCH on Google Scholar regarding the Veterans Administration. There's been a lot of ink spilled in Op-Eds and talking head think pieces: Privatize the VA. Don't privatize. The illegal wait lists.

Reading through the literature pushes my blood pressure to an unhealthy level. I listen to a TED Talk about how the VA uses metrics to lead organizational change and I'm damn near ready to start drinking.

Those metrics don't mean jack shit when people are dying. "Your mission isn't to change fucking approval ratings, asshole," I mumble.

"Do you always talk to yourself?"

I frown at a voice I haven't heard in a couple of weeks. Caleb Hollis slides into the chair that Kelsey retreated from a while ago.

"Where've you been? The Pint has been blissfully free of bar fights since you decided to fall off the face of the earth."

He shrugs and props his feet up on the low table. A blond sorority girl glances at him and rolls her eyes, a clear sign that the human female wants to mate.

I'm sorry. I don't even know where that came from. I have got to stop watching the SciFi channel in my insomnia hours.

Caleb pulls a piece of gum out of his pocket and unwraps it slowly. "Here and there. Trying to get my shit together."

I lift both eyebrows. "Really? Did you finally hit rock bottom or something?" God that was a really dickhead way to ask that question. It's like I'm deliberately trying to goad him on.

In case it's not glaringly obvious, I'm not a fan of Captain Dipshit. He's annoying as fuck and the only reason I haven't knocked a few teeth out of his head is because Eli usually runs interference between us at The Pint.

Caleb thinks we're friends. I have never met a less self-aware person in my life.

Caleb is a former officer and a West Pointer. It's so fucking difficult to believe that Caleb and Eli come from the same esteemed institution. Or that any of us have trod the same dirt.

"Something about waking up in the hospital a couple of times makes you rethink your life choices."

There's more he's not saying but for now, I'm letting it slide. I'm hoping he'll leave soon and I'll be able to get back to research.

I look up at him suddenly, ignoring his comment about life choices. He doesn't seem to notice. "Hey, have you been seen at the VA?"

He tips his chin toward me like I just asked him about life on Mars or something. "Tried. Couldn't get an appointment. Got a notice in the mail a few weeks ago that I'd missed three of them and I was going to have to personally come in and schedule any future ones."

"Did you? Miss them?"

"Unless there's someone else making appointments for me, no; I neither scheduled nor missed any. It would have been nice to be able to use them, too, because paying for your own medical crap is expensive as fuck. I've seriously considered blowing dudes for cash to pay for rehab."

I choke on a breath that's gone down the wrong pipe. "Jesus, dude."

"What?"

"Never mind."

He narrows his eyes at me, then grins. "Sure. Whatever." Like he's getting ready to start some shit in the middle of the damn library. "Why are you asking about the VA?"

"Thinking about trying to do some research about it for my

thesis." I find myself wondering if Caleb has even bothered to go to classes. How the hell is he even paying for grad school?

But that's none of my business.

"Yeah? What about?"

"I don't know, to be honest. A friend of mine suggested it. I need to bounce the idea off my advisor to see what she thinks before I go too deep into it. But it might be a really good topic for my paper. If I can stop wanting to drink every time I start researching it. It's a fucking crime what's happening there."

"Yeah, it really is fucked up. Support the troops and all that, right?"

I make a disgruntled noise. "No kidding." I look up at him, suddenly curious as to why I no longer feel the urge to get as far away from him as I can. "What happened? With the whole rethinking-life-choices thing?"

He shrugs and picks at his thumbnail. "A bunch of shit. Decided I should probably start going to classes and try to actually do something with my life, you know?"

"Yeah, but people don't just wake up one morning and go 'Hey, you know, my life is on the wrong track. Let's go out and make a difference!'" I offer my best *Deadpool* impression.

It obviously falls short: he doesn't get the reference. See, I told you he was untrustworthy.

"Never mind," I mumble.

He scowls and stands. "I just stopped by to say hi. I got a thing."

I watch him walk off, then shoot a text to Eli. Something is definitely up with his boy.

He doesn't respond right away and that's okay. Caleb is not my problem; he's Eli's.

But as I watch him walk away, I can't shake the feeling that despite how much I can't stand that fucking guy, his life is connected to mine in the strange way that all of us in the veteran community here are connected together.

And no matter how much I try to pretend I can disconnect, I really can't. It doesn't work that way. I wouldn't have made it through the first year of grad school without Nalini and Eli kicking my ass and keeping me from being eaten alive by self-doubt.

I turn my attention back to the screen in front of me, trying to figure out what-the-everlasting-hell I'm going to research for my thesis.

8

Kelsey

THE EFFECTS of not sleeping for two nights are finally kicking in. The library's silence wraps around me, taunting me, dangling sleep just out of reach. I'm so tired that my hands are shaking.

I've been staring at my computer screen for the last two hours as the sun creeps over the gothic buildings and reminds me that a new day has started. Hard to be excited about the new day when the last day never ended. I love that our library is open 24 hours. I can only imagine the bizarre stories the night shift has to tell.

I love that they don't look at me like I'm crazy when I come stumbling in at two in the morning after my shift at The Pint is over and I don't want to go home.

The articles on the Kurdish women fighters in the PKK are teasing me with these mental images of women warriors who have all their shit together. That are fighting the good fight.

I wonder if any of them have problems sleeping.

Probably. Getting shot at tends to do that to a person. But it's compelling to think of being able to come home from war and go right back to life the way it was.

What if that was possible? What a powerful fantasy.

Yet here I am in the library as dawn breaks overhead, feeling sorry for myself because I didn't sleep last night while those women are fighting for their very survival.

"Very much a First World problem," I mutter. It's funny but part of me envies those Kurdish women. Their war hasn't ended.

I wonder what they'll do if their war ever does end. Will they have trouble sleeping then?

I scroll through my inbox, avoiding real work. Maybe once upon a time I was motivated. It's hard to remember a time when I wasn't just treading water.

I stop scrolling when an email catches my eye: it's one of several replies to my Craigslist ad.

Wait, what the fuck? I never even typed that thing up.

Did I?

I actually posted it?

I breathe in deeply. Clearly the lack of sleep is hitting me harder than I thought. I was awake yesterday when I thought about putting up that ad. I never actually typed it in and I damn sure never published it.

Except that apparently, I did.

And thankfully, Craigslist responses go through their servers, so my email address is anonymous. Saving me from myself and all that.

Jesus, what if there wasn't an anonymizer on the email address? I can only imagine the toxic sludge that would be filling up my inbox right now.

And apparently there is no shortage of desperate losers asking me to let them hold me while I sleep. There are at least three responses to my ad that I find buried in all the other annoying emails that usually go straight to my spam folder.

My brain is having a difficult time wrapping around the idea that I really posted this stupid thing.

I'm suddenly trying really hard not to cry. I've worked so damn hard on getting my life back to a semblance of normal and now I'm back to graying out levels of insomnia that aren't even alcohol-induced. I blink back the frustrated tears. I will not lose my shit again. I will not.

I answer my email instead.

Or rather, I delete with impunity.

First one is a dick pic. It might be a giant cock or it might have been some weird sea cucumber that's the stuff of nightmares, but I wouldn't want that or its owner anywhere near my lady parts. I'm sure its owner is a lovely person and all that, but I'm also pretty sure not even a "hi, how are you" introductory email before sending me a picture of his dick knocks him out of the running.

Delete.

The second one is only mildly horrifying. *I'd love to hold you while you sleep. I'd watch over you all night long.*

I have a vision of this guy staring at me like Hannibal Lecter while I snore on obliviously. And well, we all know how *that* turned out for anyone Lecter invited to dinner.

Delete.

The third one is...not horrifying. I have to read it a couple of times to make sure I'm reading it right.

It has...potential:

Not sure why I'm replying to this. Sounds really weird. Like, what's wrong with you that you're posting it and what's wrong with me that I'm responding? But you know what? Fuck it. I don't like being alone at night, either.

I frown, reading it again. He sounds...human. Like me. But then that makes me suspicious because if he's like me, just how fucked up is he? Does he drink every morning just to feel normal? I wonder if he's a soldier. Has he been to war?

Does he miss it?

I'm tired enough that I'm curious, but still coherent and cautious enough not to email him my address immediately.

The temptation of being held while I sleep is alluring, tempting enough to make me want to throw caution to the wind.

I contemplate heading to the yoga studio and trying a restorative class. Maybe a yoga nidra sequence would help me sink into sleep. Yoga nidra is this really cool meditation that brings you to this meditative state between sleeping and waking.

Except that something chased me out of the darkness of my memories the first time I tried it in my new apartment. I've done yoga nidra multiple times since then but always at Nalini's studio. I'm sure the experience is not as enlightening as it could be but I'm afraid to do it alone.

My body is wired to need the physical connection to other people.

Fuck it. I hit reply. *Why don't you like being alone at night?*

My phone vibrates with the arrival of another email, straight to my spam folder. I love how my phone only acknowledges new spam emails when I actually have that folder open. Otherwise that sucker would be vibrating all the time with all the penis enlargement ads I get.

I wonder what I clicked out on the Internet to end up with all of those.

I dare to hope that it's a reply to my note and am afraid to be disappointed.

But it's him. And his response draws me closer to the idea of him:

The silence.

I read the words again. Then again. Yeah. It's the silence that gets me, too.

I tap out my reply. *I used to hear everything in my apartment. Everything. Through the walls. The cars outside. The arguing down the hall. The fucking. The fucking was the worst. Now my apartment is so quiet. I can't stand it.*

I can't believe I'm doing this. Talking like this to a complete stranger on the Internet through an anonymous Craigslist email? Is this what my life has come to?

I think about texting Eli and telling him about what's going on so they'll know where to direct the cops if my body ends up dumped out in Eno State Park.

But I'm so goddamned tired. I drop my head back in the chair.

Chatting with this guy could quite possibly be the stupidest thing I have ever done.

I've been walking a fine line since I came home. Since I left the Army.

I want to stay on the line. I want to keep walking it. To keep right on pretending that everything is fine. That reading articles about Kurdish women isn't tempting me to head straight to the recruiting station and beg them to take me back. To send me back over there where at least what I'm doing has a fucking purpose. Unlike now, where everything is endlessly mundane.

I sit there, fidgeting with my phone, reading about the end-of-the-world predictions of some preacher down in Texas. Waiting for a response to my last email.

My phone doesn't vibrate and the disappointment settles like a sour thing in my belly. It figures.

I pick up my laptop and start scanning the articles about the Kurdish women again, hoping that Professor Blake will want us to move the conversation beyond these modern-day warrior women to something less inspiring.

Because as I look at these fierce women, I see what I used to be. I see what I might have become, if the war we'd been fighting had been worth it.

But ours...our war wasn't worth it. None of the loss, the sacrifice...none of that was worth it.

I used to believe it was.

I was wrong.

Deacon

SIX A.M. COMES AROUND QUICK when you never bother to go home. I closed up The Pint hours ago, left Eli and Parker making googly eyes at each other, and waited until Kelsey had gone home before I left to wander the streets until fatigue took hold.

Fatigue never took hold. So I walked. And kept walking, unwilling to head back to my apartment.

Our shift tonight was tense and distant. She wasn't talking and neither was I. We managed to fake it, though. Just like we always do. Smile and wave, right, boys? Keep the customers happy and plied with high-end whiskey, enough to make their expense accounts weep.

I glance down at the email reply on my phone.

I used to hear everything in my apartment. Everything. Through the walls. The cars outside. The arguing down the hall. The fucking. The fucking was the worst. Now my apartment is so quiet. I can't stand it.

I read it again and again. I contemplate the life choices that brought me to this moment, when I am conversing with a stranger on the Internet. A stranger who asked someone to sleep with them, not for sex but for something far more intimate.

Sleeping next to someone is being willing to be completely vulnerable. Completely exposed.

It's something I haven't done in years. Kelsey was the last person I actually fell asleep next to in bed. If I close my eyes, I can remember how it felt to hold her body against mine. To feel her breath against the scars and tattoos on my chest.

It felt so fucking normal to just lie there and hold her and not worry about getting caught violating General Order Number One.

I've had plenty of partners. Not that I'm bragging, because

only insecure douche nozzles brag about that kind of thing. But none of them spend the night. I don't want someone there in the morning when I wake up.

I don't want someone there while I sleep.

This ad, though. The person behind this ad has been haunting me. Teasing me with a sense of familiarity that's nagging at the edge of my brain.

Finally, I find the courage to reply:

Thin walls hold no secrets. You have to assume someone is always listening.

I stuff my phone in my pocket and start walking again, down the new brick sidewalk meant to look like old brick. Past the sun rising over the upscale chocolate shop and the gluten-free bakery that are two blocks away from The Pint. Past Nalini's yoga studio where the lights are already on. A warm glow pushes away the shadows on the sidewalk.

It's not strange, wandering the streets, looking for something to pass the time. It's only strange if I think about avoiding the silence that waits at my own apartment.

Or if I wonder about the person on the other end of the mystery email. What drives someone to put up an ad that's asked for something so basic as simple human connection? I read an article about it a couple of weeks ago. About people who sign up for cuddling with random strangers. I rolled my eyes when I read it.

And then it hit me how much I miss simple human connection.

My phone vibrates and a reminder pops up. We've got a delivery scheduled for seven a.m. Looks like I'll get some manual labor done before I try to crash before my shift tonight.

I head back toward The Pint. The streets are empty and damp; only a few people are out and about at this early hour. There's a sleepy stillness to the city that seems to contain the potential of the coming day's noise and hustle.

I walk past 1984, the bookstore-slash-hippie meeting place-slash-coffee shop. The lure of fresh brew is a temptation that's too compelling to ignore. Coffee is in plenty of supply in this town and every single small coffee shop offers something unique.

I make a beeline to the counter, focused entirely on getting a badly needed cup of coffee. I'm tangentially absorbing the books and incense and the overarching feeling of calm that exists in this space.

I order a large espresso with three shots and pay the far too mellow clerk. Then I look around while I'm waiting for the coffee.

A small white elephant-headed figurine catches my eye. It's a man but with the head of an elephant. The symbol on its palm is similar to the one on Kelsey's wrist.

I pick it up, feeling drawn to it in a way I can't explain, other than that it seems like something she might like.

"Do you know who he is?" the clerk asks, handing me my coffee, then taking my money for the little statue.

"Him?"

She offers a glassy smile. "Ganesh."

I assume that means something to her and say nothing further. I'm not exactly sure what I'm going to do with it or how I'm going to give it to Kelsey without things getting incredibly awkward. I'll figure it out.

I UNLOCK the doors to The Pint and drop my jacket in the staff room, putting the statue in with the change of clothes I keep in the basement. It's always good to have a change of clothes when you work at a bar. You never really know when you'll need them. I tuck the statue beneath a clean T-shirt and take another sip from my glorious coffee.

Guess I'll get cracking on the inventory before the delivery arrives. We've got to account for all the bottles to comply with state law and Eli is incredibly anal that the basement stays organized and neat, with all of the expensive whiskies lined up and orderly. Like little alcohol soldiers standing in formation.

I think his officer brain taught him to need the order to hold back the chaos. I don't think like that. Life is a bit more immediate for me these days. Some days I'm just happy to wake up because that means I actually fell asleep.

It's amazing how little sleep the human body can run on. It's not an ideal way to live. I'd like to actually fix myself but I'm a little skeptical of docs that like to sling medicine at a problem without actually trying to fix the problem. 'Course, what ails me isn't really fixable with a pill, anyway.

The basement is creepy and cold on a good day. I plug my phone into the charger that someone left by the stairs, that miraculously fits my phone, and turn up my most recent heavy metal playlist.

Metal isn't for everyone and it's not the only thing I listen to, but I like the rawness of it: the pure primal vocals, the pounding rhythm. It's fucking primitive and right now, I need that to distract me from the cold emptiness of the basement and the boxes and crates of whiskey and liquor.

Last week's shipment needs to be moved to make room for this week's. Normally, this is a two-person job but I'm edgy enough to need the labor. Time to move crates.

I need to be distracted from the circular thoughts twisting in my brain.

Five Finger Death Punch comes on. "No One Gets Left Behind" hits all the right notes.

What did we fight for? What the fuck are we dying for? I swallow a hard breath, one that rips through my lungs and tears at my throat.

The pointlessness of the fucking war doesn't eat at me every day but sometimes, sometimes, it hits me. There was no grand cause like my grandfather's war. No Nazis to punch, no homeland to defend.

We were lied to. We fought, we bled, and we died, so that fucking contractors and DC power players could get rich on oil rights.

I can feel the anger building. The rage. The need to lash out. To release the hatred that burns in me for the so-called leaders who set us up to fail.

For the officers who looked at Kelsey and said she was fucked up before she came in. Who said the Army didn't owe her anything.

For the officers who told me to stop being a pussy-whipped puppy and leave her to do whatever she was going to do.

Have you no honor? The violence of the song pounds in my brain. Most of the officers I served with didn't know the meaning of the word.

I stack another crate onto the last one I moved.

"Who pissed you off?" Her voice shatters my concentration violently.

By scaring the shit out of me.

9

Kelsey

"JESUS CHRIST, WARN A GUY," Deacon replies.

I smile faintly. The sight of him, sweat making his T-shirt cling to his body, isn't enough to cool my relief at finding him here.

The universe is a strange thing.

Before I spoke I stood there for a long moment, in the pulsing pounding noise of the music, watching him work, absorbing the vision of the man in front of me.

His T-shirt is ripped. Just above the waist of his jeans, I can see the ridge of his hip. I remember what it felt like to run my fingers over his skin. The heat of his skin against mine, of being encased in those arms. What it felt like to be lifted against the edge of a bunker, to feel the cold concrete behind me, his strong hands on my ass as he held me open before he slid in, deep and big and smooth. God, he was so fucking smooth.

I remember him, wearing his full kit. The body armor

protecting his chest, the helmet secure around his head. A man in his full primal warrior state of existence. There is just something so goddamn raw about a man in his body armor and helmet and weapon.

Not every man. But a man like Deacon? He owned it. And it's no damn wonder that my panties got wet every time I was around him.

He clears his throat and I realize that I'm staring. Well, not entirely at him. At the memory of him.

"Sorry." But I'm not. My brain isn't working too well right now. I'm really having a hard time thinking about anything other than his hands dropping that crate and instead drawing me closer.

It would be fast. And hard.

But for a few minutes, I would *feel* again. Maybe the sensation of being alive would linger for more than a moment. Maybe the fog of not sleeping would clear and I could make a rational decision about how to get back to centered.

I know that's a lie. It never lasts. It would be a fast hit, a tease of something fleeting, like a drug flashing through my system then leaving me in need of another hit.

Something broke inside me a long time ago. And a quick fuck won't bring it back or make me whole again.

Nothing will, no matter how hard I try to keep pretending that I've got my shit together with yoga and meditation and *ujjayi* breathing.

"You're here early," I remark when I'm confident I can speak without begging him to do terrible things to my body.

He lifts one shoulder, then drops it. I'm struck by a sudden sense of him...waiting. Like a predator, stalking his unaware prey.

Except that I am very much aware of him. Of everything about him.

"Couldn't sleep; figured I'd put my insomnia to good use." He frowns then, finally noticing my yoga mat over my shoulder. "What's that for?"

"I was going to an early morning class, only to discover they'd changed the schedule." My voice breaks. The frustration at not having a class ripped at the tattered edge of my sleep-deprived brain. I may have cried about it, but I'm not going to admit that to Deacon. I've been blown all to hell and back and I didn't cry. I'm damn sure not going to cry about missing a fucking yoga class. "Nalini is doing some remodeling or something, I think."

A girl has to have some pride. But it's a close thing.

"So you decided to come here? Doesn't seem very yoga-y."

"You'd be surprised." I turn and look around the basement, glance over my shoulder at him. "I never feel alone here."

He frowns, watching me intently. "You're not. Not here."

I offer a half-smile. "Sure." I have a feeling he's talking about something else. I don't know how to tell him that I *just didn't want to be alone.*

And that I was hoping, praying that someone – *him* – would be at work this early.

But I say nothing instead. I can't admit this to him. Can't form the words that admit I'm not doing okay.

That I might need some help.

I can't do it.

"Well, since you're here, do you want to grab a few boxes and help? Or are you going to do yoga over there where I can pretend not to watch you?"

That does make me smile. "That's pretty forward of you."

He drags one hand through his hair. "Yeah, well, I'm not really known for beating around the bush."

"I remember."

He frowns, his hand braced on the back of his neck. He opens his mouth, then closes it and turns away. The suddenness of his movement snaps me out of my haze and I move toward an adjacent storage room, stacked with crates filled with empty bottles.

I step into the room and roll out my mat. It's a purple Manduka. People either love them or hate them. One of the girls at my yoga studio recommended it and while it was a pain in the ass to break in, I've been a loyal devotee ever since.

I kneel, scrolling through my phone to find the audio of the sequencing I want to attempt.

"How long has it been since you slept?"

He fills the narrow doorway, his broad shoulders cast in silhouette from the light behind him, his shadow falling against the concrete floor and cinderblock walls that remind me of some of the old buildings in Iraq. The ones that used to be office buildings or prisons before we moved in.

"I'm running on about four hours of sleep over the last two days," I admit. But I can't deal right now. Not with the raw *concern* in his voice. I don't want to need it. Or him.

I can't. Needing him is what got me to where I am today.

It's not his fault. I wish there was some solution but there's no finding my way back to Deacon. Not for anything more than a quick screw up against a wall.

And he deserves better than that.

Maybe I should get really hammered one night and come on to him. At least then I'd have an excuse to have his hands on me just once more and I could play it off in the morning when cold reality hit me once again.

When the memories came.

Because they would. They always do. They're always lurking. The pleasure so intimately tied to the fear because we were literally caught with our pants down the day our base got attacked. I've tried to forget it. To move on once we got back from Iraq. To fuck him and pretend that everything was fine. That the erotic power of his touch didn't spark the nightmares I couldn't admit to him.

I love it when you fuck me but then I freak out after you fall asleep. The fear crashes into me, seizing the air from my lungs. Ripping the calm from my veins, replacing it with frigid cold.

Deacon is still watching me. "I'm fine," I say finally. I set my phone down at the edge of my mat. I settle into place, crossing one leg over the top of the other.

The deep voice of my favorite online instructor echoes against the concrete. *We will open our practice today with the sound of three oms.*

One of Deacon's lips cocks to one side. "Are you going to do that?"

I open one eye to look at him, then close it again. "Depends. Are you going to laugh at me?"

He looks at me and I can feel heat burning through my skin. Darker than the memories of Iraq. More intense than anything I've felt since. I swallow, hesitating, wanting to cross the space between us. Needing to feel his hands on me once more.

Unable to move from the terror that might surge if I do.

"There are a million things I'd like to do with you, Kels. Laughing at you isn't one of them."

He turns away before I can come up with a smartass response, leaving me hanging, suspended in that moment, unable to break free.

Deacon

IF I THOUGHT for a second she was playing games, I'd have walked out and never looked back. But Kelsey doesn't play games. She never has.

I have to put space between us.

It would be easier if I didn't know what the problem was. If I hadn't been there when she got blown up, if I hadn't been six months behind her when we'd come home.

It would be so much easier if I could rail at the world and be pissed off at her for playing stupid games.

I hesitate near the wooden rack of expensive whiskey, waiting, hoping that she'll find the courage to make the next move. That maybe she'll step off that mat and span the gap between us. But there is only the echo of her recorded yoga class greeting my fervent hope.

I know she's not playing games.

Kelsey is too straightforward for that but I can't stand here and pretend that it doesn't hurt. That there are no ties of blood and sex and violence that bind us together anymore.

I steal a glance back at her. Through the doorway I can see she's moving, her hands and feet spread, her ass in those glorious leggings pressed into the air.

I swallow. Hard.

There are a million things I can imagine doing to her in that position. And yes, I know what downward facing dog is. I've been to a yoga class.

One, and it was on a dare. I've never gone back, either. The *om* chant at the end crawled up my spine and vibrated in my chest. I had the worst fucking nightmare that night, too. It could have been a coincidence but I never went back.

But watching her now? Yeah, I really kind of wish I had spent more time learning the language, learning the words that send her body moving as a single fluid unit.

I have the sudden urge to move with her, to feel her body arch and bend against mine, to feel the slick slide of her skin against mine.

I'm a starving man, dying for a taste, a single bite.

But I can't. Because I won't take from her. Not unless she lets me. Unless she says the words. Explicitly. Clearly.

And one hundred percent sober, which I am reasonably certain she may rarely be.

She's not the same Kelsey I went to war with.

I don't think anyone really ever entirely comes home from war. Some of us were already fucked up before we went. The scars on my chest are hidden now. Sometimes I even forget about them beneath the ink.

She asked me about them once. On one of the few nights we managed to sneak into my trailer or hers and actually spend a few hours together instead of stealing a quickie in a bunker.

I told her about the car accident my junior year of high school. Of waking up upside down, suspended by my seatbelt, glass embedded in my skin.

I told her about being alone in a car that had three of us in it before I fell asleep as we drove away from the party.

About the crow that had stared back at me from the shattered window and haunted me for years.

Once I drew him into my skin, I stopped thinking about him. About that night. I told myself I was fine. That there was nothing left to unpack with that accident.

But Kels...there's something more. She's fighting so hard to hold on to normal, she doesn't even realize how close to the edge she is. I've been watching.

I know she's lying about how much she's not sleeping. I can't blame her. I don't admit it when I don't sleep, either.

I want to help. I fucking need to.

Because I failed her so badly when we were in Iraq when she needed me most.

I glance over at the small space, watching her lift her chest into the air, her skin slick despite the cool damp air around us. She flows again, lifting one leg this time and arching it until she looks open. Ripe.

I turn away from the vision of her body moving in slow, flowing rhythm, closing my eyes and leaning my forehead against the wooden shelf, wishing. Regretting every choice I've made up until this point with her.

Wishing I could fix it.

Needing. Needing her touch. Wishing she would walk up behind me and press her body to my back, feeling her soft in places I am not. Her hands would slide around my hips, slipping beneath my shirt. Her hand would slip into my pants, finding me, squeezing me. I know exactly how good she'd feel, her fingers fisted around me.

I want this fantasy. I want her hands on my body. Her palm stroking me, her breath moving with mine.

I want this to be fucking reality. I swear beneath my breath and stalk off, needing to get away from her before she catches me acting like a twelve-year-old boy.

My thoughts for her are decidedly not childish.

The sun is sliding over the old tobacco factory east of The Pint as I step into the daylight. I drag my phone out, needing a distraction from the painful erection in my pants. I refuse to deal with it. I can't. It feels wrong, fantasizing about her when she clearly wants nothing to do with me.

I stalk away from The Pint, putting space between me and the woman who haunts my sleep. I can't do this anymore. It's been months since she moved back into my life. I've been patient, waiting, hoping she would reach out before she crashed. And every day I've watched her get closer to the edge.

I can't do this anymore. I won't.

I stood by as she self-destructed once before.

I won't do it again.

I need a plan. A war game, if you will.

And I suppose that first involves defining what winning would look like.

What do I want? I want Kelsey. I want to hold her while she sleeps. I want to be there when the nightmares come. I want her to forgive herself for the sins she couldn't control.

I want to atone for my own.

I want to help her put the war behind her. To finally come home from the war.

And maybe then, I can, too.

I walk into 1984 for the second time this morning. I love the smell of a coffee shop and books. My old first sergeant always told me I was a fucking nerd. I grin, thinking of First Sarn't Sorren. Of course, he meant it with such love.

He was such a rough-around-the-edges son of a bitch. But he loved us.

It dawns on me then that I'm a fucking dumbass.

And I pick up my phone and fire off a text.

Hoping like hell that I can figure out how to unfuck things with Kelsey.

10

Deacon

"WHAT'S UP, SHIT FOR BRAINS?"

I grin as First Sarn't Sorren's greeting burns down my spine. The phone hasn't even rung once on my end before he's picked up. "Good to hear your voice, First Sarn't."

"Yeah, well, keep your panties on. How's civilian life treating you?"

"I'm not sure," I admit.

"What do you mean, you're not sure? You either like it or you're regretting your life choices. Which is it?"

I rock back in my chair, needing a hell of a lot more than coffee for this conversation so early in the morning. And it's an hour earlier back at Hood. But as a senior NCO, First Sarn't Sorren is already at work. Probably has been for hours. Because that's just how we were wired.

"It's good, I guess. I'm working at this place in Durham. A bar. The owner does a lot for vets in the area."

"Yeah? Sounds like the kind of place I need to tell my daughter to avoid when she comes out there for college next year."

I grin, imagining him dropping his kid off at college. "Yeah, well, we have a couple of guys who need your size twelves up their ass, that's for sure."

He makes a noise. "I've got plenty of those around here." He clears his throat roughly. "So, what's up with Sarn't Ryder?"

"She pulled up here a couple of months ago."

"I figured that out already, dickhead," he grumbles.

God, I love this man. Anyone else would be terrified of him but I know him. I've bled downrange with him.

He's got a warrior's soul and... Jesus, I've been around college kids too damn much if I'm thinking about him like that.

I opt not to tell him that.

"She's not sleeping. She won't admit it. She seems stressed the fuck out and I don't know how to reach her."

He's silent for a long moment. I glance at the screen to make sure he hasn't hung up on me. "Can you get her to the VA?"

I make a rude sound. "Do you really want me to answer that?"

"Probably not."

"What do I do? I don't want her to end up as just another statistic but she won't fucking talk to me. Or anyone, for that matter. At least not that I know of."

"No family, right?"

"Not that I know of. We were her family."

He sighs hard. "Look, I'll be out there next week for a campus visit with my daughter and training down at Fort Bragg. Want me to come up?"

I try to imagine what Kelsey's reaction would be if First Sarn't Sorren walked into The Pint. I have a hard time picturing it but I imagine it would have to be good. She'd do anything for him. Just like I would. "Yeah, I think that would be good, actually." I frown into the phone. "What are you doing at Bragg?"

"Some stupid ass school the Army is sending me to in order to be a sergeant major."

"No shit? Wait, I thought the Sergeants Major Academy was out at Fort Bliss."

"It is. This is something different. Some resilience bullshit with the Special Ops community there."

I laugh. "Holy shit, they're putting you in charge of resiliency? That's like putting a porcupine in charge of free hugs at the petting zoo."

"Fuck you and the civilian horse you rode in on," he says roughly.

I'm still grinning. God, but it's good to talk to him. "Yeah well, for what it's worth, I think you'd do a damn good job. The battalion is lucky you're getting promoted. It'll keep the officers out of trouble, if nothing else."

He laughs. "You have no idea how much of my job that already is."

"We've got a good one here. The guy I was telling you about? The one who owns the bar? Believe it or not, he's a West Pointer, too. Imagine that."

First Sarn't makes a noise. "Some really great people come out of West Point."

"Yeah, I know. It's only about ten percent who are raging dick-bags." Exhibit A: Caleb the Destroyer.

"And on that, we agree. Anyway. With Ryder, just be there for her, you know? Sometimes, you have to force your way into these things. Especially when someone doesn't know how to ask for help."

I know the feeling all too well. My throat closes off. My eyes burn. "How do you do it? How do you tell someone that what we did matters? When nothing we did over there matters?"

He doesn't answer for a long moment. When he finally speaks he says, "You can't judge things the way they are now. When we left, things were getting better. When I got back, our counterparts were glad to see us." He clears his throat roughly. "You have to believe that what we do matters. In the moment. Not down the road. Not looking back on it. In that moment."

"Do you believe that?" My voice is rough. It burns, deep inside my chest, an ache that will never heal.

"I have to," he says simply.

That's not encouraging. What happens when we stop believing in what we've done? What happens when we see the futility of it all? The pointlessness when the country we lied to ourselves about tears itself apart because of what we did? The senseless loss of life for a war that none of us believed in when we went and most of us question when we come home?

"I wish I still did," I say quietly.

"I can't help you with that. But I'll tell you this much. Dwelling on how pointless everything was is a fool's journey. We can't control the larger mission. All we can do is take care of those around us. The bigger picture stuff? You're right—none of that matters. Did you take care of your brothers and sisters around you? Did you do your best to bring everyone home? That's the only thing that matters."

I want to agree with him. I want that certainty of belief. That coherence of thinking about the world that makes it easier to sleep at night. But I'm not sure I do. I'm not sure I ever did.

"That helps," is all I say instead.

"Stay with her. Tell her you love her. That you're there. Whether she wants you to be or not." He pauses. "I mean that in the non-stalker sense of it."

I laugh. "Yeah, I kind of figured that."

"Shut up, dickhead. I'll see you next week."

Kelsey

WHEN DEACON ASKED me about the VA, I could have told him about this: about the lines and the questioning and the skepticism that I'd actually been to combat.

All to get a refill on prescription meds that I can't get through school without a fucking psych eval. To get a woman's health exam that I need every year because of some stupid policy that says I have to, whether I think I need it or not.

I'm pretty sure the universe is fucking with me. Either that or the lady in the Veterans Administration office got some message from the powers that be that I kicked puppies in a former life.

I haven't had nearly enough coffee or vodka to deal with this shit at barely nine a.m. on a Tuesday.

I swallow my righteously bitchy response and smile instead. Honey versus vinegar and all that, right?

I'm not Sarn't Ryder anymore. I can't make people do what I want, especially not a civilian who looks overworked and underpaid.

"I'm the sponsor," I say sweetly, responding to her question about my nonexistent husband's social security number.

My sweetness apparently isn't enough to establish even the tiniest human connection.

She doesn't smile in return. She looks at me like I'm a burden, as opposed to the reason why she has a fucking job. Was that bitchy? That sounded bitchy. And entitled. It's probably a good thing I've kept it to myself, then, isn't it?

"Oh, do you have your DD214, then? So I can verify your eligibility to receive care here?"

My blood pressure is rising. If this keeps up, I'm going to be on blood thinners before I'm thirty. "Ma'am, you are the fifth person I've talked to this month. Every single time, I get asked for my discharge paperwork and every single time, they tell me I won't have to provide it again. So please, at what point are you going to update the system so that my service has been verified and I can start getting treatment?"

My words are tight. Annoyed.

I'm reaching the end of my patience. Again. Which doesn't get me any closer to a refilled prescription. Along with maybe getting a referral to a counselor who isn't a complete fucking lunatic like the last one I paid for out of pocket.

Her expression doesn't budge. "Do you have your discharge paperwork or not?"

I hand the paperwork over and hope my expression is blank enough that she can't read the blazing *fuck you* that's flashing over my head.

"And why are you here today?"

Same questions. Different person. End result? Me not getting an appointment. Again. "I need some referrals. An annual well-woman exam. And I'm seeking to get reevaluation of my medical records to tie certain conditions to military service in combat and to get my characterization of service changed."

It's a dirty little secret that unless you have an honorable discharge, the VA gets even more complicated than it already is.

And my characterization of service was not honorable. So there's that.

I might as well go rob a bank.

She frowns and looks down at my paperwork. "There's nothing here that says you were in combat. Or that you're entitled to services at the VA."

I hand her two sets of orders that deploy me and redeploy me to Iraq. "I was stationed at Taji, both times. I ran more than three hundred combat logistics patrols in my two tours. I am a combat veteran and therefore eligible for treatment at the VA."

She shakes her head and hands all the paperwork back to me. "You're going to need to provide verification of combat exposure before we can consider any reevaluation. This discharge paperwork says you weren't honorably discharged. I'm not sure we can help you."

I can feel the enamel chipping off my teeth. "And what does

that verification need to look like? Because I've got my combat tour award, the citation for the Purple Heart, the Bronze Star with Valor, and a letter from my former battalion commander, all verifying that yes, I served in actual fucking combat on these two tours."

She doesn't flinch at my profanity. I suppose she's probably used to it. "Let me make copies and run them through our review process. I'll call you when your case is decided."

My hands are shaking. I bunch my fists and hide them behind the counter. I won't give in to the frustrated rage. I won't. "I'm out of my sleep medication. Is there any way I can be seen while we're waiting for this to be adjudicated?"

"I'm sorry. Until we've verified that you're eligible to receive care, you're going to have to wait like everyone else."

You ever have that moment when you feel like you've been assigned to that waiting room in *Beetlejuice*? And you're stuck for eternity sitting between a dude with a shrunken head and the headhunter who did it to him?

That's how I feel, standing in the lobby of the VA, trying to convince this woman that yeah, I'm a veteran, too.

This entire organization is the biggest lie. It's a fucking fraud.

I'm trying really hard not to be bitter that the medical treatment I need is being arbitrarily denied on the whims of a bureaucrat who decides who gets to see a doctor or who gets moved onto the eternal waiting list.

That's what they should call it. The Eternal Waiting List to Hell.

But none of that bitterness gets me treated. None of it changes the fact that I got the shit blown out of me, among other things, and I can't get fixed. I've been biding my time, treading water, through legal and other means that we won't talk about, hoping that at some point I'll get seen by a real doctor.

"Could you step to one side so I can get to the gentleman behind you?" she says after a moment when I refuse to move.

"I'm not finished, ma'am," I say tightly. "If we assume that eventually, I will be deemed eligible to receive care, is this VA even capable of providing the services I need?"

She blinks, unfazed by my tone. "It's not my job to engage in hypotheticals."

I can feel it: the need for a drink. The burning grit behind my eyes telling me to try and sleep even though I know I won't be able to. I'm not even fighting it anymore. I gave that up a long time ago.

I leave the VA, barely managing to remain polite, and move out smartly. It's definitely time to start burying the day in a coffee laced with Baileys and vodka.

Again.

11

Kelsey

Walking into the classroom is like colliding with a physical wall of sound and emotion as I push open the door. The alcohol is dimming the fatigue and making the whole scene I just walked in on look somewhat ridiculous.

Maybe it helps that I finished that Baileys on the bus ride back to campus but I'm not the least bit alarmed at the cadets squaring off in the classroom. It'll make class more interesting at least.

Hopefully not interesting enough for the campus police to be called but you never know.

Ryan is carrying on about something tangentially related to the First Amendment and Jovi looks like she's ready to stab someone. Veer, who is usually in competition with me to see who can say the least, is apparently finally in the fray.

I drop my book onto the table with a bang and the entire classroom goes silent.

"Oh good, you're done," I say with a smile.

I'm no longer irritated about the shit show at the VA. I can't bring myself to care about that right now. I'm not drunk but the alcohol has dulled the anger.

Plus, I'm not an asshole. I'm not going to take it out on them. The door opens behind me and I'm hit with a sense of warmth against my back. Deacon walks in, the heat from his body brushing up against mine as he moves around me to his usual position.

"Who wants to *calmly* tell me what this argument is about?"

Veer raises his hand. His jaw is set and I can practically see the pulse beating off his skin. "Ryan made a comment about people who protest during the national anthem, that they should leave the country. I strongly objected."

I fight the urge to smile at how disgruntled he sounds. It's a nice change from the anger I've been nursing since I left the VA. This is much more controllable. "What is it that got you so fired up that you finally broke your rule against participating in the discussions?"

He frowns. "I don't have a rule. But when you have someone dominating the conversation, it's best to preserve oxygen."

I almost smile. That was a pretty good backhanded slap at Ryan. To be honest, Ryan has a lot of good points but he never bothers to just be quiet and let someone else get a word in edgewise. "Okay, but I find a generally good strategy is to figure out why something pissed you off before you just start spouting off. So take a minute and reflect, then explain why his comment got you so wound up."

It's moments like these that I miss the Army. I was only a junior NCO but damn it, I miss leading soldiers sometimes.

Ryan interjects and I can physically see everyone in the room suck in a collective breath. "I just don't see how you can live in this country and protest everything it's given you. If you don't like it, then leave it to the rest of us who appreciate the freedoms."

Veer opens his mouth to speak but I hold up one hand, stopping him. "Ryan, what's the oath you take when you commission?"

He frowns. "The oath?"

"Yeah, the actual text of it. Have you read it?"

He types something into his laptop and pauses, his eyes moving over the screen I cannot see. "So?"

I glance over at Deacon, who's watching the exchange quietly. "Read it for us."

"I, state your name, having been appointed in the grade of second lieutenant in the Army of the United States, do solemnly swear, to support and defend the Constitution of the United States, against all enemies foreign and domestic."

"You can stop there," Deacon says. He leans forward. "Why do you think she had you read that?"

Jovi raises her hand. "Because we don't get to say what rights are enforceable or not. We just do our job."

I nod slowly. This is not the conversation I expected to have today—not at all—but to hell with it. Let's see where this goes. "Ryan, why does this get you so fired up?"

"Because it's bullshit. Athletes should not be protesting the nation that enables them to earn millions of dollars. They're not political figures. They play sports for a living."

"You didn't answer the question. Why does this get you so angry?"

The pen cap he's flicking on and off rapidly screeches to a halt. He stares at me for a long moment, saying nothing.

"Think about it. You're here, on one of the wealthiest college campuses in the country, and you're getting pissed off about something that has no effect on your daily life," I say quietly. "Why?"

The cap starts to flick again. "It's not right."

Deacon sets his notebook on the desk in front of him and sinks into his chair, leaning back casually. "When I first came back from my first deployment, I'd get super pissed really easily. I remember I was standing in line at the grocery store and some woman was complaining about the long wait time." His gaze never wavers from Ryan's face. "I didn't say anything. But I was livid. How dare she be pissed about something so trivial?"

I nod and finally sit in my normal chair at the end of the table. I love listening to his voice and right then, it's so fucking smooth and calm. "I had a similar reaction for a while. Stupid things would set me off."

Veer is picking at his watch. "What does being irritated post-deployment have to do with some dumbass comment about who gets the right to protest in America?"

I hold my hand up to keep Ryan from jumping in. "Because leadership isn't about scoring points. When you get angry, no one is listening to you anymore. You lose credibility. So you can get angry. Or you can stay calm and figure out a better way around the obstacle that your emotions just erected." I glance between Veer and Ryan. "No one is perfect. But especially in today's environment, you have to be able to lead all of your soldiers, not just the ones you agree with. You call someone a dumbass and, well, it's a pretty safe bet you're not leading them anywhere any time soon."

I swallow and flip open my notebook, uncomfortable that all eyes are on me. Deacon clears his throat and leans forward. "So. Reactions to today's reading?"

I look up as Ryan starts talking about the insurgency in Syria. I don't hear what he's saying. Sitting there, gaze locked with Deacon's, I'm reminded of all the ways things used to be good between us.

And wishing intently that it wasn't something as mild as fear keeping us apart.

It would be easy, so easy to fall into step with him after class. To walk with him to wherever he would lead. And slip into the dark comfort of his touch.

Deacon

"YOU HANDLED CLASS BRILLIANTLY TODAY, you know."

Kelsey isn't leaving class as fast as she normally does. Something happened today in class. A connection. A moment. I'm not sure but something changed when she started taking charge of the argument between Ryan and Veer and Jovi.

It was like she was Sergeant Ryder again and was once more in her own element. It was a thing to behold watching her with her eyes bright, her shoulders back, her voice confident and sure.

Watching her control the room, watching her connect with each of those future officers, I was both aroused and enthralled. Not necessarily in that order.

Reminded of the confidence she'd lost somewhere in the desert sands. I've always been attracted to her strength. She had a way about her in uniform that was always just a little out of sync with everyone around us. She was energy.

A flame.

And I was drawn to her, despite every rule and norm that said it was a bad idea to get involved with someone at work.

She lets me fall into step next to her. I offer up a prayer of thanks for that simple milestone.

"Thanks. I'm just glad I didn't blow my stack at some of the comments myself."

"Yeah, Mr. First Amendment Ryan has some growing up to do."

She grins and it strikes me how much I miss seeing her smile. She doesn't do it nearly enough anymore. I didn't even notice until right then. "Don't we all?"

I make a noise, not missing the fact that she hasn't bailed on me yet. She's still walking with me.

That's a hell of a lot more progress than I'm used to with her. "Do you feel like an old man in there?"

She laughs and runs her hands over her breasts even as I realize what I've said.

"Nope, haven't felt like an old man recently." She elbows me gently. "But I get what you mean. I feel like...I feel ancient next to them."

I stop then and look at her. "Have you been drinking?" I can't say what's made me ask.

I fully expect her to tell me to go fuck myself but she doesn't. "You ever have one of those days where you have to give up fighting because being pissed about it isn't going to fix a damn thing?" She glances over my shoulder, avoiding my gaze. "I may have had a stiff one before class. I needed to relax."

It hurts then, thinking that this brief moment between us is because she's not fighting something. Warning bells go off in my head.

"Do you think things like this matter?" I step close, into her space. Needing to be closer. Afraid to let her go.

"Matter how?"

"Like, do you think any of them actually walked out of there thinking about things differently?"

She shifts her bag to her opposite shoulder. I notice the stiffness of her movement and the way she rolls her shoulder after the bag is transferred.

"I don't know." She stops walking and looks up at me. "But isn't that why we do any of this? We have to hope that what we do matters, right?"

Her question stops me in my tracks. "That isn't what you said when you first got back," I say quietly. "You said nothing we did matters. That everything was meaningless suffering." I tip my chin, studying this woman who draws me to her with such fierce need. "What's changed?"

She looks away, nudging dirt with her shoe. "I don't know. A lot of things."

It's an opening, a fleeting hope that maybe other things have changed, too.

But fear and history are a potent combination.

"What things?" Because I cannot help myself, I step closer to her. To the need to feel the heat from her body, the desire to capture her strength. The pure need to feel her body against mine just once more.

Her lips are there, just there. They part a little, the tiniest breadth of space, then close.

The barest distance separates us. If she offered the slightest encouragement, I could span the gap, brushing my lips against hers. Tasting her again after the longest drought.

"It's complicated," she whispers.

"Isn't it always?"

I move then, slowly, achingly slow, to slide a lock of hair out of her face. My thumb brushes her cheek. A current arcs between us, a living pulse of energy that binds me to her.

She doesn't look away. The noise of the crowd disappears around us, leaving only her and only me, standing impossibly close, immensely far apart.

My entire world tips beneath my feet when she doesn't move, doesn't pull away.

"Kels." Her name is a whisper. A plea.

A promise.

To do better this time. To somehow make things from the past right again or to beg her forgiveness for not being there when she needed me most.

Something shifts. I couldn't tell you what it is but for a moment, nothing more, she tips her cheek, nuzzling against my knuckles. She is smooth and soft and a thousand points of heat flash through my entire body from that single connection.

"I miss this," she whispers. But then she closes her eyes and the connection ends. She takes a single step backward.

"I spent a lot of time picking myself back up after...everything," she tells me. Her throat moves as she swallows, her neck tight and tense. She cups my cheek. "And as much as I wish it were otherwise, anything I may want to do with you could put everything I've built at risk." Her fingers slip away, my skin cool now where she touched. "I'm sorry."

She takes another step backward, and then she's gone, leaving me alone.

Empty.

Just like always.

12

Deacon

MY BODY IS HUMMING with latent energy as I climb the narrow staircase to Professor Blake's office. I can still feel the heat from Kelsey's body, the brush of her hair against my skin.

For an academic space, Blake's office isn't nearly as intimidating as it could be. Oh, don't get me wrong: she's got a hundred-pound brain and she's scary smart, but she's not an asshole about it. She doesn't have to talk down to you to make herself feel better. That's one of the things I love about her.

And her office is homey and welcoming. She's got an old sable leather couch that you can just kind of sink into and she's got these lamps that look like something from a museum with glass shades that reflect soft light throughout the room.

"If I worked here, I'd be asleep all the time," I say from the doorway.

She looks up from her MacBook and closes the lid with a smile. "You, young man, are late."

I frown. "No, I'm not. Our meeting was at ten, wasn't it?"

"And I changed it to nine thirty last week. And you responded to the email so don't try to play the 'I didn't know' card."

I pull out my phone, searching for her message...and there it is. "Shit, I'm sorry, ma'am. I didn't change it on my calendar."

She lifts one brow as she comes around her desk. "You're lucky my other engagement canceled; otherwise you'd be staring at a closed door."

"Let's be grateful for small miracles." She walks around her desk and pulls me into a warm hug.

I close my eyes and hold her close for a moment, as long as I can before I have to break free. It's hard for me to see her as an academic. She's so much more than that. A mentor. A friend. A connection to another life that I'll never give up.

There are limits to how connected I can be to that life. And some days, I walk a tighter edge than others. I'm walking that edge today.

Having Kelsey close enough to touch and having to let her go again...it's enough to break a man.

"How was class today?" she asks, circling her desk to sit across from me in the polished black wooden chair in front of it.

"Good, I think. We had to navigate some pretty tense politics today so that was interesting."

"Oh, really?"

"Yeah. Instead of discussing the role of women in the Kurdish forces, we ended up having a discussion about the Constitution."

She taps her pen against her thigh. "Interesting. Do you think it was helpful?"

"I don't know. I guess I'm questioning whether you can really change some people's minds once they've staked out a position."

"Well, if we don't believe we can change people's minds, then what are we doing here at an institution of higher learning?"

I release a tight breath. It's such an obvious thing. So simple. So easily overlooked. "Good point."

"So. Your thesis. What's this idea you have?"

My lungs are still tight. It's amazing how vulnerable you have to be to talk about a research proposal. Like the whole world is just waiting to laugh at you. "There's not much published work done on the current generation of veterans and their getting treatment at the VA. I was thinking I could do some qualitative research and look at their experiences. What they're trying to be seen for. What challenges they're having. That sort of thing?"

She tips her chin at me. "What's your research question?"

I pull out my notebook and hope that what I'm about to read doesn't make me sound like an undereducated asshole. "How do younger veterans see themselves and how does that impact their willingness or ability to use traditional veterans' services."

She nods slowly. "That's very good."

"Really? Because I haven't slept in about a day and I was pretty well convinced it was total shit."

She laughs. "No, it's pretty good. I think we need to do some refinement but it's a good place to start. Have you thought about finding research participants?"

"Other than recruiting out of The Pint? Not really."

"We can work on that." She pauses and you can almost see the wheels in her brain turning. "As you write, as you interview people, I want you to focus on capturing the authenticity of what your subjects say. I want your readers to hear the commonality of shared experiences you have with other veterans. Regardless of where they're from."

I look down at my coffee cup. "Isn't that a bit grand? I mean, no one is going to read this but you."

"Not necessarily. After we talk about your thesis, I want to start working on a veterans' panel on campus. To build on the initiative with the ROTC program and link more of our students to the veterans around them. Think of it as a step toward building the bridge over the military–civilian divide."

I frown down at my notes. "Don't most students just want to yell at us about being tools of the evil hegemonic empire?"

"'Evil hegemony' is so 2010," she says, leaning back in the gleaming wood chair. "'Storm Troopers of the New World Order' is the current flavor."

"Wait, isn't that the right-wing term?"

"Funny; you go far enough left, you encounter the right." She smiles patiently. "In all seriousness, I think there's something compelling about your shared experiences that draws you all together, long after you've left the military service. You can tie this to your thesis as well. Talking about how you all navigate after you leave the service offers an interesting perspective for the students to hear from you." She pauses, long enough for me to look up at her. "I think you need to ask Kelsey to participate in your research."

I try to keep my expression neutral even as my stomach tightens in knots. "I can ask her." But I must look doubtful.

"She might be more open than you think. I also recommend you talk to Caleb Hollis as well. I think he has a very interesting story. And I think you have more in common than you realize."

I suddenly very much need something to do with my hands. I know exactly how much Kelsey and I have in common. "Do you really want me talking to Caleb for this? He's pretty much every bad veteran stereotype we can come up with." I try not to choke on my hypocrisy. But at least mine is deeply hidden.

The best hypocrisies often are.

"His is a victory that just hasn't happened yet."

"And the rest of us? You want us to talk about the things we did to kill the boredom on deployments?"

She laughs and it surprises me. "No, I do not want you to talk about that. I'm not sure our students would find that nearly as funny as all of you would." She pauses. "I want you to talk about coming home. About how you learned who you were after you took off the uniform. And about whether that journey impacted your willingness to use the VA."

I grin. "You sure I can't just talk about how I taped the cover of a *Hustler* onto a *Playgirl* for my squad leader? It would be significantly less traumatic than unpacking all the taking-the-uniform-off stuff."

She shakes her head, still smiling. "I'll pass, thanks. But I think if you can find some inspiring stories from downrange, stories that draw you all together into a common narrative, your research could have a significant impact."

"Impact on what?"

Her smile is mysterious in only the way a professor's can be. "I'm working on a few things that I'm hoping to tie your work with the cadets and your research to. I want to expand our veterans' programs here on campus, and to do that I need to bring in donors." She holds up her hand. "Don't give me that look. Our donors have been very generous in their support of veterans' programs here on campus and in the community."

"Too bad they can't be generous and fix the VA," I mumble.

"Several of them are working on it. It's complicated."

"Isn't everything?"

I'm not really sure how Kelsey will react when I ask her to participate. Even if she agrees, which is definitely not guaranteed, I wonder how she'll feel about these questions.

But I'll ask. Because Professor Blake's asked me to. And she's one of the few people on campus genuinely committed to helping bridge the gap. And she's not asking us about *Call of Duty* or PTSD, so I suppose that's progress.

Isn't it?

Kelsey

HOW DO you sleep when you're out of Xanax?

I wonder if my Internet pen pal will answer me. I have to admit this is the strangest thing I've ever done, but after my shit show inability to get an appointment at the VA and the disaster in class, I'm grasping at straws, trying to keep things in perspective.

To keep calm and all that.

It doesn't help that Deacon knocked my world off axis right after class. I needed space and time to move everything back into the correct box. But instead, I ended up standing far too close to him on the quad. I could have moved. Or I could have slid my mouth against his and tasted the pleasure of his touch once more.

The more time I spend around him, the more I'm reminded of everything we lost downrange. And fear, when mixed with arousal, is a dangerous thing.

I have a few hours before my shift and no more cadets or class today. Hours before I have to face the end of my shift and the emptiness of my apartment.

I head to 1984 to do some research or browse aimlessly or do anything to keep my mind off the approaching darkness.

Maybe I'll be able to find some books on sleeping without medication, since I'm clearly not going to be able to get any new prescriptions any time soon.

It's absurd that the insurance I have through school won't treat issues that should be covered by the VA. Why didn't I lie on my intake forms and tell them I wasn't eligible for treatment at the VA? Then I wouldn't be having this problem. They'd give me a nice little prescription for Xanax or Ambien and I'd be sleeping like a champ and walking back from the edge of madness.

I love this bookstore. The moment I walk through the doors, I'm hit with the smell of incense and warmth. And there are more than just mainstream books here. There's a fantastic international section that carries books by Indian authors on yoga. It's refreshing to study different perspectives as Indian scholars work on reclaiming yoga from colonialism, but it takes work to find indigenous Indian writing on the subject. Everything that comes up when you Google it is usually by some generic perky blond woman who means well but often just repeats harmful inaccuracies about the Hindu traditions.

I've done my own share of harmful things as I've gotten deeper into my practice. I'm sure I will again. But I'm working on doing better.

"Can I help you find something?"

I look up at the clerk, who looks more like an escapee from Woodstock than a bookworm. She has a head full of white-blond, twisted dreadlocks and bright, happy eyes behind her horn-rimmed glasses. She smells faintly of patchouli and roses. She feels...friendly, and there's something about her that puts me instantly at ease.

"I'm looking for books on insomnia." It's an easy admission. It doesn't involve anything deeper than that.

"You're in luck. We just got in two new books on that."

I frown, mildly surprised. "Really? Hot topic these days?"

Before I started yoga, I would have considered that a coincidence. Now? Now I'm always amazed at how the universe works. I don't believe in coincidence anymore.

I don't necessarily believe that everything happens for a reason because that...that's a level of cruelty that I can't accept. But I do choose to believe that I'm where I need to be and that the universe has placed certain things in my path.

"With all the politics surrounding insurance lately, we've had a lot of increased interest in nonmedical treatments for all kinds of things."

I swallow, wishing that comment didn't hit as close to home as it did. "Yeah, well, I can relate to that."

She motions for me to follow her to a nearby shelf, and pulls a book from it to show me. "There's some really interesting stuff out there. This one is published by a medical doctor out of Colorado. I'm not sure how you feel about marijuana but she's claiming that she's got several patients who have benefited greatly from it."

The part of me that will always be in the Army jerks away from the idea of smoking pot. But the part of me that remembers I'm a civilian now and really needs to fucking sleep is intrigued. "Really?"

"She's got some other possible treatments. Chamomile tea is popular if you're worried about getting arrested for trying to score some weed."

I laugh at her statement. "That's a really sad commentary on so many things."

She smiles and it is warm and welcoming as she chooses another book. "It really is. Check these out and if they don't work for you, I'll see what else I can figure out. Lack of sleep is not something to ignore."

She hands me the books and I can't miss the flash of a pearl-white scar slashing down her forearm and disappearing beneath her brown leather wristband.

She catches me staring. "It was a long time ago," she says quietly. "But trust me when I tell you that sleep is important."

I swallow hard as she moves away to help another customer. I buy a cup of coffee and sit in a corner, beneath some wind chimes decorated with moons and stars swaying gently from little silver strings.

1984 is an oddly comforting space. The music is something New Age-y and the warm scent of sandalwood mixed with coffee and tea fills the air. There's a quiet buzz. Something magical, if I believed in magic.

I may not believe in magic but the connection of us to each other...yeah, yoga has taught me a lot about just accepting the things that happen for what they are.

I smile to myself, remembering an argument I had with one of my squad leaders back in Iraq, about whether or not there was a God. She'd been so certain in her faith. So, sure.

Looking back, I envy her faith. It must be so comforting to believe that every bad thing in this world happens for a reason. That there's ultimately some good that will come of it.

I wish I had her faith. I wish I could have that certainty. I don't.

It's not that I don't believe in God. It's that I don't know what kind of God would allow this much evil in the world.

I shove those thoughts away and crack open the spine of the first book. The jacket is a brilliant white, with a pot leaf sitting in a mason jar resting on a concrete countertop. *The Skeptic's Guide to Medical Marijuana.*

"Well, at least she's not promising miracles," I mumble.

Introduction: Why You Should Be Skeptical of this Book.

I smile. Parker would have a field day with this opening as a marketing plan. It's kind of brilliant. Telling people why they shouldn't buy the book is probably the fastest way to get someone to buy what you're selling.

My phone vibrates and I look down at an email from my Internet pen pal.

I don't use Xanax. It gives me nightmares.

It's odd the way his stupid email makes me feel. Connected. Like there's someone out there who might not judge me as harshly as I judge myself.

How do you sleep then?

His response is pretty damn fast, seeing how it has to hit the Craigslist servers then come back to me.

There's no way this doesn't make me sound like a weirdo—and I know your ad specifically stated no weirdos—but sex helps a lot.

I grin, thinking about Deacon and his tendency to go home with women from the bar. Someone should write *that* self-help book: *Fuck Your Way Out of Insomnia.* I don't think they'd stock that one on the shelves at the local Barnes & Noble.

Don't you worry about catching something? Or stumbling into the next Fatal Attraction?

I flip back to the pot book, needing something to fill the time before his next response.

One, I'm selective. I only sleep with people who know what they're signing up for: a one-night stand of mind-blowing sex. Two, I always, always wear protection.

Heat traces through my veins at his words. Mind-blowing sex sounds pretty amazing. It's been far too long since I've had my hair blown back.

Well, I'm not having sex with you. I don't sleep with strangers.

If I tell you my name, then we're not strangers.

I shake my head at this last note.

How do you know you'd even want to sleep with me? What if I'm hideous and deformed and covered in tattooed scars?

A very legitimate question. Some men don't like women who have tattoos. Or scars.

This time, he doesn't respond immediately and I'm once more afraid I've run him off.

But when he does, his comment thaws a little bit of the ice around my heart.

Everyone deserves to have someone to hold them at night.

13

Kelsey

"YOU LOOK GRUMPY."

I look up from the bar towels I'm folding. Parker is pecking at her laptop, looking nonchalant, like she's not even paying attention to what she's typing. Probably designing the next social media campaign for The Pint. She's a damn genius on that thing.

I envy her brain in more ways than one.

I bet hers doesn't keep her up at night replaying a nightmare that's way past its expiration date.

"I'm just tired." I slap a towel down on the counter. "I take that back. I tried to have an appointment at the VA today. But part of the wonders of modern bureaucracy is that it's unable to deal with things that it's not designed to deal with."

"Like women veterans?"

"Like women veterans. I mean, it's not like our grandmothers weren't kicking ass in WWII or anything. But they still can't seem to get it into their heads that there are a lot of us out there."

"You weren't seen?"

"Nope."

"So go to a different doc."

I reach for my drink. It's all so simple in Parker's world, where you can throw money at a problem and solve just about anything. "It's not that simple. I have to be seen at the VA for...service connected stuff." I don't want to go into what service connected stuff.

Not interested in tearing the Band-Aid off that wound tonight.

"Don't you have insurance through school?"

"Let's just say the first time I asked for a referral to get a refill on some medications they sent me to a geriatric urologist. That was fun, trying to get the insurance company to acknowledge that billing error."

"Wait, they charged you for the visit that never happened?" She seems honestly shocked.

It's cute.

People like Parker used to annoy me. People who thought the world was a good and just place and that some people were just misunderstood. I used to resent people like her and think they were naive for not seeing the world the way it really is.

But then it dawned on me that her world really is like that. She really lives in a world that is safe from violence, safe from hunger. Safe from all the terrible things lurking at the edges of civilized life.

Now, I'm glad that world exists for her. I'm grateful that people like her get to live in a world that's a little better than the one I spent too much time in.

I mean, that's why I enlisted, right? To defend her world so she didn't have to?

And wow, am I feeling melancholy this evening.

"Until I managed to point out their error. That was at the first VA I went to back in Texas. I've been fighting with the new one since I moved here. So yeah, just because I have insurance doesn't mean I can go to any doc I want."

"I had no idea how complicated this all was. Is."

"You should try to get a pap smear at the VA. That's a new level of hell right there."

She opens her mouth to say something then closes it, opting to say nothing. My deflection has paid off, so at least I've got that going for me. I pick up my phone, considering my alternatives while I'm still thinking clearly.

It's amazing how desperation for a decent night of sleep will make you consider doing Very Stupid Things.

And my definition of "Very Stupid Things" is somewhere between "Things You Go to Jail For" and "Things You Don't Want Your Mom to Find Out About."

Scrolling through anonymous social media looking for a place to score some Xanax is up there on the list of things I don't want to get caught doing but am seriously considering before my brain starts to eat itself from lack of sleep. It would probably be easier to try and find weed on campus than Xanax. Might get me less jail time, too, if I get caught.

I'm not really sure what's going to happen tonight when I try to go to sleep. Or how I'm going to get through until this shit with the docs gets sorted out and I get another appointment.

The last time I ran out of sleeping pills, I drank so hard my liver packed her shit and went to live with my Aunt Rachel in a dry county in Kansas.

No really. I ended up in the hospital because my liver decided to go on strike and get an infection. That was fun.

It turns out, having a liver infection that lands you in intensive care isn't nearly enough to get you to stop drinking when you can't sleep. Neither is yoga. Drunk yoga is surprisingly transcendent, but there are risks associated with falling on your face because your balance is shit.

And I don't really get drunk anymore.

Guess my liver decided to toughen up. It's a small victory.

I'm still thinking about that book on medical marijuana. I'm not sure how I feel about it. And it's just as illegal as scoring some black market Xanax.

Eli walks in, talking to someone I don't recognize. I catch Parker watching them. Not them. Eli. She's completely drawn into his orbit. Just like all of us. "Hey, what's the deal with that guy?" I ask.

Parker glances over. "Sam? He's moving to the area. He owns a barbecue joint down at Fort Bragg and I guess he's opening one up here or something."

I lift both eyebrows. "Is all that on his business card?"

She smiles and laughs. "No. Eli was talking to him last night up in the apartment until long after I fell asleep."

"Really?"

She frowns. "Which part of that is surprising? The guys sitting up drinking part or the me falling asleep part?"

"The part where Eli leaves you sleeping to drink with his buddies." It's my turn to frown. "Never mind. I forgot who I was talking about."

Her smile is warm as she watches him. I guess that's what love looks like? "Yeah, he's kind of good like that."

She doesn't have to say it. It's one of the things we all admire about Eli.

Eli provides a kind of structure. A place to call home that feels...familiar. I used to have such a negative feeling toward West Point officers. The only ones I'd met were giant dickbags. But Eli, he managed to convince me that all officers aren't the devil. Which is good since he's my boss and I would like to keep working, as I'm somewhat partial to food and housing.

Evening bar traffic is starting to pick up and one of my least favorite people in the world walks in. Apparently, I've made a noise because Parker looks behind her at Caleb then back at me.

"You don't like him?"

"Cheers, Captain Obvious." I tip a glass in her direction.

"Why?"

"Oh, where to begin... I don't like that he fights all the time. He drinks way too much and he talks about what a badass he is." I toss back a shot. "He's what we call Full Hoah. As in 'you never go full hoah.'" She looks confused and I remember that she hasn't served in the military and we have a unique way of talking about folks. "A good rule of thumb is if a guy has done something he won't generally talk about it, and Caleb won't shut the fuck up."

"Ah. That makes sense." Parker pauses, looking down at her laptop. "Eli worries about him," she says after a moment.

"I know he does and that's why we all love him." I pour another drink. "But his loyalty is going to bite him in the ass some day. He should be more careful where he leaves it lying around. Guys like Caleb end up hurting everyone around them."

I turn away, not wanting to deal with Caleb's shit today and hoping he'll pretend I'm not here. I don't want to listen to his bullshit war stories or be the one who has to pour him drinks all night long.

Of course, he doesn't take the hint. Because my life is a goddamned reality tv show with orchestrated moments of friction perfectly timed to fuck up the rest of my night.

Deacon

It's hard to miss Kelsey's reaction to Caleb when he walks in. I slide behind the bar, leaning into her briefly. "I've got him."

She shoots me a quick look of gratitude as she takes another customer.

After this morning's class, I don't have the courage to ask her about letting me interview her. I know her story from downrange.

I'm pretty sure she's not going to just open up and tell me how wonderful life is as a civilian. Some of us have rougher transitions than others.

I do need to figure out who I'm going to interview but that can wait until I get through the night without nailing Caleb's ass to the wall.

"What's on the menu for creative drinks tonight?" Caleb leans on the bar like we've just completed the Bataan Death March together or something.

"What are you in the mood for?" I ask him, trying to keep things easy and praying that he doesn't start in on the turn-the-Middle East-into-a-parking-lot bullshit.

I'd rather hear about his latest obsession with CrossFit. Or get a root canal.

He's that level of fun.

"How about a rum and Coke?"

"Sure thing."

"So, did you get a chance to talk to your professor about your research? What did he think?" he asks as I slide his drink across the bar and snag his credit card to open up a tab for him.

"Yeah. She thought it was a great idea. Now I just have to figure out who I can talk to about their adjustment to being a civilian."

He frowns as he takes a long pull off his drink. "I thought you were going to interview people about the VA."

"I am. But she wants me to get into people's sense of identity, too."

He swirls his drink. "What does that even mean?"

"It means how you see yourself. Like if I asked you to describe who you were, what would you say?"

He swallows another long pull off his drink and motions for another. "I don't know how to answer that question," he says quietly. He's drinking tonight but at this point, he's usually five or six drinks in. I have the impression he's only just getting started.

I watch him as I mix his drink. "Are you okay?"

On a normal day, I never would ask. But something isn't right about him tonight. Combined with our random meeting in the library, something isn't sitting right with me.

"Yeah. Like I mentioned the other day, I'm just spending some quality time reflecting on my life choices."

"What does that mean?" I repeat.

He shrugs and turns away, leaving me to wonder some more about what's going on with him. I don't want to care. But I find myself curious. And I try to remind myself that not everyone has all their shit together.

Maybe there's a hell of a lot more depth to the Caleb story than I thought.

But I keep the peace mostly for Eli's sake and the fact that I don't want The Pint to devolve to the level of drama reserved for groups of middle-aged men in bass fishing clubs arguing about who stole whose fishing hole.

There's no place for that kind of drama here.

I glance up as a pair of business school bros walk in, sporting Brooks Brothers button downs and Vineyard Vines flip flops. And then I do a double take at one of them.

Holy. Shit.

I grin as a wave of memory rushes out of the past. Sam Rossi. I knew Sam Rossi back in the Cav on my second tour in Iraq when he was a hell of a lot piss and vinegar, especially for a logistics guy. He was one of our platoon leaders in our forward support company and damn if he didn't move mountains to make sure we got the bullets and bandages we needed when we were in the thick of it.

He meets me halfway between the bar and before I know it, I'm pulled into a brutal and overzealous man-hug. "Holy shit, when did you get into town?" I ask when I can breathe again.

"Couple of weeks ago. Sort of." Sam grins at Caleb and grips his outstretched hand. It's the first time I've seen Caleb interact with someone without it turning into a dick measuring contest. "Still surfing unicorn porn websites?"

Caleb grins back and flips him off. The utter normalcy of the exchange – for soldiers that is – isn't lost on me. "No, that browsing history was destroyed when the servers got blown up in that mortar strike."

Sam laughs quietly. "Some things never change."

"What are you doing here?" I ask Sam.

"Trying to expand my empire." Sam leans on the bar, his dark skin split into a wide grin. God but he used to get us in so much trouble with the commander because he was such a smart-ass. "Right now, I'm trying to close up a couple of deals there so I can relocate here permanently."

"Doing what?"

"Well, real estate, for one. But I'm also trying to hire a manager for a restaurant I just bailed out."

Caleb perks up. "Yeah? I could probably help you with that," he says. "I've been doing some managerial consulting in business school."

"That would be awesome. I'm definitely outside the loop here in Durham so I could use the help." He hands Caleb a simple business card. Damn this guy has his shit together.

"Business cards? You always were mostly civilian," I say. He always wore his hair too long and he was one of those guys who had a five o'clock shadow before nine a.m. His mere existence sent first sergeants everywhere into apoplectic fits.

"Yeah, well, looking like one and feeling like one are two different things," Sam mutters.

Caleb tips his glass in Sam's direction. "Tell me about it."

"So, what brings you to The Pint if you're between states?" I ask. Still, it's good to see another familiar face. And, it's a nice change to see Caleb not being a self-aggrandizing dick for once.

Guess miracles can happen after all.

"Just out for a night. Thought I'd finally try my hand at socializing." Sam rubs the back of his neck. He frowns as he pulls his phone out as it vibrates in his palm. "A night that is apparently going to be cut dramatically short. Sorry. One of my distributors. Back in a few."

Sam steps out of the bar and Caleb takes a long pull off his drink then shifts around on his bar stool, drinking quietly for once. I've never seen him like this and it's disconcerting how dramatic and sudden the change is. I find myself curious about what the hell's happened to the asshole I used to hate.

I don't want to care. I don't want to know anything about him other than that he's not causing problems at The Pint.

But in that moment, his sudden shift guts me with an unexpected sadness that rises up out of the abyss, reminding me of the ties that bind us together, whether we want them to or not.

I glance over at Kelsey, who's smiling and flirting with a customer as she pours their whiskey and mixes another drink.

Wishing that the ties that bound us were tighter.

14

Kelsey

"I DO NOT GET PAID ENOUGH to deal with this shit."

I grin over at the pure disgruntlement in Deacon's voice as he taps the iPad violently to ring up the latest tab.

"What's happened?"

He doesn't want to tell me. I can see it written all over his face. But he's going to. Because he's Deacon and no matter how much we may both try to pretend there's nothing but rampant hostility between us, once upon a time, we used to be friends.

It hits me suddenly, violently, like a wave of light and heat: I want that again.

Maybe I just need to sleep. Maybe I'm starting to hallucinate feelings instead of little dancing unicorns.

But in that moment, the sudden want crashes over me.

He glances over at me and sighs heavily. "Promise you won't laugh?"

"I won't," I promise.

Deacon makes a face. "Guy just hit on me. Asked me to dinner at The Durham Hotel."

"You should be flattered." I'm trying really hard not to laugh at his irritation.

It's not working.

"Yeah, well, it would have been if he'd genuinely been interested in me but he offered to buy my time for the night, if you catch my drift."

And just like that, the laugh escapes, ripping free of my best efforts to keep it contained. I slap my hand over my mouth but it's too late. "He wanted to pay you for..."

"Don't say it," he snarls. "You said you wouldn't laugh."

"Oh, that's so priceless. We should have Eli put up a sign. 'Not for sale', maybe?"

"Ha ha ha. You wouldn't think it was funny if it was you." He turns back to his customer, handing over the iPad for them to sign.

I pour another round. "What are you talking about? I get offers like that all the time. Along with random dick pics from pathetic losers who think that's the same as asking someone for coffee."

Deacon shakes his head, his lips pressed into a hard, flat line. "You're too nonchalant about that stuff. Guys should not be sending you pictures of their junk. It's fucking rude."

Because I can't help myself, I reach over and pat his cheek. I blame the lack of sleep and the alcohol mixing in my brain for the sudden courage to shatter the barriers I've kept between us.

I'm tired of fighting. So fucking tired.

His skin is warm, his stubble rough against my palm. I play it off but it burns where I touch him. "Not everyone is as chivalrous as you."

He stills beneath my touch. The world falls away, the noise from the bar suddenly distant.

It was a mistake to touch him. To dance that close to the fire.

He snags my wrist, even though he's got to be fully aware that everyone in the bar can see him.

We've done this before. Flirting behind the counter, making the customers think we're repressing violent sexual feelings for each other.

But tonight, it's not a show.

Maybe it never has been.

Maybe I've been lying to myself all along.

He lowers our hands, drawing me closer until I'm a breath from him, until I can feel the heat from his body. "I'll show you chivalry," he whispers against my mouth.

The move is stunning in its simplicity. One minute, we're putting on a show for the customers. The next, heat arcs between our bodies and mine is craving for him to touch me.

It's amazing how much my body still remembers how good we were together.

All of the good is gone, though...isn't it? Tainted and dyed in blood and waking nightmares.

There are a thousand things I want to do in this moment. Press my lips to his. Lean into his touch. Or maybe let his hands wander over my body. I don't even care that people could be watching. My body aches for him. For the way things used to be.

"You shouldn't touch," I whisper. I can feel all the eyes in the bar on us. Watching as all of my feelings for this man escape in wild abandon. "I might fall for you. And I hate falling."

I don't know what's drawn those words from my lips. I really couldn't say.

"I'll catch you," he whispers, suddenly more serious than I've seen him in a long, long time.

The moment wraps around us, luring me closer to the temptation that he represents. The risk to the carefully drawn boundaries I've had to erect to stay sane in this new world of yoga pants and lattes.

I want to take the leap.

But fear is a powerful thing.

"I've got to get a bottle from the basement." A convenient lie. I back up, searching for my escape path.

One he accepts as he releases me, saying nothing.

I slip away from the bar. Not heading into the basement, but just moving away from the bar for a moment to catch my breath and lock away the emotions that are threatening to rip free.

We tried this once before. When I first saw him back in the States. Everything was raw and wrong and ragged. The sex was different. Hotter. Less urgent. More powerful.

And then the dam broke and everything I'd been avoiding for fifteen months crashed into me.

I look over at the pictures Eli has on one of the walls. He asked all of us for pictures.

I never gave him any.

"Hey."

I look up. Deacon is there, just there. A little too close. A little too worried.

I smile sadly. "Who's watching the bar?"

"Eli. He's showing Parker how to make a martini."

I smile at the image. Parker is good at many things, but mixing drinks does not seem to be one of her strong suits. "That's probably not going to go well," I say quietly.

Deacon takes another step closer.

Something has changed tonight. I can't say what it is.

But he steps closer, until he's right there, his palm pressing against my cheek. "There are so many ways things could have been different between us."

"They can't be," I whisper. "You know that."

This is the most honest I've ever been with him.

"I wish I didn't know. I wish I could just hate you and call you terrible names."

My brain detours sharply. "What, like 'wheezing bag of dick tips'?"

He laughs quietly. "I was thinking more 'wilted cockthistle.'"

I laugh with him over our shared love of *Deadpool*. And I don't pull away. This interlude won't last. Even if I went home with him tonight, I'd run. I always do.

I'll have to leave. I'll have to face the silence of my apartment and wait for the sleep that won't come.

But here and now, I simply stand and savor the feel of his hand on my skin. Breathing into the sensation and drawing his warmth into me.

"Why is everything so complicated with us?" he whispers.

"The universe hates me." I smile sadly, savoring the absolute normalcy of this moment. "I think I must have kicked a puppy in my former life."

He chokes back a laugh, lowering his forehead to mine. "I miss you, Kels."

It's those words that have me backing away.

A stark reminder of the aching, needing, wanting truth.

I gave up on a lot more than just us in the weeks and months after our first deployment.

And so did he.

The space between us grows, until I am standing at the edge of the stairs leading into the cellar. I stop there, facing the darkness below. "It's terrifying how close to the edge we can get."

I rub my hand absently over my stomach, avoiding the scars hidden beneath the roses and lotus flowers etched into my flesh.

The scars remind me. The past happened. It's not just a memory.

Deacon is dangerous to me.

As I am to him.

And we both need to remember that.

Deacon

I SHOULDN'T HAVE FOLLOWED her into the dark but I'm glad I did. I can hear First Sarn't Sorren's voice in my head: *Let her know you're still there. That you'll always be there.*

But as much as he knows both of us, he doesn't know her like I do. That following her right now could be the wrong thing to do. That it could send her running. Again.

It was a risk, following her, but one I'm glad I took.

And if she's here, I can be near. As near as she'll let me.

My palm burns where I touched her. She's a fire, a flame I can't help but want to touch.

Eli glances over at me when I walk back behind the bar. "She okay?"

"Yeah." I shrug, trying to play it off. Eli has never dug into our history. The trust that man places in those around him is astonishing. He doesn't even Google new employees to make sure they're not secretly Internet trolls. He's got a faith in humanity that I lack.

He makes a noise and pours another drink, something with mint and grenadine and triple sec.

Caleb is talking to a girl beneath one of the low-hanging lights near the pool table. There's something simultaneously surreal and normal in watching him talk to her. Sam is hanging out, holding a beer and talking to someone who looks like they belong in a Harley Davidson commercial. Truth be told, Sam looks like that, too. Hard to picture him as a skinny, awkward, West Point cadet once upon a time.

God, but the fucking normalcy of the moment hits me hard.

I toss back a shot of whiskey, needing the burn to unlock the tension in my chest.

I glance over at Eli. "So, ah, you know how I've got to write a thesis?"

He lifts one brow and keeps mixing the drink in front of him. "That's the normal requirement for graduating, last I checked."

"So anyway. My advisor wants me to interview a bunch of veterans and see if how they transitioned to civilian life impacted whether or not they used the VA."

"Yeah? That sounds really interesting. You need me, I'm in. What questions are you going to ask?"

"Man, you're one of a kind," I say beneath my breath. Have I mentioned that I'd take a bullet for him? Because I would. "I don't know. I think I want to just get people to talk about what transitioning was like for them and work out questions from there."

I wish I'd had an officer like Eli when I was in. I might have stuck around longer than my initial enlistment years.

"Seems reasonable. I mean, I didn't really have a tough time of things but someone like Noah or Josh? Yeah, they had a hell of a time." He jerks his chin toward Caleb. "A guy like Caleb has been out longer but is still very much figuring out who he is without the uniform."

"Why do you think some of us have harder times than others?"

He slides a shot of tequila down the bar toward me. "Why was it easier for you to get out than stay in? You landed on your feet, right?"

I toss back the shot and it burns the entire path down my esophagus. "I had a rough time at first. Did a lot of bartending in New York before you called."

"Bartending doesn't exactly sound like a rough spot."

I grin. "You weren't there to see how much I was drinking."

"But you didn't become an alcoholic. You adjusted."

"Because you called and asked me to come down and Noah sealed the deal for me. And I decided to get my ass back to school and use those GI benefits Uncle Sammy promised me before he changes his mind."

Eli laughs and lifts the shot glass in mock salute. "Well, see?

So what's different about how you got to where you are and how Caleb is doing? Or how Noah and Josh did?"

I pour another drink for a customer and slide it across the bar. "Good point. Guess that's where I start, isn't it?"

"Are you going to see if Kelsey will let you interview her?"

"It's complicated." And thinking about asking her makes me think I need another drink.

"What's complicated?" Caleb has extracted himself from the woman he was talking to and sidles up to the bar.

I turn away, pretending I don't hear him. Caleb is not someone I want to interview, no matter how much Professor Blake seems to think I should.

"Where'd the girl go you were talking to?" I ask Caleb instead.

"Bathroom break. I think I may have some company tonight," he says easily.

I can't shake the feeling that something has changed with him.

And that maybe I should stop holding his past shitty behavior against him.

I RING up another customer as Kelsey reappears from the basement, carrying a bottle of Johnny Walker.

Damn me for being a judgmental prick.

It's an uncomfortable feeling. While I have personal history with Caleb being obnoxious, he's not right now...and hasn't been for a while.

Which makes me an asshole. I want the elements of my life designated, with clear lines between good and evil. People I like and people I don't. I don't want complicated emotions toward people I don't like.

I toss my towel onto the bar and walk out, hating that things aren't as cut and dry as I would like them.

15

Kelsey

I WATCH Deacon walk out of the barroom and head for the basement. Parker glances over at me from where she's standing behind the bar, attempting to make another bastardized version of a martini.

"Is he always like that?"

I'm watching the shadows where Deacon disappeared. I'm still distracted, not fully in the moment. "Yeah, cycles of the moon. He gets his period when it's full."

She chokes and laughs, covering her mouth with her hand. "That's terrible."

I smile, hiding my worry, though. His was not an angry departure but one that was more reserved. More troubled.

I'm chopping up fruit. We're running low on lemons. It's Friday night and we're bound to be busy. There's a local whiskey festival coming to town in two weeks and we've been running specials, trying to get more people through the front door.

Because once they're through the door, they almost always stay for a drink. I wonder if I wanted to finally cut the cord between Deacon and me, whether I'd be able to leave him fully behind.

"You knew Deacon before you both worked here, right?" Parker asks, reminding me that she's there and that I'm not alone.

I breathe out sharply: didn't really see that question coming. I should have. But I've never been very clear-headed when it comes Deacon. Nothing is clear about him. It never has been.

I toss back a shot of Jack, needing the burn of normalcy to slide down my throat before I start talking. And believe me, I'll change the subject as quickly as I can. "Yeah. We were in Iraq together."

Parker perks up, sitting up even straighter than you'd think her perfect posture allows for. It's hard not to hate the woman for her posture. She makes it look so damn effortless. But I like her.

She's had an interesting life. Don't let anyone tell you that rich kids don't have real problems. The poverty in her life had nothing to do with material lack and everything to do with love. But that's all changed now that Eli's drawn her into our circle here at The Pint.

Like I said, there's something about this place.

"Really? How on earth did you end up in the same bar in North Carolina?"

"Small Army," I say with a smile. "You'd be surprised how small the world really is."

She smiles and twists her hair up on the top of her head, then jams a pen into the messy bun. "I'm learning." She nods toward the basement door. "Was he like that before? When you knew him in the Army?"

I shrug. "Repressed childhood trauma," I mutter as I write down the next bottle I need to bring up from the basement. "That or his penis hasn't been let out to play recently. He's a pretty carnal guy."

She chews on the edge of another pen. "'Carnal'? I've never heard anyone described as carnal before." She tips her chin at me. "That sounds...erotic."

"Tell me about it." I glance toward the stairs once more. I'm running on a serious buzz and an overtired high that feels like a million bucks.

I feel loose. Like I can function well once the doors are opened and the crowds start coming in. I'll flirt and smile and tease. I'll hint at the promise contained in my smile.

None of it is real. It's all a masquerade, a polished, perfected lie that keeps the world turning while I avoid uncomfortable things.

Like the uncomfortable things I'm avoiding as I avoid Deacon.

"You know, it's not nice to keep secrets," Parker says, watching me watch the stairs where Deacon disappeared.

"No secrets. Just complications."

I look over at her when she doesn't respond. "You're not going to ask?"

She smiles softly, tucking her hair behind her ear. "I learned a while ago that when you all are ready to talk about things, you'll talk."

I swipe the lemons I've been cutting into a small bowl and slide them into the fridge beneath the bar. "You have been paying attention."

It's nice to not have to be on guard constantly. I'm working on my first real female friendships—Parker. Nalini. There weren't a lot of women in my units when I was active. I was always one of the guys.

It took coming home, though, to realize that no matter how hard I try, I will never be one of the guys. I never was. It was all a convenient lie I told myself to feel like I was fitting in. The more I work on building my circle of female friends, the more I realize how much I've been missing out on.

"I'm working on my people skills," she says, raising her glass in a mock salute.

"It's working." I toss back another shot and grab the empty bottles, heading toward the basement, trying not to feel like I'm walking into an ambush.

Deacon

I LIKE THE Pint's basement. It's always cool, and most of the time it's a place where I can have a drink in private when things start to get twisted.

And tonight, they're getting all kinds of twisted.

I hadn't been planning on not hating Caleb. It's funny how random acts can screw up how you view the world. Maybe tomorrow night I won't feel like the world is rocking beneath my feet.

Except it's so much more complicated than that. I sit on one of the crates and lean my head back against the wall.

I know why this shit with Caleb is bothering me. And it has nothing to do with him and everything to do with me.

My regrets.

I pull out my phone, checking to see if my pen pal responded. She never responded to my last remark.

Funny how I'm convinced she's a she and not a he.

No comment? Are you afraid?

I'm feeling peevish. I want the mystery woman on the other end to fight back. To show some fucking spine.

To take the dare.

I crack open a beer and take a long pull, rubbing it against my temple, resisting the memories that circle every time I start to think seriously about breaching the wall that Kelsey has erected around her. Around her past.

Around *our* past.

Funny, I never really spend much time thinking about my part of our shared history. It's so much easier focusing on hers. But tonight, watching Caleb, unpleasant things started circling around the edge of my mind.

Reminding me of the cost of being a fucking asshole. You might not get tomorrow to apologize.

I'm supposed to ask Kelsey if she'll participate for my thesis. And asking her might be the most difficult thing I've had to do in a long damn time.

The more I think about it, the more the words lodge in my throat. In the vicinity of the space that used to hold my heart.

I take another long pull off my beer. I'm going to need something a hell of a lot stronger than beer to broach the subject with her. Maybe I should take a few muscle relaxers and get really loose before I attempt to talk with her about it.

Jesus, is that what it's come to?

"Oh, how far the mighty Sarn't Hunter has fallen, eh?"

I look up to find Kelsey leaning against one of the crates of California wine. "When did you become a ninja?"

She frowns. "Huh?"

"How the hell did you sneak down here? Those stairs aren't exactly quiet."

"Maybe that's a sign you're either half in the bag or distracted by whatever you're looking at on your phone."

I lean back, killing the rest of the beer. The glass clinks against the concrete as I set it down next to my foot and grab its twin, pulling it out of an open crate that Eli leaves down here for us for when we need a break from upstairs. "Neither."

"Cryptic much?"

It wasn't always this way. I didn't always have to look at her and know I could never touch her again.

"Does Caleb seem off to you?" I ask her suddenly.

She frowns for a moment. "Yeah. He's normally super obnoxious. Tonight, he was only mildly so."

"You think he's okay?"

She rubs the bridge of her nose. "I'm too fucking tired to try to psychoanalyze my least favorite person in our little tribe."

I grin and extend the beer toward her.

"Thanks." She takes a step closer and snags it, taking a long pull. "You worried about him?"

"I don't know. It just feels...off without him being the resident pain in the ass. Like I don't know how to function without having to break up his fights."

She hands me back the beer. "I overheard him talking to Eli. Something about an anniversary coming up. The way it sounded, it's not a good one and it's maybe hitting him a little harder than normal?"

"Jesus, I feel like an asshole now." I take a long pull off the beer, then lean my head back, closing my eyes.

"Complicates things, doesn't it, when the people in our lives don't fit into neat little boxes of good and evil?"

"Definitely." She kills the rest of the beer and cracks open another one, taking a pull from it and handing it to me. "Are you okay?"

"Mostly." I should present to be a rational adult and have a reasonable conversation. Anything is better than the status quo, right? "I guess...sometimes things get to me that shouldn't."

"Yeah. I get that." I look up at her words, the frustration in her voice echoing the tension clawing at my heart, locking the words I need in my chest. "It's hard, though. To say when something hurts."

I say nothing for a long moment. Letting her words sink in. Letting their possibility wrap around me.

Then I move. Silent and slow, I back her up against the wall. "You don't have to be strong all the time," I tell her softly. Her mouth is there, just there. She is soft against me, soft in all the ways I remember.

Soft in a thousand ways that will torture me for the rest of a lifetime.

"Neither do you." She's goading me tonight. Crossing boundaries I know she's set in place. I can't figure out what's changed. If it's the fatigue I see in her eyes or the mixture of that with too much to drink. I don't know.

And part of me doesn't care. Part of me only cares that she's here. That her body is pressed to mine. That I've penetrated the space around her and she has not pushed me away.

God, this woman is fierce and amazing. She doesn't back down, doesn't break against the threat anyone else would read in my body.

"I will never forget what happened between us in Iraq. Or when we came home." I reach for her then, cupping her face. Sliding my thumb along her full bottom lip. Wanting so badly to taste her. To end this unnecessary distance between us. "But we don't have to keep suffering alone. Apart. It doesn't need to be like this."

And goddamn her, she presses her lips to my thumb. A gentle kiss. A thousand sensual memories slash through me, ripping away any shred of my composure.

It takes everything I have not to lift her, to urge her legs around my hips and grind against her. I'm hard as a fucking stone. I know she can feel me, solid and hard against her.

She's my addiction. The one woman I dream about when I'm with someone else.

And she knows it. She has to know it.

Her barriers hurt us both.

"We spent four weeks together when we got home and I don't remember any of them. Except the nightmares." She cups my face, brushing her lips against mine. "I can't do that again. I can't get lost in the alcohol and the sex. Because it doesn't help me forget. It only makes it worse."

I lower my forehead to hers, her quiet admission gutting me, ripping through me. That's why she's kept us apart. That's why she's walked away and pretended there was nothing between us.

Her words hurt; they slice at me, reminding me of how fucking self-centered I was when I first got home, wanting to do nothing more than drink and fuck, then drink some more.

I had no idea how much she was hurting. Because I didn't bother to look.

"I didn't know." It's a pitiful confession. So insufficient. I step back then, releasing her from the wall.

Letting her go when it's the last thing I want. She disappears up the stairs, quiet as a ghost.

I lower my forehead to the wooden shelf holding parts of Eli's extensive and very expensive whiskey collection. We're a long fucking way from that bloodstained container where Kelsey used to live.

But we might as well never have left.

A piece of my soul stayed back there, mixed in with the sand and the bullets and the blood.

Forever entwined with hers.

16

Kelsey

I WISH he hadn't done that.

I could practically taste him. The warmth of his breath against my mouth. It would have been so easy to slip my hands into his pants pockets and pull his hips toward me. To let him draw me into one of the dark corners of the cellar and do what we used to do under the stars in Iraq. Sometimes the nights were utterly quiet except for the hard sounds of our breathing.

Sometimes there were distant gun battles echoing across the desert, but the war had seemed so far away when Deacon had been touching me. Hard and rough. God, there was nothing like it. Not before and definitely not since.

It's been so long since I've had such a raw, human connection...tangled with so much alcohol and sex and history.

My body burns. I can almost feel the cool sand beneath my palms as I braced and offered myself to him. The feel of his fingers digging into my hips as he pushed inside of me in one of those bunkers that no one was supposed to be in unless we were taking indirect fire.

They had been perfect for forbidden trysts like ours. "Fuck me," I mutter. I slip back behind the bar, needing a drink or three to put out the goddamned fire between my thighs. Because if I don't, I know what happens next.

The memories from Iraq were good.

Until they weren't.

But for a moment in the dark, cool basement of The Pint, surrounded by thousands of dollars in whiskey, I was able to remember the feel of his cock inside me, the feel of his hands on mine. All without thinking about blood dripping onto the sand. Even if it was just this once, I could practically feel his cock filling me, his hands dragging my hips closer.

I toss back a drink as more customers wander in off the streets. The upcoming whiskey festival is drawing a lot of foot traffic earlier than we're used to, but these are good problems to have.

Parker has vanished back to Eli's office. That's probably a good thing. I don't think I'm going to be fit company tonight, despite working on my girl friendships.

Maybe I should get on social media or something. See if any of the guys from our old unit are still around. I swallow another shot.

"Girl, you keep drinking like that and we'll be carrying you out."

I lower the shot glass and look at the owner of the voice. "Been a long time since anyone called me 'girl.'"

The man in front of me might be a god. A fallen one with a smile as dark as sin that promises all sorts of wickedness. I'd noticed him earlier talking to Caleb and Deacon. Now that he's talking to me, he seems to have swallowed all the light in the room, consuming my attention. "Does the girl have a name?"

"Isn't it a little early for a *Game of Thrones* reference?"

"It's never too early for a *Game of Thrones* reference." He leans on the bar.

I nod toward where Caleb is sitting at the end of the bar. "You know Deacon and Caleb?" I ask.

"Yeah, we were in the Army together. I'm Sam. Sam Rossi."

His hand crosses the space between us. I'm used to being hit on. Used to being flirted with, but his direct approach is a little... unusual. There's a casual arrogance. Like he's not used to people turning him down.

I wait a little too long. He lifts one brow, then lowers his hand. "I promise I don't bite. Unless you want me to."

"You are quite the forward one, aren't you?" I fold my arms over my chest and lean back against the counter behind me. Putting space between us just in case he turns out to be a serial killer or a werewolf.

"My mom raised me to introduce myself. I was attempting to be polite."

I can't help but smile. He's quite the distraction. He's a big man, bigger than Deacon. And the kind of well-built that just screams a lot of time in the outdoors and a penchant for grilled meat. Pounds of it.

Jesus, what the hell is wrong with me? I should be jumping all over the opportunity this guy presents.

"I'm Kelsey."

"Nice to meet you. You always drink that hard?"

I lift one shoulder. "Doesn't really phase me."

I brace for a lecture about *the first step to recovery is recognizing that you've got a problem* but it doesn't come. I motion toward the bar. "What can I get you?"

"How about a glass of Jack Daniel's Monogram?"

Jesus; moneybags. No matter how long I spend around The Pint, I can't get used to the levels of wealth around me. "Sure thing. Got a firstborn to put up for a down payment?"

He grins. "It's expensed."

"Of course it is." I snatch the key from near the register and open the locked cabinet beneath the bar, pulling out the leather-bound bottle. Eli's gamble on the high-end stuff is paying off.

I pour his drink, put away the bottle, lock the cabinet, then slide the glass toward him. "Starting a tab?"

He hands over a black card. Someone is working a little too hard to ensure I notice the wealth he wields like a weapon.

I suppose he's used to it causing panties to drop.

And I'll be honest: Mine might have, except that they were already set on fire a while ago by another man who all the money in the world could not replace.

"Are you new in town?" I ask. It's part of my job to be chatty, even on nights that I don't feel like it.

"Yeah. I'm opening up a new business. And possibly reno-vating a property I inherited out at Jordan Lake."

I lift both eyebrows. "You have carpentry skills for that?"

"My dad's a contractor, so yeah. Well, sort of. I figure there's a lot I can figure out and hire out the help I need otherwise. I got my degree in engineering at West Point, so I know a little bit about building things."

I feel like I missed an inside baseball joke somewhere but I don't ask him about it. "Did you like the Army? Or West Point?"

"I liked the building and blowing shit up more than the officer part. It's one of the biggest reasons why I'm a civilian now."

"Makes sense. Excuse me, I've got to take another order." I drift off to help another customer, amazed that Eli's bar continues to act like a magnet for veterans around North Carolina.

No matter how much this guy drinks or talks shit with that whiskey-smooth voice, I'm not interested. At least not in what he could be offering.

I've got bigger problems waiting for me at the end of my shift tonight, problems that involve a lack of sleep and clear decision-making ability. Problems that could be solved with a little shot of Deacon.

But that's the problem with addiction. One shot is all it takes to draw you back in.

Deacon

"You always carry around a bottle of whiskey with you when you're skulking around in dark corners?"

I lift said bottle of whiskey in mock salute at Eli. He's sitting on the small couch in his office, feet kicked up, reading a report Parker's prepared. Or at least I'm going to assume she prepared it, based on how smugly she's looking at his expression.

I am not going to think about all the things done on that couch since she became a part of his life. Nope. Not going to do it.

"When you work at this place, yes."

Parker pats his shoulder and stands. "I've got to run upstairs for a few minutes. I'll be back."

She slips by me, her palm brushing my shoulder as she passes, then melts into the dark hallway, heading toward the stairs that lead up to his loft. She hasn't moved in. Not completely. But she's there often enough that I'm pretty sure she's got at least a toothbrush up there. And maybe some clean underwear.

And Jesus, I need to redirect my thoughts somewhere other than underwear because tonight everything is leading me down the path to temptation, with Kelsey waiting at the end of it.

Because it's not Parker's panties I'm thinking about. Not in the least.

Eli drops his feet from the table in front of the couch and leans forward, bracing his elbows on his knees. I wish I had something to do with my hands but the whiskey seems to be the last thing I have to hold on to. I breathe out hard. "You ever...had someone you care about a whole lot but you can't be around each other because of the fucked-up things that happen when you're together?"

Eli picks up his pen, tapping it end over end against his palm. "Kelsey?" He frowns. "This has to do with your first tour, doesn't it? The tour when you were downrange with her?"

"Yeah." The word is a brick, lodged in my throat. I look down the hall toward the bar, hoping to catch a glimpse of the woman who fucking haunts my sleep. When I sleep, that is. "She's got me in a box. And I'm not enough of an asshole to force my way out of it."

"Force doesn't really strike me as something that would go over well with someone like Kelsey anyway."

I scoff quietly. "You don't know the half of it. Her platoon sergeant tried a little quid pro quo with her when she was a private. She kneed him in the balls and told him that if he touched her again, he'd be mailing his balls home to his wife in a baggie."

Eli lifts one skeptical brow. "How did she not get court-martialed? Doesn't seem like the kind of thing a private could do with impunity."

"She was her company commander's driver and he'd tried the same thing with her."

Eli drags his hand over his beard. "What the hell kind of unit was she in that a senior NCO was trying that shit with anyone, let alone a company commander?"

"A screwed-up one, at least until we got First Sarn't Sorren in. He cleaned that shit up quick. But to your point, Kelsey isn't one to take threats or force lightly."

"Have you tried just being alone with her and talking with her?"

My mind detours back to the basement. To the feel of her body, soft and smooth against mine. "Yeah."

"Well then, you are well and truly fucked, my friend." He

reaches for a glass on the low table in front of him. "Look, you're obviously not ready to talk about whatever it is that's going on with you and her. Go drink a beer. But get whatever is eating at you out of your system before it rips you apart. I'm not up for any more visits to the emergency room, if it's all the same to you."

And with that, our conversation is over. Mostly because he's hit a sore spot that he doesn't know he's hit. I touch the tip of my index finger to my forehead and duck out of his office.

It's so simple in my head: *Kels, we need to talk. About Iraq. About everything. And I'm not leaving until you do.* Such simple statements.

And I can practically hear her response. *Which part? The blood-covered walls? The indirect fire that shook those same walls?*

I stop at the edge of the hallway, watching her flirt with Sam. I am suddenly feeling quite peevish about my dark and far too sexy friend.

I want him about as far away from Kelsey as I can get him.

But Sam isn't the problem.

I swallow a hard lump. "Or how about we talk about the fucked-up night that we both keep pretending never happened?"

The words disappear into the din of the music and the noise and lights of the bar, unheard and unanswered by an uncaring universe.

17

Deacon

I'M ALONE in the bar, long after last call. Kelsey dipped out a couple of hours ago and the only reason I'm not raging with jealousy, worried whether she went home with Sam, is that I saw him staggering out with Caleb. Which was odd because usually, people don't like drinking with Caleb.

We didn't speak the rest of the night. No flirting for an audience. No teasing touches that could go too far, too fast.

It's my turn to shut things down tonight. I don't mind being alone and closing things up. My phone vibrates on the counter.

I can't sleep.

I stare at my phone for a while; I guess I'm surprised that my pen pal is still talking to me. This is by far the strangest thing I've ever done, but right now, it's comforting. Like talking to an old friend.

Me either. Nights like this can get really long, really quick.

Do you want to meet?

This could be an elaborate scam to steal my money or milk me for sperm to sell to a fertility bank. Or maybe my pen pal wants my kidney. Those are in high demand these days, aren't they?

To hell with my kidneys. I'm curious now.

Shouldn't we meet somewhere public and well lit, first?

She sends me the place: 42 North, an all-night café a few blocks from here.

What if I get there and we decide that meeting in real life is super awkward?

The email response is back almost before I can blink. There's a desperation in the speed of the reply, and with everything else that happened tonight it's got my Spidey senses tingling.

We'll have to figure it out, won't we? Do you like to play games? Like Monopoly or something?

That response I don't have to think about: *Not particularly.*

The response is delayed this time. As if she's thinking.

I'm assuming the person on the other end is a she. Could be a dude. Which would be awkward because I don't hit for the same team.

No games. No sex. I just...I don't want to be alone.

The worst part is being alone, isn't it? But I don't text that to her. Because that would mean I'm going to admit there are things I don't like about being single. Or that I'm still not used to being a civilian. That there are unfulfilling aspects to civilian life that I never thought I'd hate.

I'll be there in fifteen minutes.

She doesn't respond. I suppose this could be a catfishing scheme. There are a thousand other things that could go horribly wrong.

I close up The Pint and start walking. There are a few bars that stay open later than The Pint, and I know Eli has toyed with the idea of staying open later, but given we're a little short on staff he can't swing it right now.

The warehouse district is just a few blocks from The Pint. It's busier than normal from the Summer in the Streets festival that'll be gearing up over the next week. The festival's our small North Carolina town's attempt at a smaller version of South by Southwest.

It has raised the hipster and starving artist population density in our town by six hundred percent. I may have to start drinking in the mornings again if it gets much bigger.

I turn toward the old warehouse district behind the tobacco building district that has been reclaimed and fully gentrified into loft apartments.

I stop before I step inside the café, which has a pretty busy crowd inside for three in the morning.

I'm not afraid, just uncertain about how this is going to go.

I don't really know what I'm dealing with. The person on the other side of this email chain could have massive issues that I'm not equipped to handle.

But there's something so unbreakably human in her request to just have someone hold her in the dark. It's so terribly sad that she doesn't feel like she can get that from any normal interactions, only from a stranger on the Internet. I lean back against the cold brick wall outside the café, looking up at the overhead streetlights. Wishing there was some way to fix the world. Wishing there was some way to stop the hurt that I'm avoiding just as much as the person I'm about to meet is.

Okay, fine. I'll admit that I'm afraid. Afraid of this connection. Afraid of crawling into bed with someone and holding them. I've never fully spent the night with anyone. Not since Iraq, when I would sneak out of Kelsey's trailer before dawn to get back to my own.

I take a deep breath. I can do this, right? It's something simple. Something human.

It's a single night. If it doesn't work, I can sneak out and delete the emails and pretend I never crossed the line from Are-You-

Fucking-Kidding-Me to Today-in-Shit-That-Only-Happens-in-Movies.

What's the worst that could happen?

42 North is a small café tucked in between a head shop and a New Age bookstore that's been around since before the tobacco district was the cool place to be. The walls are covered in black chalkboard paint, the menu written in bright pastel chalk behind the register.

There's a group of college bros sitting in a booth near the bathroom. They're flirting harmlessly with the waitress, who appears to be flirting back. The cook is behind the counter, flipping what's probably some exotic grained pancakes with goji berries or the random-ass super food of the week.

And of all the people who could be sitting in a small booth near the door, is the dead last person I expected.

She doesn't notice me at first. She's tapping out something on her phone.

It's got to be a coincidence, right? I mean, the universe doesn't work like this.

But then my phone vibrates.

It's her.

I don't even have to look at it to know it's from her.

She looks up then, aimlessly scanning the café.

And she stills when her gaze finally settles on me.

Her throat moves as she swallows. I can see the leading edge of panic and fear mixing in her dark eyes.

I have one chance at this. One chance to not screw this up.

One wrong word and she'll bolt. She'll run. And this time, she may run to where I can never find her.

I swallow hard and search for the right words.

And stumble into the void. Praying I can find my way out again.

Kelsey

WHY IN A THOUSAND years and with a couple million people in the Triangle did it have to be Deacon who answered my email? The Internet is a vast, wide open space and somehow, it was him all along.

What are the odds? "I didn't know you liked piña coladas." His words are light but the emotion beneath them tense. Tight.

"Or getting caught in the rain?" I stand then because I need to be on equal footing with him. "We both know I'm into yoga."

"How do you feel about making love at midnight?"

My throat tightens. "It's already past midnight."

"I think we can figure something out."

I latch on to the first clear thought that surfaces, braced and prepared to head for the door. I can't do this. Not with him. Suspicion is easier to feel than the vulnerability that threatens to choke me. "Did you know it was me?"

"How could I?" There's hesitation in his answer. He's not lying.

It would be easier if he was. If he'd cracked into my phone somehow and known it was me, too, all along.

But he didn't. And now I'm going to have to try and explain writing an ad I don't remember writing. Explaining how I haven't slept in far too long.

I don't have the words I need. I don't have the ability to give voice to the emptiness inside me.

I chew on my bottom lip and search for something, anything, to fill the awkward silence. Fuck it. The most direct path through an obstacle is to charge right through it, right? "So on a scale from walking in on someone taking a piss to finding your uncle fucking a piece of fruit, how awkward is this?"

He scrubs his hands over his face and laughs, releasing the tension threading itself between us.

"Holy shit, I didn't need that visual," he says finally. He shoves his hands into his pockets. "But to answer your question, it's pretty damn awkward."

I glance toward the door, still thinking about making that run for it. Unsure how this ends.

But I'm so tired of fucking running. "Well, at least I know you're not going to murder me in my sleep."

He looks down at his feet, his body tense, angled toward the door. Is he thinking of running too? "Look, we don't have to do this," he says. He's giving me an out. An escape. My heart melts a little more for this man. This big, powerful, quiet man.

"I'm not really sure that's what I want," I admit quietly. I'm trying not to cry in frustration. Deacon represents every complication in my life that I've been trying to avoid since I left the Army.

Everything is coming apart, no matter how hard I try to hold on. I wanted to prove to myself that I could be around him, day in and day out, and not lose my tenuous grip on reality.

I was wrong. I can't do this. Not alone.

He rubs the back of his neck, his T-shirt stretching tight over his biceps, distracting me from the aching silence between us. I have to smother the happy dance that's going on in my panties right now. Arms have always been my thing. And Deacon has really great arms.

I'm overtired. That's my story—about why my hormones are suddenly, deeply interested in a man I can no longer deny my feelings for—and I'm sticking to it.

"I don't really know how this doesn't get more awkward." His voice is deep and low.

"Oh, it can get plenty more awkward," I say dryly.

He grins sheepishly. "I guess it can. But we don't have to test this theory, do we?"

I look up at him. At the bright blue eyes that melted my

willpower five years ago and the wide, full smile that filled my heart once upon a time. "No," I say softly. "I guess we don't."

He steps into my space. He's there, close enough that I can feel the heat from his body. He's watching me the way he used to watch me, back when we were in Iraq. Before we were both more cynical. And much less scarred than we are now.

"You look tired." His voice is low, caressing my skin.

"Hence the Craigslist ad."

"Do you do this kind of thing often?"

"What, solicit complete strangers on the Internet for no fucking?"

There it is, the frustration I've been careful to keep cultivating. In order to keep the distance between us.

He laughs softly. "Things you never expect to hear at a company commander's safety briefing, right?"

I motion to the door behind him. Without the need for further discussion, we step out into the well-lit night.

"For what it's worth, I don't remember writing the ad," I say once we've started walking. "I was really tired. I'd thought about it in a sarcastic kind of way, and then I started getting replies."

"That's never good." There's an amazing lack of judgment in that simple sentence.

My apartment is one block away. I lead him inside, to the foyer right outside my door. "So, listen..." he starts. I cut him off before he can say the words.

"Let's not do this here." I open my front door. "My crazy cat lady neighbor is probably standing at her door right now, watching us through her peephole, slowly stroking her pussy. She never sleeps."

"Fuck me, that's a terrible visual." He chokes and laughs and steps into my apartment.

I shut the door and can't really avoid the sense of finality I feel hearing the click of the lock. It sounds nothing like I imagine a tomb would sound when it's scraping closed, but it's what it feels like to me, to have that door shut behind me.

"Maybe we should have coffee or something first." I move to the kitchen, needing to put some distance between us. "Do you want some? I got a Keurig at the thrift store."

"Don't you feel guilty about the pods filling up landfills?"

I set a can of beans on the counter and pull out the refillable pod. "Nope, I use a refillable one."

"Smart. And frugal. I think I'm aroused."

I smile over my shoulder at him. "Is there something wrong with saving money?"

"I love *Deadpool.*" He leans against the counter and it's enthralling to watch the cotton of his T-shirt stretch across his chest. "If you're tired, are you sure you should be drinking coffee? Isn't that going to be counterproductive?"

"Coffee calms me down."

"Yeah? So what's keeping you up then?"

"PTSD? Childhood trauma? Pick your favorite damaged-veteran stereotype and let's see if we can come up with an interesting back story that's doesn't consist entirely of bad clichés."

I can feel him the moment he steps into my space. The heat from his body wraps around me a moment before his hands settle onto my shoulders.

He says nothing, letting the silence speak for itself.

I close my eyes. I'm standing on the edge of the abyss. I've been staring into the darkness for so long, I've forgotten there is light in the world.

The heat from his body is brilliant and bright and warm. Drawing me closer to my need. Drawing me closer to the memories.

The good and the bad. All powerful, though. All overwhelming.

The need inside me is powerful, and fighting the fatigue. I focus on the good. The memories of him making me laugh the first time our base got hit with mortar fire when we'd snuck away for a quickie in a bunker.

It was odd to be aroused and terrified at the same time.

I lean back into his embrace, into the solid wall of his chest behind me. "Of all the men who could have answered that ad, I'm glad it was you," I finally whisper.

He says nothing, but his hands slip from my shoulders and slide around to my belly, drawing me fully, completely against him.

And for once, for the first time since I came home from that terrible deployment, I am completely at ease.

I'm home.

18

Deacon

In her bed, I have found perfection. In what feels like one simple move Kelsey is in my arms, her body relaxed against mine, our breathing in sync, her back rising and falling with her breaths in time with the way my chest moves with mine. I could stay here forever, just feeling her breathe. Her sheets smell like her. I'm surrounded, engulfed and more aware than I've been in a long, long time.

"When did you start doing yoga?" My mind is wandering. I'm focusing on the sound of her breathing, the rhythmic rise and fall of her chest.

She strokes her fingers over my forearm. Soothing. Soft. Sensual. This body-to-body contact completely consumes every ounce of my consciousness.

"The first time I ran out of sleep meds. About six months after I got out of the Army." I hear what she doesn't say: six months after I left her. "I tried drinking through the problem and it didn't really help. I was staying with a friend down at Benning, trying to figure out what the hell I was going to do with my life and she dragged me to my first class. It was super weird at first but I got hooked on it." The sound of her voice, throaty and deep, vibrates against me, drawing me in deep.

"What was weird about it?"

"Being still. Getting my brain to stop racing." She makes a noise. "The first time I tried yoga nidra, I had a full-blown panic attack."

"That doesn't sound like a good thing." My fingers tense against her ribs. "What's yoga nidra?"

"The easiest way to explain it is being halfway between sleeping and waking. They call it the yogic sleep. It's guided meditation where you focus everything internally, except your hearing."

"And you think it helps you? How?"

"Well, yoga teaches us that our bodies store all our bad memories. Yoga is a way of coming to terms with them by releasing all their stored energy through practice."

"I thought yoga was more cleansing and releasing toxins and all that shit."

She laughs and the vibration massages my heart through the wall of my chest. "Some of the time. But other times, it's about accepting where you are and what you've been through. About not fighting the darkness."

"That sounds like something you need a counselor for."

"Yeah, well, I can't afford a hundred bucks an hour for a counselor. Yoga is cheaper."

The bitterness in her voice hits me hard. I lean forward and nuzzle her cheek with mine. "It seems like a hell of a lot of faith to put in an exercise routine."

"It's more than an exercise routine. It's something...sacred. It's important to millions of people. And I damn sure don't have any faith in the VA." She breathes out deeply. "I don't want to talk about the VA. It would require hours of meditation to get rid of the anger."

"Yeah. I get that. I haven't even tried to get seen there for my knee."

She turns in my arms, resting her cheek on my chest. "I'd forgotten about that. You never got the surgery while you were active duty?"

"Never had the time. When I finally decided to get out, the process came really quickly."

"So you're walking around with ripped tendons because you refused to make time to go to the doctor?" The sarcasm drips off her words, thick from the sleepy edge in her voice.

"Well, when you put it that way," I say dryly. I stroke her hair out of her face and press my lips to her forehead. The need to keep touching her is a compulsion. A drive. I can't stop stroking, petting. I'm just reveling in the sensation of her body next to mine, exchanging heat and warmth and oxygen.

She's silent for a while. Her breath is warm on my neck, steady. I almost want to check to see if she's fallen asleep.

"In yoga, there's this meditation called *trataka*." Her voice vibrates through her body and into mine. "The flame meditation. You stare into a flame until your eyes water, then you close your eyes, focusing on the mental image of the fire."

I have no idea what this has to do with anything but she is still lying in my arms. She could read a fucking cereal box right now and I would still listen. She's falling asleep but still talking to me about yoga.

I'm so fucking grateful that she's not alone right now. That she didn't turn me away when she realized it was me on the other end of that email exchange.

"The first time I did it, I cried the entire time." Her voice thickens. I tighten my arms around her. I don't have the words I need. I'm trying to tell her with my body, my touch, that I'm here now. I wasn't, but I am now. That she's safe. "It was overwhelming. I almost quit yoga forever. Again."

"But you didn't."

"But I didn't." Her palm slides over my forearm, resting there. "The more I did it, the calmer I felt." Her fingers tighten, digging into the black ink on my skin. "I guess I wasn't prepared for it to stop working. I haven't slept in months." She doesn't stiffen. Doesn't pull away with the admission that she didn't have everything under control like she thought.

"I'll stay," I whisper. "If you need me, I'll stay." It's a promise I can make. For now. In this moment, she is everything I need, the fulfillment of every promise I broke to her.

She slides her arm over my chest, resting her palm against my heart. "I want to sleep with you."

"By 'sleep', do you mean sleep or screw?"

When I look down toward her, her face is tilted up. She smiles faintly. "I hate feeling like this. Like I'm teasing you. Using you."

I arch one eyebrow. "Honey, you can use me any time."

"Somehow you managed to make that sound filthier than I think you meant it to be."

"Only if you want it to be."

God, but it feels good to be flirting with her, even if she's half asleep.

To be fucking *alone* with her.

I cup her face, nibbling on her lips. "Kels, I don't need to have sex with you."

"Jesus, thanks for that ego-smashing let down," she says mildly.

"I mean, not right now." I lower my forehead to hers, smiling because I can't help it. "I want you sober." She flinches at the word *sober* but I press on, needing her to hear me, to really hear the words I'm speaking. "I want you to do filthy things to me. But I only want that when you're ready for it. When it's not going to spark the nightmares that had you running away like last time."

She closes her eyes. For a moment, I feel like she's going to ask me to leave. That she's going to get up, open the door, and tell me she's changed her mind.

I don't move. Don't speak. I slide my thumb over her cheek and offer myself to her. For whatever she needs. For however long she needs.

Kelsey

"STAY," I whisper.

His body physically relaxes beneath my touch. His heart is slow and steady beneath my palm, his breathing smooth and slow.

We lay in the quiet for a long moment. I'm somewhere between sleeping and being awake. Except that I feel everything about him, his body, his touch. The warmth surrounding me. Connecting me. Threading our energies together.

"How did you end up in North Carolina?"

The sound of his voice is deep beneath my cheek, soothing. The beating of his heart is a warm comfort. There's a lazy arousal sliding through my body. A sensual need tinged with old, never forgotten fear.

This is Deacon, I remind myself. I don't have to be afraid. I shouldn't be.

But I am. Because the nightmares are there, always there. The shame of being weak. Of being unable to handle everything the Army threw at me.

"Because I had nowhere else to go after I got kicked out of the Army," I finally admit. There's no sense in hiding it.

"Wait." He goes deadly still. "When did you get kicked out of the Army?" His lips are warm against my skin but his body is tense.

He kisses my forehead gently. His fingers leave tiny heatwaves behind each stroke. His attempt to calm me doesn't break through the shame burning over my skin. After a second or two he adds, "You don't have to tell me. It doesn't matter."

I smile, savoring the drugged feeling of being so close to sleep. "I popped hot on a urinalysis. The Army changed the medication policy so that you couldn't take anything you'd had longer than six months. My brigade commander had a zero-tolerance policy for any drug use. My company commander managed to get me separated as opposed to court-martialed."

His body tenses. It's a subtle shift but it's there, just there. His fingers continue to move, sliding over my skin, stroking softly. "Motherfucker."

I make a noise. "Yeah, he really was. Always droning on and on about being a professional and if you couldn't take care of yourself, how could you lead soldiers? This from a guy who spent the bulk of the war at the Pentagon." I release a deep breath, tightening the back of my throat in a cleansing *ujjayi* breath. "When I went to his office, he told me I was a disgrace and I should consider myself lucky I was being administratively separated. That the Army didn't need NCOs like me in the force who couldn't handle their personal issues."

Deacon swallows hard, practically vibrating beneath my touch. "I'm having a hard time not being violently angry right now," he whispers. His voice is tight, thick. Ragged in a way I haven't heard from him in a long time.

"I've made my peace with it. I can't change it. And I knew the rules but I took the meds anyway." I press my lips to his throat. "I needed to sleep."

He shifts in a sudden burst of energy and pulls me tighter to him. Our bodies are flush, chest to chest, thigh to thigh. He's warm and pulsing and alive. So very alive.

He's my personal flame. I stare at the pulsing of his heartbeat beneath his skin at his throat, then lean in, feeling the beat beneath my cheek.

"Does not being alone really help you sleep?" he asks after a long silence.

"It's not a cure all. But it helps."

I close my eyes, focusing on the memory of his pulse in the darkness.

"I wish you could have come to me," he whispers, so softly I almost don't hear him.

I nuzzle his throat. "Fear is a powerful thing."

His fingers slow along my back, then pick up their soothing rhythm once more. "I know."

I shift, wriggling against him, and then I feel him hard and stiff against my belly. Heat bursts through my veins, warming between my thighs. I fight the urge to arch against him. "That feels uncomfortable."

He makes a noise deep in his throat. "I'm practicing delayed gratification."

"Really?"

"No. I'm actually thinking about all the times we used to sneak out to that bunker in Iraq."

The heat flashes to a fire. I press my thighs together, remembering the urgency, the rapid way we'd both struggle to free each other from our body armor and uniforms. The urgent way he'd slide between my thighs, filling me.

"You were always so wet whenever I touched you." His voice has changed now. Deeper. Richer. Aroused.

The fear is there, nestled against the boundary of my erotic vision. Close, so close to breaking through. Like the fear of getting caught, it adds a sharp edge to my arousal. A poignancy.

"I used to count the hours until I could sneak away and see you."

His body is pulsing now with a new energy. A new heat. Old

memories collide with new. I'm recalling how he felt when he pushed me back against the cellar wall at The Pint.

"I've been dreaming of this, Kels," he whispers. "Just holding you again. Hoping there'd be some way we could get back to what we were."

"We weren't much more than fuck buddies in Iraq, Deacon."

He tenses again. "You know that's not true." There's a violent edge to his words. His fingers bite into my skin before they release me, stroking over the spot. "It was more than that for me."

"It didn't start out like that for me." I close my eyes against the hurt buried in his anger. "But I grew attached to your penis."

The laugh slides out of him, rich and needed, snapping the tension between us. "Yeah, well, he's missed you, too."

"Not that he's lacked for company," I grumble.

He makes a strangled noise. "We all do what we have to do to avoid the nightmares."

It's really hard to hide my skepticism. "Sex with strangers helps you avoid the nightmares?"

"Sleeping with strangers on the Internet was going to help you?" he shoots back but there is no venom in his words.

"Touché." I press my lips to his throat again, breathing in the scent of his skin. I give in to the temptation and arch against him, rubbing my hips against his erection. "We could..."

He rolls me then, faster than I'm prepared to react. He settles between my thighs, his body hard and stiff and unyielding against me. "I want you. More than anything, I want you, Kels." He kisses me then, soft and sweet and demanding all at once. "After you've slept."

19

Deacon

I LEAVE her when she's finally asleep. It's around eight a.m. when I sneak out, leaving a note for her on the bathroom mirror. As much as I want to stay, to be there when she wakes up, she was right about her apartment. The silence is too much, crawling over my skin, drawing me closer to the edge of panic.

It felt so good holding her, talking. Remembering the feel of her body, the tight way she'd grasp me, drawing me into her. So quick and urgent, always afraid of getting caught for violating General Order One that forbade all the fun sins.

She'd been worth it then and she's worth it now.

I'm not going to risk my own issues colliding with hers. She's barely able to deal with her own bullshit. I'm not going to dump anything more on her lap.

I've got a bottle of Jim Beam that can handle those problems.

I let myself into The Pint and toss back a couple of shots. The immediate burn spreads out from my throat to my entire body, dulling my senses. My brain is fuzzy, like it's floating on pure cotton. A couple more shots and I'll be ready to start working, losing myself in inventories for Eli.

Work has always been an escape. A place for me to avoid the noise in my head when everything else fails. The latest shipment is only partially sorted and unboxed. I crank up some smooth country music and start moving, sorting, unboxing. An extra crate captures all the packing materials.

The sun has long since crept up over the skyline outside. Inside the basement, the air is damp and cool. I'm slick with sweat, the work soothing the angry edge of my memories.

She's probably going to be pissed that I left her. But the silence started crawling around my head, bringing with it darkness and fear and too many memories that weren't the kind I wanted to recall.

I remember too damn well how it felt to touch her. To hold her. Then to hear her screaming on that godawful day when everything went to shit. It was the last time I touched her in Iraq.

I felt the scars on her body last night. Thought about my own from that same day.

I can still hear her screaming as I held her back from going into the wreckage of her CHU. I can still see the blood and smell the sulfur and the deafening acoustic echo that slammed around us when that mortar began the twelve hours that would mark the beginning of the utter destruction of our lives.

Twelve hours of fighting back an assault on our base. Twelve hours of defending ourselves against a ferocious violence that, had we failed, would have been broadcast to the world.

All of it slammed back into me around four a.m. It's been a long time since those particular memories hit me so hard, and I don't know what to fucking do with them. Normally I'd find a willing partner and take her home. Bend her over the bed and lose myself in a sexual haze for a few hours of deviant pleasure.

But that doesn't feel right, now that I've finally reconnected with Kelsey. And even though we're not together again, part of me feels like I should be loyal to her.

I finish unpacking the shipment. Move the boxes to one side and look at the disorder around me. The shelves need to be reorganized. Maybe by year? I bring down an inventory sheet that itemizes what we have and I start comparing it to consumption rates. I can see that the expensive stuff moves slower but turns a much bigger profit.

The numbers are a good distraction. A break from the memories hammering through my brain.

"You think you're funny?"

My heart slams against my ribs. "Jesus Christ, how do you keep doing that?"

I turn in time to see her advancing toward me. "You think you can just sneak out and leave like that?"

I lift one eyebrow. "Your reaction is a little over the top right now." It's never going to end well when you're trying to explain to someone who is acting like a fucking insane person that they are acting...like an insane person.

"Really?" She pushes me back against the wall and my temper flares.

"What did you want from me? You wanted me to fuck you senseless when you were barely conscious from being so goddamned tired? Is that what you wanted? Me to fuck you while you were vulnerable? What the hell does that say about me? Or you, for that matter."

"Nothing that hasn't been said before," she snaps. "You think it's over the top to wake up, dreaming about your hands on my body, dreaming about feeling you inside me, only to wake up alone?"

I fight the urge to smile as realization slams into me. It's a superhuman effort. "Wait, you're pissed because...you're horny?"

She narrows her eyes at me. "You think that's funny? You think I wanted to wake up alone? When I fell asleep this morning, I wanted you. I wanted this." She reaches for the front of my pants where, yeah, I'm already getting hard. This is the most erotic fucking thing I think I could have ever imagined. I pinch myself.

She glares at me, her hand fisting my cock and driving me fucking wild. "What are you doing?"

"Making sure I'm not dreaming." The pain is sharp and bright and yeah, I'm not asleep. I close my eyes and grind into her palm, the pressure sweet and dark and tight where she grips me.

She pushes my pants open, freeing me. The air is cold against my cock but then her fist is tight and hot. "You don't get to leave me like that," she whispers against my lips.

"I'll never make that mistake again." She slips her thumb over the sensitive tip of my cock. "Sweet Jesus, do that again."

I'm definitely on board with this little fantasy. If I close my eyes, I can smell the desert around us, and the basement encases us like the bunker where we used to sneak away.

I grip her hair, tipping her mouth to mine. She's open and moist and hot, her mouth warm and wet. "Please," she whispers against my lips.

I know what she wants. I know how she wants it.

I turn her away from me, pressing her against the wall. Sliding her pants down her hips, exposing her where I can see the smooth wet silk of her body glistening on her thighs.

It's what I need. What I crave. I may never get another chance at this. I need this. I need her.

Open. Exposed. Swollen.

And waiting. For me.

Only me.

Kelsey

THE WALL IS cold against my palms, the air a cold contrast where I'm aching and wet. I need this.

I couldn't walk down those stairs and say the words I needed. I latched onto the anger, the frustration, finding the courage in the blur of emotion and arousal to ask him for what I needed.

He knows what I need. What I'll always need from him.

He's behind me, his erection pressing against my rear as he tips my neck back. I'm fucking aching for him to fill me. I arch, trying to urge him home. To please fill me, complete me. End the burning ache inside me in the way that only he can.

He nips at my neck, his fingers sliding around the crease of my thighs to stroke me where I'm swollen. He's teasing me, his fingers slipping through the silky wetness to circle me. "Please, Deacon." I rub against him where he's silk and solid heat against me.

I reach behind me, urging him lower, between my thighs. The friction of his cock through my heat is enough to break me. I shiver against the movement and slide my hips against him, riding him in an erotic twisted dance.

I grip him then, holding the tip prisoner at the entrance to my body. I shiver at the sensation—just there.

And then he moves, slowly, a little deeper. My body stretches to accommodate him. It's been so long since I've felt this delicious pleasure. I groan as he takes his sweet, agonizing time. His fingers stroke me as he fills me, drawing the erotic sensation deeper in my body.

"You're so fucking tight." A growl near my ear, his breath hot on my skin. His breath is rough on my neck as he fills me completely, a sharp, biting pleasure. I rock, needing him to move, to fucking *move*.

He pulls out then, slowly enough that he's driving me goddamned wild. I push against the wall, shifting to drive him deeper.

He grips my hips, his fingers dragging me against him, and he finally pushes into me. Hard and fast, it's exactly what I need. What I remember. The quick burst of pleasure that drags me under, away from the world, away from the nightmares and into a writhing mass of sensation and heat and sexual need.

I close my eyes, meeting him thrust for thrust, arching against him, opening, drawing him deeper into me. Harder—the world falls away until all I can feel is Deacon, his body, his fingers, his breath, his cock. Surrounding me, filling me, taking me away from this life and into something else. Something wild and raw and complete.

He drives into me until my arms are weak, until his skin is slick against mine, until my release starts as a shudder then spirals wide to drag me into the void. It spirals wide to pull him under with me, a bright, shuddering nirvana in a burst of color and sensation.

His breathing in is the only sound, the feel of him pulsing deep inside me the only sensation. I rest my cheek against the wall; his fingers thread with mine.

Complete.

Deacon

"THAT'S ALL IT TOOK?" she asks after a long silence.

I'm not really sure what she's talking about. My brain is foggy and I'm not sure all my limbs are going to keep working at the moment. I want to stay here, to never move. I'm already softening but I don't want to slip free of her body.

She shifts, though, and turns in my arms, and I can feel the cold slap against my cock as her warmth leaves me. I lean against her, fixing her pants, then drawing my own over my hips. I feel drugged. Heavy.

I want to sleep.

She cups my cheek and brushes her lips against mine. "Thank you," she whispers.

I lift one eyebrow, coming back to myself slowly, as if I'm waking from a dream. "For..."

"Letting me use you."

"I thought we discussed this." I kiss her softly. "You can use me any time you want."

She smiles against my mouth. "Did you get everything out of your system with your rage stacking?"

"Is that what I was doing? Rage stacking?"

"I've never seen anyone stacking alcohol so violently. You're lucky you didn't break anything."

"This shit's expensive. Eli would kill me if I broke a bottle."

I step back, putting space between us, unsure of where things are heading at the moment. It's an odd sensation, being wrapped in a cloud of latent arousal and cautious uncertainty all at once.

"Yeah, well, he's forgiven a lot worse," she says, tucking her hair behind her ear and adjusting her clothes. She finally looks up at me. "How did we used to do this in Iraq? I don't remember it being awkward."

I rub the back of my neck. "I think it involved making sure no one would spot us coming out of the bunkers at the same time and sneaking back to our respective sleeping quarters or duty."

"Should we sneak upstairs and make sure no one suspects anything?"

I grin then. "I don't think anyone is here this early."

The silence is a live thing between us. "So, ah, I slept really well last night," she says after a moment. "Did you?"

"A little bit." The truth, for once. I didn't sleep at all but it was better than climbing the walls in my own apartment, praying for daylight. "Don't we have the cadets today?"

"Yeah. Which reminds me that I have to scramble to do the reading before class. Can't discuss it if I haven't read it." She takes a single step toward me. "So listen, I, ah, I'm happy to repay the favor tonight, if you, ah, need help sleeping."

I slip my hands over her hips, tracing her hipbone beneath my thumb. "Yeah?"

Her palm is warm on my stomach.

"Yeah."

"What about...everything?" I cup her face, sliding my fingers through her hair. "The last time..."

She presses into my palm. I can convince myself she needs the connection as much as I do to retread this old terrain. "The last time, neither of us was really dealing well with anything from Iraq. Staying drunk for a month isn't really healthy, no matter how much we tried to lie to ourselves that we were both fine." She closes her eyes. "I'm willing to give it a shot. And hope that maybe, the nightmares will leave me alone."

I lower my forehead to hers. "One day at a time then?"

She nods. "One day at a time."

It's the best we can do.

It's more than I ever hoped for.

I'll take it.

20

Deacon

IT'S strange sitting across the table from Kelsey, watching her, knowing that I'll be going home with her tonight.

Somehow, I've got to survive sitting in class with the cadets, listening to them argue about leadership and women in combat and everything else they think they know about while trying not to think about her naked in my arms.

I do my best to pull my mind out of the gutter and back to the conversation. I'm letting Kelsey lead it today, mostly because all the blood in my body is still trying to make its way back to my brain.

Ryan isn't in class today. I'm not sure where he is but it doesn't bode well that he didn't drop either of us a note to let us know he was going to be absent. I know the ROTC commander is strict about that stuff. I'll get in touch with Professor Blake and the battalion commander after class if neither one of us hears from him before then.

"The reading this week is on tribes. The author isn't a soldier but he's spent significant time with soldiers. What do you think of his argument that we are lacking modern tribes?" Kelsey asks.

Veer raises his hand. "I'm not sure I agree with him. It seems awful simplistic to dismiss PTSD like he does."

"How do you mean?"

He flips open his notebook. "I think it's a compelling argument but it seems like it's romanticizing the past as some ideal where everyone felt like they were part of something. I'm pretty sure that past doesn't exist for everyone."

Jovi raises her hand. "I don't know. I think it's a really interesting argument. I can't imagine what he's describing. The idea of sleeping in austere conditions, getting shot at and bombed, and sleeping better than you do back home in the comfort of air conditioning and showers? I don't buy it."

"Why not?" I ask.

I love listening to Jovi work through her thoughts as she's speaking them. She's so fucking smart.

"Because I just...I can't imagine it. How? How on earth does that make any sense?"

Kelsey is flipping her pen cap on and off. I'm not sure she's even aware that she's doing it. "Well, if you think about it, our American standards of so-called wealth are very odd. At the most primitive level, we used to sleep and live and die in packs...tribes. It's only been since the industrial revolution that we began to segregate ourselves as part of moving up in the world. Maybe we need each other more than modern society is able to admit?"

Iosefe has said very little in the class so far but I've been watching him. Even though he looks like he's not paying attention, he's hearing every word.

Today he raises his hand. "I'm from American Samoa and when we moved here, the kids at school said we were poor because I lived in a house with my cousins and my aunt and uncle. We were crowded but we were happy. But my father always told me to push harder so I didn't have to live like we did growing up." He clears his throat. "He never asked me if I was happy."

Jovi looks like she's thinking hard about his statement. "Were you?"

"Yeah. It's family. It's big and it's messy and it's loud but there is no one who loves you like family. I never felt alone until I got here and had my own room."

Veer nods. "I agree. My grandparents are from India. Everything I grew up believing stems from the fundamental idea that we are all connected. The reading really speaks to the lack of connection in American life."

Kelsey swallows hard. "So what do you do about it? How can you apply this to your future as lieutenants?" She pauses and she's still avoiding looking at me. "How do you build your tribe?"

Veer looks at me. "Shouldn't we be asking you that? You've actually done this, haven't you? As sergeants." I smile at the way he says the full word *sergeant* as opposed to abbreviating it to *sarn't* like anyone who has been in the Army for a minute does.

I take a deep breath. I figured we'd only get them to talk for so long before they put us on the spot. "There isn't a formula. You have to be genuine. You have to really care about your people. You can't expect them to assume risk without assuming the same yourself. You have to protect them, but that doesn't mean making life easy on them. You have to train them. And that's uncomfortable. But it's better to bleed in training than die in combat."

Kelsey tucks her pen into her fist. "I think the only thing I would add to that is to not trivialize things. Something that may be very basic to you may be a very big deal to someone else. Everyone has a different threshold. Protect your people but also hold them accountable. Don't let things slide. We have standards. You have to uphold them. That's part of your job."

She finally looks up at me. The bitterness in her eyes, the frustration, hits me in that moment. Everything we're talking about, both of us failed to do when we got home from Iraq.

The hypocrisy burns.

Kelsey

I KNEW the discussion was going to be rough after I read the chapters for class today. Reading about leadership and risk and bonding during war was far too real, far too potent a reminder of all the things I lost when I left the Army. All of it hit home, hard. Really hard.

It's never easy to look back and know you failed your soldiers. But I did. And I can't change it.

The guilt comes back every now and again. I think it's worse today because of...things. Things that involve Deacon and the memories of coming home to a home that wasn't.

"I'm not sure I can have this conversation right now," I tell him as he falls into step alongside me.

"Who said anything about talking?"

"So we're going to walk to The Pint in awkward silence?"

"Why not? We're both heading to the same place; we might as well, right?"

I glance over at him. His jaw is flexing so hard I feel bad for his teeth. "You still grind your teeth."

He relaxes his lips but it's not enough. The tight line of his neck doesn't relax. "Bad habit. They wanted to give me meds for it when I went for my last checkup at the dentist."

"You turned them down?"

"My inner hippie doesn't like taking medication unless I need to. Grinding my teeth doesn't seem like a big enough problem to suffer through pharmacy lines for. And my liver gets enough work every day."

I stuff my hands into my sweatshirt pockets and say nothing.

"I'm really glad that Iosefe brought up his background today," he says after we've walked a block without speaking. "I wish Ryan had been there to hear it."

"Yeah, I think Ryan could have really benefited from Iosefe's story." I make a noise. "It's funny how Ryan's got such strong opinions about what the military is like."

"He's watched *Full Metal Jacket* too many times." Deacon makes a noise that might be a laugh but I'm not sure.

"It's hard sometimes," I finally say.

"What is?"

"Looking back." I release a breath, clenching the back of my throat with a deep cleansing breath. "These readings about belonging were harder to read than I thought they would be."

"Why?"

"Because the author is right. Because I miss it. I miss the stupid pranks in the motor pool, I miss the three a.m. phone calls. I miss going to the field and listening to soldiers play stupid-ass 'what if' games. I miss all of it." I stop walking beneath a tunnel that's decorated with the emblems of clubs from around campus. There's no art for a veterans' club. Because we don't have one. "Because what I did mattered. Because I had a fucking purpose. And then I went and fucked it all up because I couldn't sleep."

It's hard to meet his eyes. I'm trying so hard not to be a fucking coward these days. Trying to be the person I envision when I'm on the yoga mat.

Trying to pretend that everything I hope to be can ever outrun the person that I was.

"That is such a load of bullshit. Did you see the way those kids were looking at you when you were talking today?"

"They don't look at me the same way they look at you."

He shakes his head and steps into my space in the cool dark shadows beneath the bridge. "Yes, they do."

I back away, colliding with the chalk-covered stone behind me. I'm trapped. "There's nothing to tell."

"Why do you do that? Why do you downplay your own accomplishments?"

"I didn't do anything special. I did my damn job, Deacon."

He moves into my space then. His hands are rough where they grip my shoulders. "You did more than that and you know it. The Army doesn't hand out Bronze Stars for Valor for showing up at head count at the chow hall." His mouth is there, just there, his body pressing against mine.

But this isn't sexual. This is more intense. Something more raw. Something primal.

"They just wanted to put a female face on the attack."

"Bullshit," he snaps. "Stop doing that. Stop acting like you didn't lead the defense after our perimeter was breached. Stop acting like you didn't take over when the LT refused to get out from behind the tire he was hiding behind. Stop downplaying what you did."

I shove his hands away but he snaps them back into place.

I shove them off again and this time, he stops. "What do you want me to say? You want me to get up in class and beat my chest about what a badass I am? What kind of badass drinks herself to sleep every night if she can't sleep? What kind of badass was so fucked up by everything that happened downrange that she took meds she shouldn't have and got herself thrown out of the Army? You want me to tell *that* story? Because that's not fucking heroic."

He's shaking his head slowly. "You don't see yourself the way I do."

"All you want to do is see me naked." My quip falls flat, like an egg cracking on the sidewalk.

He doesn't smile. "There's so much more to you than you give yourself credit for."

"I fell apart. For more than a year after you left, I fell down. And I couldn't get back up." The words break me, shattering like a lightning strike slashing down the middle of a tree, burning in my chest, squeezing my throat and blocking out the air I desperately need. "Heroes don't fall apart."

"But you got back up." He cups my face and I don't push him away this time. A dark part of my heart needs his touch. Even if it's only for a moment. I wish the heat from his palms, the abrasion from his fingertips, could warm the cold dead space inside me. "Why can't you see how that makes you strong?"

I cover his hands with mine. Then draw them slowly away from my face. "Because it doesn't. If I was strong, I never would have broken in the first place."

And then I'm gone.

Because that's what I do. I run. I always run.

I ran away from home. I ran away from the Army. Away from Deacon.

Away from the fragile peace I thought I'd found.

It was a futile hope. All of it.

I leave everything good behind because all I ever do is fuck things up.

21

Deacon

I LET her go because I have to. I saw the fear in her eyes but laced in that fear, I saw the truth that she believed.

It's not an objective truth, not by a long shot. But it is the truth to her, the internalized belief that she never should have broken. That somehow, the bravest among us never break.

It's the bullshit lie that the Army has forced upon us since basic training. That a warrior is brave and courageous and loyal and that because we fight the good fight, that we are the righteous.

No one tells the idealist privates about the sleepless nights. About the pain of losing our friends. About the last emails we received before we find out that one of our buddies died, not from an enemy's bullet but from their own. Or from a prescription screw-up.

Or from just plain giving up on finding a purpose in this life after the war has left everything else flat and colorless.

I walk because I don't want to be around people. The idea of being crammed into the campus bus strikes me with revulsion. It's a painful thing to admit you don't want to be around people.

It's a short walk to The Pint, to the place where I can at least do something productive with the irritation built up inside me.

Eli's inventory is going to be done in record time this quarter if I keep this up. I've managed to make my way through fifteen crates. Only forty-two more to go.

She's not at The Pint when I get there. I guess I would have been surprised if she had been. I start unboxing the expensive whiskey that Eli has made the cornerstone of his brand, trying to pretend that everything is fine. That I'm not worried sick about her.

It's fine if I keep checking my email every few minutes, right? Totally normal. It's a long shot but I'm hoping Kelsey will play along.

I send her a note from the anonymous response email I used before I discovered it was Kelsey on the other end of the insomnia email chain.

Please don't shut me out. I can handle anything but that.

I hit send before I can talk myself out of it.

"Kelsey's not going to be here tonight," Eli says, sitting down on the bottom stair.

"I know."

He's watching me as I stack the Talisker neatly on the shelf, replacing the date with the grease pencil we use to keep things current.

Eli says nothing. Waiting.

I'm stalling, searching for the words that will give Eli enough information without violating Kelsey's confidence and privacy.

We all have demons we'd rather not share with the world. And while I was there when some of them were made, hers are not mine to share with him.

"We got into an argument today," I say finally.

"About what?"

"About her not being honest with the cadets about who she is."

Eli frowns, rubbing his hand over his mouth. "What does that even mean? It's not like she's got a secret identity as Wonder Woman or anything."

"She kind of does. She's got a fucking V device and she acts like she pushed paperwork in the Army." I slam a bottle beneath the counter. "We've got this little shit-stain cadet, Ryan. He's like a younger version of Caleb, if you want the truth. A latent ammosexual all hopped up and dying to go infantry with all that *hoah* bullshit they feed you officers. Oh, by the way, he's branch detailed so he's going to get his feelings hurt when he has to go be a signal officer. And he's spent a good amount of time in class arguing why women shouldn't be integrated into combat arms. And she's sitting there like she's not a living, breathing refutation of his argument and she doesn't say a goddamned thing." I release a hard breath. "It just pissed me off today, that's all."

"Well, that explains why you're extra sandpapery but not why she's not at work," Eli says, like I just gave him a shitty weather forecast.

"We argued about it."

He lifts one eyebrow and in that single gesture, I am reminded of how it felt to get called on the carpet for fucking up when I was a soldier. I sigh. "I may have yelled a little bit."

"Still doesn't explain why she's not here."

"I don't fucking know." I slam a crate into the corner and the wood splinters from the shattered edges. "I don't know. I don't know why she's afraid of really living. I don't know why she genuinely believes what she did was something trivial and not worthwhile. Or why she continually downplays who she is and what she's capable of." I turn away from the man who saved me. Who saved all of us by bringing us together. By making us his tribe, whether we wanted to be or not. "I wish I did," I whisper. "I wish I could fix this."

"You and Kelsey are two sides of the same coin." He gets up and his strong hand grips my shoulder. I look over at him, prepared to call bullshit. He shakes his head. "You just hide it better than she does."

"I'm fine."

"You don't sleep sometimes. You have a bad habit of fucking anything that moves. And don't think I don't see how much more you've been drinking since Kelsey showed up."

"It's a coping mechanism. Better than mainlining black tar heroin."

"True." He frowns. "Is that even a thing anymore?"

"I don't really know and I don't want to Google it to find out. I have enough problems sleeping."

"Look, all I'm saying is maybe by focusing on her issues you're using it as an excuse to avoid unpacking all of your own." He grips my shoulder, over the dog tag tattoo surrounded by the branches of the tree that spread across my pec, hiding scars I pretend aren't there.

The crow on my chest pulses over the scars. "That's some seriously mystic woo-woo mind reading shit you've got going on."

He smiles quietly and he suddenly looks tired. "Maybe I've been listening to Nalini a little more these days." He squeezes my shoulder and turns to the stairs. "Finish up whatever you need to do down here. But figure out a way through this with her. Because I don't want to lose either one of you."

I'm off balance by how easily he's called me on my bullshit. I thought I had everything well-concealed. I don't miss work like Kelsey. I don't disappear for days on end.

But he's right. As much as I hate it, he's right.

I head upstairs, taking orders and making drinks, and making small talk behind the bar. I glance over at Eli as he leans across the bar to drop a cherry into Parker's mouth. It's a ridiculously sensual gesture, one that makes my body tighten thinking about Kelsey's lips around a bright red cherry.

But it's too late. My mind has already detoured away from the bar, to the warmth of Kelsey's bed, to the feel of her body pressed against mine.

I want to feel her breathing as she sleeps. I want to thread my fingers with hers and hold her against me, have the cool silk of her dark hair spread against my chest.

It's such a simple want and yet, it is infinitely complex.

The Army taught me how to plan. How to develop courses of action, how to accomplish an objective.

But here there's no grand scheme, no grand strategy.

Just a deep breath and the courage to knock on her door long after my shift has ended.

To ask if she's okay.

Kelsey

I SUPPOSE I shouldn't be surprised to find Deacon standing outside my door at two a.m.

"What if I'd been sleeping?" I ask, leaning on the doorframe. There are deep slashes beneath his slightly bloodshot eyes and a dark shadow along his jaw. The urge to pull him against me and draw him into my bed is pulsing through my body with every beat of my heart.

His lips pull into a faint half-grin. "Well, then I'd have to assume you found some other rando from the Internet and I'd be a little put out."

I curl one side of my mouth. "Maybe I just decided to smoke some weed and relax."

He frowns and looks at me sideways. "Did you really?"

I'm not sure whether his question contains judgment or curiosity. "No, but I've been seriously considering it. I was looking to see if there were any medicinal marijuana studies being conducted around here." I rest my head against the door. "And no, I wasn't sleeping."

He runs his hand down the back of his neck. "Look, can I come in?"

"It's two in the morning."

"Is that a no?"

I smile faintly and step aside. "No; it's not a no."

He slides by me and I lock the door behind him. I'm not sure if he's going to stay or if he'll leave after her says whatever is on his mind.

The fact that he's shown up after a long night at The Pint warms my blood with something sweet and erotic all at once. It's sexual but also something more. Something deeper.

Something...intimate.

"So, hey, I, ah, got you something." He pulls a small statue from his pocket. "I saw it and I...I don't know; I felt like you might like it."

My eyes widen as I take the small figurine from him. "It's Ganesh." There is a brilliant burst of light around my heart. "Do you know what he represents?"

"Not really." He looks embarrassed that he picked it without knowing anything about it.

"He's the Remover of Obstacles." I set the statue down on the counter and step closer to him, sliding my arms around his waist. "The first time we did a chant to Ganesh at Black Stone Yoga back in Texas, I was like, 'this is really strange.' The next day, I got a call that I was approved for an exception to policy on my GI Bill."

"That's a pretty cool coincidence."

"Maybe it was. Maybe it wasn't. But the shorter version is that I was able to start school." I shift. "And you giving me this... thank you."

He kisses my forehead, and I am ensconced in a moment of pure trust. "I'm glad you like it."

"A lot of people are wigged out when they find out I'm actually serious about the spiritual side of yoga, not just the fitness."

"They shouldn't be. It's none of their business."

"Yeah, well, we are in the South and people get a little funny about the Hindu gods and all that." I brush my lips against his again, needing the connection, the touch. "This is absolutely perfect. Thank you."

He nuzzles my mouth, urging me to open and I do, taking the sweetness of his taste into me. "Eli fed Parker a cherry tonight and I could not stop thinking about you."

I hop up on the small island in the kitchen. "I'm confused."

"The whole time, I had this erotic little fantasy of you doing terrible things to that cherry." He takes a step toward me, resting his hands on either side of my thighs. Not touching but close enough that the heat from his body wraps around mine. He smells smoky and warm, like a being wrapped inside a blanket sitting in front of an open fire.

"That's an interesting fantasy," I say, unsure how to untangle us from our current stalemate.

"It's my way of saying I missed you at work tonight."

He's just there, at the edge of my knees. It would be so easy to part my thighs and slide my feet around his hips and draw him closer until he pressed against me where I so badly want his touch.

It's hard to meet his eyes but I do. Because I'm trying really hard not to be a coward these days. "I needed some space."

"Did it help?"

I slide my finger over his bicep, over the edge of the dog tag tattoo. "Considering I was wide awake when you knocked on the door, I think the answer to that is obvious."

"What did you do tonight?"

The conversation is innocent, safe. It's the kind of conversation that normal people have when they have normal relationships and not fucked-up histories that involve a six-month bender where you don't remember your own name.

"Worked on a paper for one of my classes. Might as well use my insomnia for something productive."

He inches forward. I shift to make space for him and my knees brush against his hips. "What are you doing it on?"

"I still don't know. Mostly, I'm just reading right now."

"Have you talked to Professor Blake about it?"

"Briefly. I need to get on her calendar again. I'm avoiding the stunning disappointment she's bound to have when I tell her that despite spending two years working with her on military–civilian issues, I am no closer to figuring out an original research idea."

"I talked with her the other day. She actually pointed me in a really interesting direction."

I can hear the hesitation in his voice. "Yeah?"

"Yeah." He clears his throat and looks down. "She wants me to interview vets and talk to them about their transition to civilian life. And whether that's impacted their willingness and or ability to use the VA."

I'm quiet for a moment, studying him. His hands are fists by my hips but when he looks up, he slides them over my thighs, cradling my body in his palms. "It's a big project." He bites his lips together. "I could use some help. A sounding board, maybe." His thumb brushes over one hipbone. "I'd like to interview you, if you're willing."

There it is. There's the thing he was afraid to mention. I breathe in deeply, holding my breath until it burns, then release it slowly. "At my yoga classes, we've been working on the concept of obstacles."

"Ganesh?" He nods toward the small figure.

"Yeah." It warms my heart that he's not making fun of me. "So, tonight, when I went to class, the instructor talked about the things we're holding on to. The stories we tell ourselves." I swallow a hard lump. The words are jammed in the back of my throat. "And it hit me that I've been telling myself the same story since I got home from Iraq." Another breath. "It's not that the story isn't true. But I've gotten stuck on it, too focused." Release. "It's why I ran today after class. Because I don't know how to let go. How to forget and move on."

"Maybe you shouldn't be trying to forget," he says softly. His hand slides up to cup my cheek. "I don't want to forget Iraq. I don't want to give up the memories of the good."

I touch my forehead to his. "But the good brings the bad with it. I can't separate the two." A quiet release. "It's why I've run from anything to do with you. The bad overwhelmed everything. It felt like dying."

"Even this time?"

I close my eyes. "No. This time...the bad hasn't surfaced yet."

"But you're waiting for it."

"Yeah." I inhale deeply. "I hate that I'm telling you this. I hate that I'm so fucking weak that I have to admit a few panic attacks and a couple of nightmares kept us apart."

His fingers tense on my cheek.

"Look at me."

And his words are not a request.

22

Deacon

IT FEELS like an eternity passes before she finally opens her eyes. It takes everything I am to remain calm, to keep the anger and frustration out of my voice.

I don't think I'm successful.

"Stop doing that."

She tenses beneath my touch. "Stop doing what?"

"Stop downplaying everything. You were involved in a major attack downrange. You defended our base. You evacuated our wounded when you were hurt yourself." I brush my lips across hers. "You're allowed to have nightmares. You're allowed to have panic attacks. All of those things are incredibly normal reactions to completely abnormal situations."

She closes her eyes again. "It's not that easy."

I want to shake her, to repeat my words until she internalizes every single syllable. But I don't. Because I know how that choose-your-own-adventure can end.

"I know," I say instead.

Her lips press into a humorless smile. "It's not the same for you."

"I know that, too." I swallow. "I never noticed how things were different for you back at Hood. How when guys wanted to buy a round of drinks, they always assumed you were just the waitress, not one of us." I release a deep breath.

She frowns. "When did you get so perceptive?"

I nuzzle her nose with mine. "I notice everything about you, Kels," I whisper. "I didn't before and I lost you. I don't want to make that mistake again."

She closes her eyes and lowers her forehead to mine. An impossible silence stretches between us but it's a good silence, something warm that binds us together.

"I'll concede that it's been a teeny bit difficult being around you and not being able to touch you."

"You could have touched me any time you wanted."

"Pretty sure you set some pretty clear boundaries," I say dryly, reminding her of the no-touching rule. I close my eyes against the hurt of that memory. My mouth goes dry, the kind of dry that you get after an all-night bender when you forgot to drink anything non-alcoholic along the way. "I don't remember much about that night. Other than the you-never-want-to-see-me-again part."

She is infinitely still. We've never talked about that night or the month leading up to it. Or the deployment that led up to that.

"I woke up," she admitted softly. "I couldn't remember what we'd done. I couldn't remember where I was or what I was doing. I spent a month with you and I don't remember any of it. Except the nightmares. Those I remember." She scrapes one thumbnail along the top of the other. "I thought I was fine after Iraq. But spending thirty days drunk off my ass wasn't normal."

"I shouldn't have reacted the way I did." Regret grips my throat tight, closing off the air I desperately need.

"The Army put you on orders for Fort Bragg. Pretty sure they would've frowned on your going AWOL to keep your crazy-ass fuck buddy from losing her shit."

I swallow and fight the urge to tell her to stop talking about herself that way. I remember this from Iraq. This crushing sense of self-doubt she carries with her like an added weight in her assault pack, making the load that much heavier to haul.

She won't hear me. She never heard me downrange. She won't hear me now. But maybe I can convince her in other ways.

I have to try. Because I can't keep living like this, close enough to touch her but still frozen out of real connection.

I need that with her. I can't do half measures. I can't do just good enough. Not anymore.

I need all of her.

I slip my fingers into hers, threading them together and lifting them between us. "I wouldn't be standing here today if I didn't think what we had was worth fighting for. Even the fucked-up shit we did in Iraq and afterward. I want all of it. The good. The bad. I want to be the person you trust with that." I press my lips to our fingers. "Don't ask me to walk away again. Because I don't think I can do that."

Her fingers spasm beneath mine. It's a physical thing, this slight pressure moving *away*. It's a terrible thing, being vulnerable.

"Is this what normal people do when they're with someone else?"

I smile. "I have no idea. Mostly because I don't know what 'normal' really means."

She curls the edges of her lips in that way she does that drives me up a fucking wall. "I've heard it's very boring."

"After getting blown up and shot at and dealing with crazy-ass soldiers, I'll take normal. Or whatever variant of that we end up making."

She makes a noise. "Making 'normal'? Is that what we're talking about?"

I slip my hands around her waist, drawing her closer to the edge of the counter until I press between her thighs. "I'd like to take you back to that bed and show you what making 'normal' looks like in my world." I lean in, my lips close to her ear. "It involves a little..." I trace the edge of her ear lightly with the tip of my tongue, then blow gently on it.

She shivers and tilts her neck in silent offering.

"I think I'd like to see what you call a little normal." Her voice is throaty and deep. Arousal tightens my skin against my bones and I press against her some more. She rocks against me, her thighs tensing around me as I pull her close, grinding slowly against her.

"Challenge accepted."

Kelsey

IT TURNS out it's easy to fall back into this with him. To feel his body press against mine as he backs me slowly into the bedroom. To pretend that the intervening years since Iraq haven't happened and that everything between us is, well, normal.

It's not. And it never will be. But for a little while, I'm going to close my eyes and pretend.

He turns me and his body is strong at my back, hard edges rough against my skin. He slides his fingers over my stomach, just below the edge of my T-shirt, stroking, soothing. Petting. Until they slip against my lower back, my spine. Soft. Firm. A thousand sensations as his fingers continue to slide over my body.

I feel him shift but don't open my eyes. Not even when he presses his lips against the small of my back. "Tell me about your tattoo."

I'm distracted by the vibration of his voice up my spine. I want him to keep talking, to feel the juicy sensation arc between us. "The lotus...it grows in mud and dirty water." His tongue traces over the outer edge of the ink and my knees nearly buckle with the intensity of the connection. "It grows into something beautiful. In yoga, it symbolizes being grounded." He scrapes his teeth over the dimples at the base of my spine. Heat floods my body and I bite back a groan. "But also reaching toward the divine." The last word is a gasp, riding on a hit of pleasure.

His fingertip traces the edge of the flower once more, dipping below the line of my panties to the upper crease of my ass. Teasing, his touch is electric. Like the feeling of *om* in yoga, I can feel my body vibrating with his every touch.

"I like it," he whispers against my skin.

"Mmmm. Please do that again." A groan, just short of begging.

"Do what?"

"Talk with your lips against me. I can feel your words vibrate through my body."

He makes a deep noise in the back of his throat that I feel in my breastbone. I'm burning for him in a way I haven't burned in...since him. No one has ever touched me the way he does.

"You want me to talk dirty to you?" His voice travels up my spine and down between my cheeks to throb against me where I am swollen and aching.

"You could read a cereal box." I clench my hands by my sides, wanting badly to reach between my thighs and stroke myself where only his voice has been so far. "Just keep talking."

I press them together, the pressure on my clit intense and electric. My sleep pants are thin. Barely any barrier between us and he knows it. His fingers slide down the small of my back, pressing into the crease between my cheeks. Slowly drawing closer to where I need his touch.

"I could tell you about my thesis," he says. I try not to laugh and I'm distracted by the erotic vibration of his voice that's going straight to my core. "But I don't think that's very sexy."

Close his fingers slide, a very gentle pressure against the opening of my body. I push against his hand, wanting more. Needing his fingers, his voice.

Needing all of him.

He presses his cheek against the small of my back, nudging my thighs apart with one shoulder. His palm traces up my inner thigh, skimming close but not close enough.

"I was worried about you tonight. I worry about you when you don't come in to work." A gentle kiss, revealing the skin beneath my pants as he pushes them down. My body feels like pure fire and heat. Burning and needing more. "Other times, I think about you like this. Or on your knees in front of me." My pants draw down, over my hips. "I love the way you look when you're like that. Hips up, your thighs revealing your beautiful pink pussy."

Hearing the word is jarring, laced with erotic power. I've never had a lover talk dirty before. The emotional hit of it being Deacon, telling me what he sees, what he wants...

He urges me to the bed, to the position he's describing. I'm happy to oblige but he doesn't kneel behind me.

Instead, he folds around me, resting his cheek on the curve of my ass. His palm slides up my inner thigh, closer. So close.

"I love seeing you like this. Open. Trusting."

And then he touches me. His palm is hot against my thigh and his thumb circles the slick opening of my body. Gently, but each stroke is pure electric current.

My body spasms as he strokes me, circling the entrance, creating heat and energy. Light bursts behind my closed eyes. I press back against him, begging him with my body to fill me. Sounds are locked in my throat, trapped whimpers. I am primal need contained in a mortal shell. Burning. Aching. Needing.

Still he circles. And talks.

"Do you know how good it feels to slide inside you, Kelsey? How it feels to have your tight body squeeze my cock?" He presses against me now, his thumb barely sliding inside me. I shiver, the closest I've been to orgasm denied in...ever. My entire body is tuned to the vibration of his voice.

He shifts his index finger, running it the entire length of my clit as he presses his thumb more deeply inside me.

I am completely undone. Exposed. Vulnerable.

And more aroused than I've ever been by a simple touch. A few words, laced with meaning and depth.

I spread my thighs, opening more, parting for him. Begging him to take me over the edge. To send me into the next life.

To complete me with his touch. His words.

I rub myself against his fingers. "Please."

There is no pride. Only pleasure, only need. Raw, aching pleasure.

He slides his finger against my clit again, increasing the pressure, increasing the tempo. His thumb slides more fully into my body; not the completion I need.

But I'm too far gone. I rock against him, urging his fingers where I need them, urging his touch to finish the journey started by his voice.

And then he shifts and he is behind me, filling me, stretching my body, claiming me. Completing me. He's big and tight inside me and then he taps my clit, slipping his finger through my slick heat. One caress and I fly apart, shattering around him even as he starts to move, joining his own pleasure in mine.

His pleasure, linked to mine. One spirit. One body, connected by more than physical touch.

Reunited in absolute serenity.

23

Deacon

SHE IS WARM AGAINST ME, pliant and soft, and definitely not sleeping. I imagine the vibrations between us are what it would feel like if humans could actually purr.

"That was definitely not normal," she murmurs.

I smile against her hair. "It could be."

She makes a noise and nestles back closer to me. "I'm tempted."

"You're welcome." It's hard to keep the preening sense of pride out of my voice. I had no fucking clue if what I'd tried was going to work but apparently, it worked like a goddamned charm.

I pull her closer, sliding my arms around her and feeling her breath rise and fall against my chest.

"Thank you for checking on me tonight," she whispers. "And not being mad."

"Worried is a better description." I nuzzle her neck. "Can I ask you something?"

"Sure."

"So how did you get deeper into yoga? I know guys that do it but they swear it's just about the fitness. For you, it seems like it's more than that."

She makes a noise that sounds like a laugh. "Well, when I first started yoga, it was really just to try to stop feeling like shit all the time. It helps my shoulder not ache all the time and my back. But we had one instructor who started talking about the sutras and how yoga was more than just exercise and wellness."

I close my eyes, enjoying the sensation of her voice vibrating through my chest and through my entire body. "So you started to learn more."

I remember her being hungry to learn and to be challenged when we were in the Army together. She was always volunteering for things, trying new fitness trends.

"I did. It felt...like I was connecting with something when I practiced. I started going deeper and learned about breathing and meditation and right living. There's actually eight limbs of yoga." Her fingers tighten over mine.

I lift her wrist, tracing the symbol just behind her palm. "Is this part of it? Your practice?"

"This is the *om* symbol. I debated a long time about adding it to my body. I didn't want to just slap on a pretty symbol and I was afraid of being called out for cultural appropriation."

"Use smaller words."

"There's a strong argument that Western Yoga is stealing Hindu traditions and stripping them of their meaning and then making a shitload of money off of them. Which is true, in a lot of ways. Yoga is tied to India and Hindu tradition and culture. But you get over here and you've got these fitness instructors who ignore all of that and say, 'oh it's just exercise, it's meaningless.'" She takes a deep breath. "And that's really bullshit. It's fundamentally dishonest." Another deep breath. "So anyway, I'm trying to be respectful in my practice and honor the tradition that it comes from because yoga... This sounds super cheesy but it really saved me."

Her body tenses as she talks. It's as if a physical barrier slides between our bodies, the warmth and vibration gone. I roll then, slipping between her thighs and cupping her face. "I don't care what you've done or who you've prayed to. If it helps you get back to being fully you, that's all that matters. And if anyone judges you for that, they're not worth your time or energy."

She shifts, wrapping her legs around my hips. "Were you always like this and I just missed it?"

"You were too busy gripping the edge of the bunkers we snuck into to notice how awesome I was." She laughs and I nibble on the edges of her lips. "But I like to think I'm a bit improved over the previous edition."

I cup her face. "Have you gotten your sleep problem figured out?"

"Not really. I'm waiting for an appointment at the VA that I'm likely to never get." She scrapes her fingers over my chest. I love watching the ink on her arms move with her. "What about you?"

"I should sleep tonight."

She swallows and presses her lips against the notch at the bottom of my throat. "Will you stay?"

"I'd like to. Will it keep you awake?"

"No. I don't think so." She arches against me where I'm half erect and nestled in the moist heat between her thighs. "This might make it tough to sleep, though."

I slip against her heat, my cock hardening with the intense friction. "Now look what you've done."

"Is that for me?" She lifts her hips and draws me deep inside her. She's tight and warm and impossibly wet, the sensation electric and pure. She clenches herself around me and I damn near drop dead from the pleasure. "Jesus, do that again."

She does, rocking against me as she urges me to move, to slide deeper into her, to time my strokes to build the pleasure between us. She is vibration and energy and sexual heat. She is my everything.

She just doesn't know it yet.

I close my eyes, dragging my teeth over her ear as I push deeper into her, chasing the pleasure with every stroke.

Knowing it's temporary. Knowing I have to come clean with her at some point.

And not caring as the climax bursts behind my eyes, blinding in its intensity.

Kelsey

HE IS STILL in bed when I wake up. His arms are tight around me, his body rough and warm and solid and real.

I've slept.

I never appreciated sleep as much as I did when I stopped getting it. And as much as I credit yoga with saving me, it doesn't always help when it comes to sleep. I wish it did.

I don't move for a long moment, content to lie there in Deacon's arms and feel the heat from his body seep into mine, the beat of his heart pulse against my skin.

I'm okay. For now. I've managed to sleep. Even if it's only been for a few hours, it's better than nothing.

I really don't want to get out of this warm cocoon. I close my eyes and just lie still. Savoring the sensation of just being.

I still have to get my meds taken care of.

I guess I could try to tackle that problem again but I'm really not up for the ass pain of dealing with the VA.

I slip from his arms and pad into my tiny kitchen. It's really sad how much I don't cook. My kitchen has vegetarian meals in the freezer, and a container of milk in the fridge that I'm reasonably certain is expired.

I'm such a bachelor.

I glance over at the tiny figurine of Ganesh on my counter, a smile spreading over my lips. I lift him into my hands. He's pure white, the details painted in gold and red and turquoise. His trunk twists to the left, one palm holding his broken tusk as a pencil.

I stroke his smooth head. It really is funny how the universe works. I'm constantly amazed at those who say they don't believe in a higher power. I don't know what's out there but I know that yoga brought me out of the dark.

If you start really thinking about the obstacles in your life, it's pretty powerful what happens when you can let go of them.

I have to find the proper placement for the statue. I know he's not supposed to go in the bedroom unless you can't avoid it. I settle on the window in the northeast corner of my apartment, where he can watch over everything.

I hear Deacon a moment before I feel his arms around my waist, his lips pressed to one shoulder. "Found him a home?"

I make a noise. "I can't explain it but it feels like something that was missing isn't anymore."

"I'm really glad you like him."

I turn in his arms, pressing my lips to the base of his throat. "Did you sleep?"

"Yeah. A couple of hours at least." He presses his lips to my hair. "Thank you for letting me stay."

"Thank you for letting me borrow your penis."

He laughs out loud, his body shaking into mine. "You're welcome to that any time."

"So listen, I'm getting ready to head to yoga. You can stay here if you want while I'm gone."

He draws me close, his arms wrapping tight around me. "Want some company?"

I lean back to look up at him, skeptical of his offer. "Have you ever done yoga?"

"Once. Enough to know what downward dog was when you were doing it in the basement the other day."

"You were watching me?"

"Maybe. But I had to stop because it was turning me on."

My lips twitch. "Which part?"

"The part where your glorious ass was in the air and all I could think about was standing behind you and...well, you probably get the idea."

Heat flashes between my thighs. God but I'm so needy these days. I rub my hips against his. "That probably wouldn't work unless I had really, really strong shoulders to hold myself up."

He lifts one eyebrow, his lips parted. His breath is suddenly ragged.

"You're thinking about that right now, aren't you?" I whisper.

I can feel his response pressing against my belly. He leans in, nipping at my earlobe instead. "I can't seem to get enough of you."

I tip my head, offering myself to him. "There's another pose we could try, though, that would probably work."

"You have my attention." His voice is guttural, his cock hard against my belly.

I back away from him slowly, toward the doorway to my bedroom, stripping my T-shirt over my head and dropping my panties.

I turn away from him, kneeling on the edge of my bed, watching his reaction over my shoulder.

Watching his hand slide down his belly to grip his cock beneath his boxers. Watching him stroke himself as he watches me.

I could watch his hand play over his cock for hours. The way he grips it hard, squeezing. Stroking.

I lower myself onto my knees, arching my hips and stretching my arms out in front of me, still managing to twist enough to watch him watching me.

My heat is exposed to him, open and inviting.

Still he stands there, stroking himself. Making me wait.

I reach back between my thighs, slipping my fingers through my heat. My body is ignited, an electric fire of pure sensation as I touch myself.

His stroke quickens.

I slip a single finger inside of myself. The pressure is slight, teasing, not filling me the way I want him to. But I continue, hoping he'll take the invitation.

Hoping he'll fill me and take his pleasure with me.

Frustration tightens in my belly. I'm close. I want to come with him inside me.

"Please, Deacon."

And he finally moves. Pressing against me where I'm sensitive and primed for him. Drawing my hips back as he fills me.

And I shatter with him as he slides into me. A perfect union.

Complete.

24

Kelsey

"You don't have to do this, you know." I hand him one of my extra yoga mats before we walk to Nalini's studio.

It's a short walk, about six blocks in the opposite direction from The Pint. It's an old brick building that she's painted white. The lobby walls are brick, lined with shelves. It's funny how I notice the space with Deacon with me. The chalkboards that announce the class schedule. The books propped up near the register. Behind the register a black bow with a notched arrow, pointed to the sky.

Nalini has created a sacred space here for us. A space for community. For peace and growth.

I glance over at Deacon as he fills out the insurance waiver required to attend class.

He's wearing shorts and a T-shirt and looking quite pleased with himself after our earlier episode. He hands the tablet back and follows me into the studio space.

"I want to. This is something that's important to you."

I glance at the mala beads hanging in the bright sunshine. I've never purchased a set but Nalini wears them.

"We're doing yoga nidra at the end of class. Are you going to be able to sit still for that long?"

"We'll find out, won't we? If I run from the room doing a Muppet flail, we'll know it's probably not a good idea to repeat."

"You're awfully nonchalant about this whole thing. Most people are really intimidated by yoga."

He lifts one shoulder. "I'm sure it'll be fine."

I take our mats into the studio and snag spaces for us, then I drop a blanket for each of us before I pop into the bathroom quickly.

I step back into the studio to see him lying flat on the mat, covered entirely by the blanket. One of the other regulars is looking at him like he's crazy.

"I paid for a nap?" His grin is pure mischief.

I yank it off him, grinning like an idiot and folding it back up. "The blanket is for after. You'll get cold doing the yoga nidra because your body will relax a lot."

He scowls and sits up, his legs crossed awkwardly in front of him. He's stiff but trying to play it cool. "Why is it so hot in here?"

"It's a heated class."

"What the hell does that mean?"

I sit next to him, crossing one leg over the other and twisting in his direction. "Have you heard of hot yoga?"

"I guess."

"Well, the guy who started that trademarked it so no one is allowed to do Hot Yoga. But studios can do heated yoga without violating his trademark. The studio is set somewhere around ninety to a hundred degrees and we do flow yoga in that."

He looks mildly horrified, as if I've just told him we'll be handling live snakes or something. "Why would anyone want to do that?"

"Oh it's amazing. The first time I did it, I thought I was going to drop dead. But now that I'm used to it, I prefer it. You get deeper stretching and poses with it. You have to hydrate though. I sweat like nobody's business."

"I know something else that makes you sweat."

"Shhh!" The studio is starting to fill up as other people start placing their mats. Some are meditating, some just sitting quietly. "No talking during class, either."

He mirrors my pose, crossing one leg over the other and stretching. "No sarcastic comments? No swearing?"

"No. People are here for a lot of reasons so you have to respect people's ability to get into their flow."

"I assume that was English."

I narrow my eyes but can't stop the smile spreading across my lips. "Are you nervous about this?"

He scoffs quietly. "No." Like the suggestion is absurd. "Why would I be?"

I smile at him. "You'll see. Bodhi's a pretty intense instructor."

"I thought you said this was an easy class."

"It is." I fold over my legs, stretching the back of my quads. The burn and pull against the muscle is juicy and delicious, a hint of what's to come.

I look forward to this. To the flow. To the movement. To the tuning in to my own body and my own strength. To focusing on what I am, not what I used to be or what I could be. To be utterly and completely immersed and connected to everyone around me.

The instructor comes in and closes the doors, drawing down the blinds. "What's going on?" he whispers.

"Shhh. Just take your cues from him."

Bodhi is new but I've fast become a fan of his restore classes. He opens the class talking about the new moon and the power of new beginnings. I close my eyes and fold my hands in front of my heart, trying not to watch Deacon out of the corner of my eye.

He looks around at everyone then he rests his hands on his knees.

And then we *om*. A deep inhale and then I raise my voice with the sound vibrating in the air around me. It penetrates the bones of my chest, the center of my spine, running through my vertebrae.

I savor the sensation, the complete surrender of being connected with everyone around me.

We stand and Deacon follows.

I raise my arms overhead, reaching for the sky, then fold forward at the waist into the first sun salutation.

And try not to laugh as Deacon makes a noise somewhere between pain and surprise as he bends over.

Halfway lift. He's a beat behind everyone, his jaw set, his expression focused on keeping up.

It's a beginner flow class. Nothing too intense.

The instructor calls for *malasana*, the yogi squat. I ease down into it, balancing on the balls of my feet.

Deacon...I'm not sure what he's doing but it's something that resembles a dying stork. He wobbles badly and swears under his breath, his T-shirt already soaked. The room isn't even that hot yet.

He catches me watching him and he waggles both eyebrows and mouths something that might be *I'm going to die*.

I try not to laugh as I move into crow pose, trying to forget that my lover is next to me doing everything he can to keep up as he suffers through the next few poses. I hear something that might be *no fucking way* and try really hard not to laugh.

My soul warms with the connection, though, in knowing he's here with me because he wants to be.

And that, for the moment, I'm okay with him being here. I'm not afraid.

Maybe we're not as bound by our past. Maybe there's hope that the past...just is. That it will stay where it is.

That maybe, for once, I can be in the moment and savor it, without the fear of it rising from the dark.

I move into downward dog, my body releasing an unsettled feeling I've been carrying for far too long.

My bends are deeper, my arms stronger. I feel alive. Awake.

Whole, for the first time in years.

Deacon

I FOLD for what seems like the thousandth time and seriously try not to die from a heart attack. The last time I can remember being this covered in sweat was in Iraq after an eighteen-hour convoy security mission for a logistics patrol.

I am going to fucking die.

I started the class, watching Kelsey out of the corner of my eye. Watching how she seems to fall into the whole thing, like a well-worn pattern that's familiar and comfortable.

Then the instructor did the *om*. I wasn't going to do it. It seemed way too weird. But I found myself actually joining in and the vibration echoed through my ribcage. Not like the first time I did it, where it freaked me out. Maybe it's because I'm with Kelsey but this time was...kind of neat. The way my sound blended in with everyone else's?

Okay, so I think, *I have this.*

We move into something called warrior one. Okay, this is doable. Right?

Oh fuck no what are we doing now? Arms back overhead. Kelsey drops her back arm and lifts her front arm over her head in a graceful bow shape.

I feel like a deformed pretzel that got dropped on the floor, all jagged elbows and knees. There is nothing smooth about any of this.

Now what is warrior two? Okay, arms stretched. Upper thigh does what? Mine doesn't bend that far. Kelsey's front leg is parallel to the ground, her body straight and somehow soft.

We keep going through the different motions. Two seconds into this monstrosity called chair pose that I already hate, my thighs are screaming, threatening to amputate themselves and go on strike.

Half moon? Kelsey has one leg kicked out behind her, her upper body parallel to the floor, one arm stretching into the sky, the other barely skimming the earth. It's graceful and poised. My legs don't separate like that and I'm damn sure not reaching the ground with one hand. I can barely lift my back foot off the ground.

The instructor takes pity on me and brings me a block. I notice I'm the only one using it but at this point, I have no more pride left. I balance precariously on it, lifting my back leg as high as it will go, which isn't very damn high.

I've never felt more inadequate in my life.

Kelsey glances over at me and I give her a wobbly thumbs-up. I'm pretty sure I look about as cool as a cat dunked in a swimming pool.

Oh, what the hell is this? Dancer? Kelsey grabs her back foot, lifting it into the air, raising her other arm out in front of her. And she's barely freaking wobbling.

I can't even grab my back foot. *Humbling* isn't even the word for this.

The instructor moves on to something called wide-legged forward fold. That sounds benign.

Until I face the same direction as Kelsey and she folds over right in front of me.

And now I've got a semi looking at her sweet ass pretty much right in my face. Given that we were in a shockingly similar position not even a couple of hours ago, I'm now officially hard. I smile, imagining a juvenile Beavis and Butthead laugh in my head.

This is definitely not going according to plan. Damn it. I sneak my hand between my legs, flicking my cock. The pain is blinding but does nothing to take my erection down.

Kelsey gets down into something called side crow and I'm trying to stay upright. Jesus, there's another dude in here who's bare chested and holding the same pose.

How in the hell...?

I'm not even going to attempt it. I'll just hold twisted whatever it is that I'm doing at the moment. The only good part about this madness pretzel shit is that it made me lose my erection, which is good because now I won't be embarrassed, looking like the stalker weirdo in the class, walking out with a hard-on. Pretty sure that's a good way to get arrested.

Oh yay, now we're sitting. This should be easy.

And...nope. Not good. We're not sitting, we're kneeling and leaning backward. Because the human body is meant to do this. What the ever-loving hell?

Kelsey's legs are bent beneath her, her torso folded back, her shoulders flat on the ground.

That's a level of flexibility that I could seriously get behind. Or in front of.

Or holy crap, I need to stop watching her. This is too erotic by far.

Oh shit, child's pose. Yeah, that's pretty much exactly the pose she did earlier with her strip tease.

Shit.

Wait, we're lying on our backs now.

Everyone is under a blanket. Okay then, lying down is definitely something I can do.

Kelsey is lying on the floor, her eyes closed, her body draped in a multicolored wool blanket.

I do the same, closing my eyes, grateful my public humiliation is at an end.

And then the instructor starts talking. About breathing. About feeling your body, lying on the floor.

How long is this going to last?

I'm twitchy, lying there. Trying to listen and not distract anyone. The bottom of my foot starts itching something fierce. I don't scratch but it's so intense my damn leg starts shaking.

And just as suddenly as it starts, it stops. I have the oddest sensation of floating somewhere between waking and sleeping. It's strange because I can hear Kelsey's quiet breathing next to me. It's comforting, not being alone in this strangeness.

Lights flash behind my eyes. I frown but don't flinch. It's reminiscent of lightning streaking across the night sky. Quick streaks across my eyelids. My heart starts beating faster. I try to focus on the streaks and flashes but the harder I try to watch them, the faster they disappear.

And then they're gone, leaving only the blank space behind my eyes. I find myself looking for them. Wanting them to come back. The black shape morphs and twists, a shadow that reminds me of the crow that sat on the edge of the broken window that night, long, long ago.

Not wanting to be alone and still. I shiver suddenly, like someone walked over my grave and I am suddenly, achingly cold.

It feels like an eternity before the instructor's voice snaps through the silence, telling us to move our fingers and toes.

To roll onto our sides, then slowly sit up.

I feel slightly out of it.

Like I'm waking up a little bit drunk.

I steal a peek at Kelsey, whose palms connect at the center of her forehead as she bows. I quickly follow; something tells me this is the most important part of the class.

The whispered hush of "Namaste" slides over my skin. Something soothing. Calming.

Serene, even.

I've never felt anything like it.

25

Kelsey

"WHAT DID YOU THINK?"

"It was an experience," he says, dragging his hand through his wet hair. "You do that all the time? Willingly? You look exhausted."

I smile and stretch my arms overhead until my spine pops. "I love it. Most of the time, I leave class feeling amazing."

"And when you don't?"

"Usually it's because I can't focus and my mind keeps wandering on me."

He opens the bottle of water I filled up and tossed at him before we left the apartment, chugging it hungrily. "That was seriously intense. I already thought you were a badass but now it's confirmed."

I open my own water bottle and drink deeply. I'll get a headache if I don't drink enough. "Drink the whole thing," I tell him. "I usually pound down a full thirty-two ounces immediately after class to rehydrate."

"I can see why," he says dryly.

"What did you think about the yoga nidra?"

He looks away, taking a long pull off his water bottle. "What happened?" I ask, pressing him ever so gently.

He takes a minute to answer. "There were all these flashes behind my eyes. It was like, hypnotic and unsettling. I felt the strangest urge to keep staring at them, though."

I brush my fingers against the back of his hand as we walk back to my apartment. "It can open you up to strange emotions. I've had a variety of experiences with it."

"Why do you do it?"

"It's part of my practice. Part of being still, in the moment and just feeling your body and connecting with something deeper."

He frowns for a minute. "If it's so good for you and you're so into this, how come you still have insomnia and stuff? Like why doesn't it cure you?"

My turn to buy myself a moment by drinking. "I think because nothing is permanent. Every day, we're a different person. The practice that released something yesterday doesn't hit the same muscles today. But it's the best thing I've done for myself in my attempt to not be a raging chaos Muppet train wreck."

He smiles down at me. "Chaos Muppet?"

I flail my arms overhead. "You know, like Kermit's Muppet flail?"

He laughs and tugs me close then, kissing me lightly. "I'm glad I went with you. It was different and disconcerting and enlightening."

I rest one hand against the hard angle of his stomach. "Will you come back?"

"I don't know. I've got a pretty bruised ego right now, watching you do all those twists and bends and folds and I'm standing there looking like a brain damaged ostrich."

I brush my lips against his. "A very sexy damaged ostrich. I almost died laughing a couple of times. You were very distracting."

"So were you, bending over like that in front of me. Do you know how hard it was to keep my hands to myself?"

I make a noise in my throat, already wanting him again. "I'm very glad you did. I would not have been able to stay silent."

"Isn't there something like sexy yoga?"

"You're thinking of tantric yoga and it's actually been horribly bastardized by the West. It's about a much higher plane of energy than sex itself can create."

He purses his lips and I can see where his mind is going. "Have you...done this?"

I shake my head. "No. It's a very advanced practice that involves a release of energy."

He narrows his eyes. "Now you've definitely got me intrigued."

"Maybe after you've gone to more than one yoga class. Hell, I'm not even ready for it and I've been practicing for a couple of years."

He tugs me close, nipping my bottom lip. It's so strange, having his hands on me the whole time, having the freedom to actually touch him without fear.

To feel that utterly human connection with him again. I return the favor, scraping my teeth against his throat. "We have the cadets in a couple of hours. Are you prepared for the discussion today?"

He sighs dramatically and releases me. "That's a hell of a way to kill a boner, thinking about that little peckerhead Ryan. Thanks. I may never get aroused again."

"Challenge accepted. Later. After class."

"What did we give them to read this week?"

"That article about the war crimes in the 101st Airborne."

"Oh, that's going to be fun," Deacon says dryly. "Fine. I'll chew some Xanax before class and keep my temper."

I pat his shoulder. "You should shower first."

He glances as his watch. "Yeah, probably right." He kisses me quickly, then releases me, turning back the way we came in the direction of his own apartment. "Hey, Kels?"

I turn back. "Yeah?"

"I'm really glad you turned out to be the random stranger I was talking to on the Internet."

I laugh and shake my head. "Yeah, me too."

I turn away, heading to my apartment to read the article and shower and get ready for class today. We're several lessons in and I still can't get used to feeling intensely nervous every time we bring them together. It's like I'm waiting for one of them to call me out for being an idiot.

I walk into my apartment and see the little Ganesh statue in the corner near the window. I smile at him, unable to resist the thought that maybe, just maybe, some obstacles are finally being moved.

Deacon

IT FEELS like an eternity until the class gets under way. We walked to campus, talking about the cadets, about The Pint. About nothing and everything.

I guess this is what normal people do? It feels very mundane.

It feels kind of perfect.

We take our normal positions at the opposite ends of the conference room table, the cadets filling the same seats they always occupy.

Kelsey starts the discussion. "You all are going to be lieutenants very soon. And whether you like it or not, you will serve in combat unless you are very, very fortunate. Will someone sum up the article for us?"

Surprising exactly no one, Ryan's hand shoots into the air. "I guess I'm not sure what we're supposed to wrestle with here. This was pretty cut and dry. The brigade commander set a command climate that led to his men murdering civilians. What's the ethical dilemma?"

Iosefe leans forward. Oh, this ought to be good. He's so quiet, sometimes I feel like he's mentally somewhere else. But today, he's definitely present. "There are huge issues here. If you're a lieutenant and your brigade commander is giving you a take-no-prisoners order? How are you supposed to fight back against that?"

Ryan frowns. "Refuse to obey? We don't commit war crimes."

I catch Kelsey's eye and she's as surprised by his response as I am. I expected Ryan of all people to be supporting the command climate in the name of self-defense.

Funny how people sometimes defy the boxes we try to put them in.

I lean back, listening and watching the future officers. It's like a fire has been lit beneath Iosefe. Veer, too, is antsy in his seat, waiting to get a word in as Iosefe launches another argument.

"It's not that simple. It's like you're that dude who says 'yeah I could never enlist because I'd totally knock a drill sergeant out when he gets in my face.' Until you've actually stood up and spoke truth to power you never appreciate how hard it is."

Veer leans in, his hands moving as he speaks. "I think Iosefe's right. I mean, we all want to believe that we'd be the one helping the Jews escape the Nazis but at the end of the day, most of us wouldn't be."

Jovi glances over at him, her expression solemn. "That's a really depressing thought."

Ryan sits back in his chair with a huff. "I don't buy it. I don't believe we can just sit around and say 'yeah, I'd totally go along with this.' It's not right. There's no moral dilemma here. We don't kill prisoners."

Iosefe mirrors his body language, folding his big arms over his chest. "My grandfather was in the Pacific during World War II. My father was in Vietnam and the Gulf War. I've heard the stories they tell. And they would tell you that when you're in that situation, it's different."

Ryan still isn't buying it.

Kelsey taps her pen on the table, drawing their attention. She's edgy, taking a deep breath before she starts talking. "I was faced with a situation like this. Our base..."

Oh shit, she's going to tell them. My heart tightens in my chest.

"Our base was attacked. We managed to push them back and keep them from overrunning it. We captured a guy in a VBIED that didn't go off." Another deep breath. She's never told me this story before. I realize I'm holding my breath. "My lieutenant wanted one of my soldiers to shoot him. To just end him. We were in the middle of a firefight. We didn't have time to take control of a prisoner." Another deep breath as she looks each of the cadets in the eye. "I refused the order. I told my soldier to disobey the order." Another breath. "And while we were standing there arguing, the prisoner grabbed my LT's weapon. There was a struggle. My LT didn't make it home."

"Jesus, Kels," I whisper.

"Do you regret disobeying the order?" Jovi asks, her voice a stark contrast to Kelsey's in that moment.

"Part of me does. Maybe my LT was right. Maybe I should have pulled the trigger myself and gotten on with the rest of the fight." She holds another deep breath for an impossibly long moment before slowly releasing it. "I don't know whether I made the right call. I regret that my lieutenant didn't come home. That his parents received a flag instead of their son." She looks at each of them again. "But I do know that I would have the exact same doubt if I had pulled the trigger."

I clear my throat softly. "Nothing in war is simple," I say finally. "The friction Clausewitz talks about has not gone away with new technology and guided munitions. Every choice you make has consequences. Every single one has a second and third order effect. Your war is infinitely more morally complex than even the one that Kelsey and I served in."

The cadets are somber now, less animated. Our words are sinking in, hopefully making them think about the choices they will have to make.

Ryan glances over at me. "How do you do it? How do you tell yourself it's worth it?"

I can hear First Sarn't Sorren's voice in my head. My gaze collides with Kelsey's. "You do it for the person to your left and right. You try to make a difference one day at a time. You try to leave the world a little better than you found it, even over there. And you hope that the people you love the most all make it home with you."

Jovi's voice breaks the quiet. "And if they don't?"

"Then you honor the life they led. You crack a beer on Memorial Day and remember all the good times, the stupid shit," Kelsey says softly, her eyes never leaving mine. "And you keep going. Because that's what they'd want you to do."

26

Kelsey

"THAT WENT WELL," he says as we walk out of class.

"Ryan surprised me today," I say, trying to shake off the feeling that we're not seeing the entire picture with Ryan. "He's wound awfully tight for a twenty-two-year-old."

"Wasn't his dad a Marine?"

"Mom, too," I add.

"That seems like it could explain a lot."

"Are we stereotyping Marines?"

He jostles my shoulder gently then holds the door for me to precede him into The Grind. "If we can't stereotype Marines, then there is nothing left to live for."

I smile and order my coffee. Deacon winces as I sip from it. "What?"

"No sugar? How is that even possible? You used to molest hazelnut Coffee-Mate in Iraq."

I smile at the memory. "Who hasn't offered up blow jobs for the last hazelnut Coffee-Mate on the FOB? And you knew exactly what you were doing, hoarding all of it." I drag my hand through my hair, still smiling. "Wow, I haven't thought about that in a long time."

"That may have been the best cup of coffee I ever had."

"I bet." We sit in a small booth at the corner of the coffee shop. The library is attached but it's not a high traffic time so we'll have relative privacy.

He takes out a notepad and pen, then stares at it for a long time. "So, um, thank you. For being willing to do this interview." A hard push of breath. "I owe you."

"Oh, I'm going to collect. You shouldn't have reminded me of the Coffee-Mate episode."

His nostrils flare just a little at my words. "Oh yeah?" His knee presses against mine beneath the table. Gentle pressure, innocent enough. But after the last few days, my mind and body are attuned to him in completely not innocent ways. "Maybe we should get a carrel?"

"Maybe you should ask your questions so you have a paper to turn in so you can graduate."

"Are you reminding me to get on task?" He picks up the pen and pulls out a sheet of paper with questions typed on it. Another deep breath. "So, I guess start with when you knew you were getting out of the Army."

"What about it?"

"What did you do to start planning? Did you start looking for a job?"

I smile sadly. "I pissed hot on a urinalysis and ninety days later, was cleared from Fort Hood by my squad leader because I was in the hospital. So no, I didn't really have a plan for getting out of the military."

He looks up from the notepad. "Why were you in the hospital?"

I look down at the coffee cup, digging my fingernail into the edge of the cardboard cup holder. "Turns out, having your lady parts removed fucks with your head."

The words are harder to say than I thought they would be. They didn't get stuck so much as they dragged a well of emotion out of the mud, like an anchor coated in weeds and dirt from the bottom of a river.

But one look at his expression tells me he's having a very strong reaction to them.

"Say that again," he says quietly.

"Which part?"

"The part about your lady parts? I knew you got hurt but it wasn't serious enough to get you evac'd out of theater. What... what happened?"

My belly aches the way it used to when I used to get my period. I don't have that problem anymore but the echo of the pain flares up every so often.

Like now.

"I didn't even realize what was happening. I got home and went for my well woman. They sent me for an evaluation. Turns out one of my ovaries had been pretty banged up during the fighting. Took a while to catch up to me but something burst and they took both of them and a good chunk of my uterus before I really knew what was going on."

God, but this hurts to talk about. To talk about the loss of something that everyone complains about until they don't have it anymore.

"Jesus, Kels... You never said anything."

"I was mostly healed when you got home. Didn't think it was important. Except that it was." I swallow hard, looking down at the coffee cup. Breathing deep, closing off the back of my throat and doing the *ujjayi* breathing I've been practicing to try and keep the anxiety at bay.

"My commander didn't believe I was actually having real

mental health problems but I wasn't sleeping. Turns out not sleeping really fucks with your decision-making abilities. I took some older meds I had, had a terrible interaction with the alcohol I'd been drinking and ended up in the hospital. When I got out of the hospital, he handed me my DD214. I've been fighting with the VA ever since."

He's not writing anything down. Not moving. Just sitting there, vibrating with energy. "This is supposed to be an interview. Aren't you supposed to be writing things down?"

"Kels."

I look up at him then because I would be a coward not to. "I had some pretty bad complications when I got blown up in that attack on the base. No one bothered to tell me to keep an eye out for some pretty heavy-duty side effects. Turns out, Army docs aren't very good at dealing with female problems. I ended up in crisis; they put me on a super strong anti-psychotic and I stepped in front of a bus. I don't even remember most of it." I take a long sip of the coffee, needing the burn to remind me that I'm still alive. That I didn't die that day or any day since. "And since my female problems are service-connected, I have to be seen at the VA because I can't get insurance elsewhere. And because I lack an honorable discharge, they won't see me."

It all comes out in a rush. I'm surprised by the violent spike of rage and frustration that burns in my chest at the words. At the utter and complete bullshit that the Army made of my life. "I was actually fine before and during Iraq. But I got hurt. And it fucked with my head and I made some really bad choices. I guess the powers that be decided I should pay for them for the rest of my life."

He's still not writing anything down. He's not flicking the pen. Or even moving. "Jesus, Kels. I..."

"Didn't know. I know. I didn't tell anyone. I mean, it's not the kind of stuff that comes up in regular conversation."

He's grinding his teeth so hard it looks like his jaw might

crack. I really wish I could distract myself away from the ache in my chest but it's pounding in time with my heart. Dark and violent and filled with anger.

I turn my wrist over, looking at the *om* symbol there. Trying to focus on everything I've learned and done in trying to deal with the chaos that is my life. Deep breaths. In through the nose. Slow. Release. Again.

But the frustration remains. It doesn't ease back.

His hands slide around mine. I breathe deep, drawing on the strength in his touch. I look up at him. Wishing I could see myself the way he sees me.

But I can't.

Because the way he sees me is built on memories of who I used to be.

Not who I am now.

Deacon

"Do you realize how amazing you are?"

She smiles but it's kind of watery and forced. "I know, I'm good between the sheets."

I laugh because she needs me to. "Besides that."

"Deacon, I know what you're going to say. But that stupid medal doesn't mean jack shit at the VA. My characterization of service isn't honorable."

I want to shake her. To rail at the system that's put her in this situation, where she needs treatment and has to deal with the bullshit at the VA to get it. "I thought they changed the rules," I say when I'm sure I can talk without letting the anger in my voice escape.

"This VA hasn't gotten the memo. Something about they're

waiting for guidance from higher up. But that's even assuming they have me in the system. I've been fighting with the VA for months about just trying to get them to keep me on file." I scowl, confused. "They keep deleting me from their database. Or never adding me. One way or the other, I don't exist for them."

I push out a hard breath, rubbing my thumb over the *om* tattoo she'd explained to me the other night. She shivers beneath my fingers.

I close my eyes at the rage and frustration and utter helplessness that claws at me.

"There's nothing to do," she says after slipping one hand free from mine and taking a sip of her coffee. "Well you've got at least one story to put in your paper that ought to punch people in the guts."

I'm still stuck, locked in the past. Remembering.

I am absolutely still.

She's tossing her stuff into a reusable grocery bag. Her bra is hanging from the lamp near the bed. My bed is filled with the warm smell of sex and her shampoo and tequila.

"What are you doing?"

She doesn't look at me.

"Leaving."

I try to stand up but I'm still drunk. The room spins wildly and I sit back hard on the bed.

I try again and succeed this time, staggering toward her. "Why?"

"Because."

I'm drunk enough to get pissed.

"That's not really an answer."

She doesn't say anything.

I grab her arms. "What the fuck is your problem?"

She yanks away. "Don't." Snatches up the small bag. "I need some space. I can't do this anymore."

"Is this about me leaving? I don't have a fucking choice. The Army put me on orders."

She snatches her bra off the lamp and slaps it into the bag.

"I can't do this right now."

"Are you fucking kidding me?" I wheel away, spinning wildly and slam my fist into the wall by the bedroom door. "I'm so sick of these fucking games." My words are a shout, violent and tainted with hard liquor.

She slings her purse across her body.

"You're just going to leave?"

She pauses by the door. "It's what you're doing. I'm just doing it first."

The door closes behind her.

Just before the bottle of tequila explodes against it, shattering into a thousand golden shards of liquid and glass and pain.

"Hey."

Her voice penetrates the memory but the hurt is still there, tight around my heart, squeezing my lungs.

I rub one hand over my mouth. Shame rips at me, tears at my heart.

"You're not really processing this very well, are you?" Her words are meant to soothe but the rage beneath my skin is too hot.

"No, not really."

I rub both hands over my mouth now.

"Which part?"

"All of it?"

"This isn't yours to be upset over. It's in the past. I can't fix it. I can't change any of it."

The rage crawling beneath my skin snaps free. "So you're going to just do fucking yoga and hope that the VA eventually lets you see a real doctor and hope that you don't get really fucked up in the head in the meantime?"

"I've already been fucked up in the head. Spent eighteen months getting acquainted with it, thanks very much. How I chose to try and put the pieces back together was rather a matter of necessity."

"Kels, this is a fuck-ton more serious than chanting in some yoga class can fix."

She holds up her palm. I see the little *om* symbol at the base of her wrist. Her voice is as steady as her hand. "You can be angry at the Army, the VA. You can be frustrated with the system and with me, for that matter. But don't attack something that is fundamentally really fucking important to me because it's something you don't understand."

Part of me, the part of my brain that realizes I'm falling into old patterns and terrible habits, is screaming at me to shut the fuck up before I drive her away.

But the rest of me is really not being rational right now. "This is your solution?"

"It's the best I've got," she says quietly.

I look at her, dumbfounded at the shit show she's managed to overcome. At the calm way she told her story, as if it had happened to someone else.

At the calm way she walked away, protecting herself from the toxic hurt I brought back with me from Iraq.

I can't do this right now. I walk away. Leaving my notebook. Leaving my backpack. My feet carry me away, but the weight of my sin is lead pressing on my shoulders.

She's always needed more from me.

And I was never man enough to give her what she needed.

Fuck, I never even noticed any scars. Not now and definitely not when I first came home.

All I wanted to do was keep fucking like we'd done in Iraq.

The memory of the night she left slams into me. I never asked if she was okay after the attack. We never once talked about it.

How I expected her to fuck my brains out until I moved away. How I expected no attachment sex. In Iraq. Back at Hood.

How I failed her in every single fucking way possible.
And she still let me back into her life.
It hits me then. Powerful and raw and ragged.
It's not her who hasn't let go of the past.
It's me.

27

Deacon

IT'S BEEN FAR TOO LONG since I've sat in the silence of my apartment. Walking away from Kelsey in the library was a dick move but sometimes, space is the only right thing to do.

Sometimes, shit is too raw, too overwhelming to put into words.

For the second time in my life, the magnitude of my selfishness has hurt someone I care about.

I rub the scars on my chest, hidden beneath the branches and the crow tattooed there.

I was drunk that night. Just another junior in high school who thought the rules didn't apply to him. I still wonder if Kyle would be alive if I hadn't dared him to race Mitch on that old strip of road.

I never talked to Mitch about that night. I just graduated and joined the Army, getting the fuck out of that Michigan town as fast as I could.

I heard he died a few years ago. A toxic mix of pills and alcohol.

I wonder what would have changed if I'd had the fucking courage to talk to him about that night. To just say I'm fucking sorry.

I guess maybe that's why I don't talk to many people from high school any more. The memories kind of suck.

Guess it's true that those who don't learn from the past are bound to repeat it.

I never asked Kelsey if she was okay. Never asked her to talk to me about the firefight.

I was so used to her having her shit together downrange, I assumed she wanted the same thing I did.

I assumed she was fine with drinking and fucking and me leaving her behind when the Army put me on orders.

I scrub my hands over my face.

And despite all of that, she let me back in. Once again, she was the stronger one. She had the fucking courage to let me back into her life.

I didn't mean to lash out at her about the yoga. I was just too overwhelmed that it was something she could seriously use to work through...all of that. The VA needs to do its fucking job. It can't keep using bad paper to keep denying vets services.

An idea slams into me and I pull out my phone, dropping a note to Professor Blake. I finally know what I'm doing for my thesis. I just need her help to maybe pull this off.

Because Kelsey deserves better than what the VA has given her.

She deserves better than what I've given her.

She is everything I want.

She's so much better than I deserve.

Kelsey

Despite the terrible ache in my chest, I go to work. I don't want to. I don't want to see Deacon.

I don't have the energy to process why he walked away, leaving everything behind. He's lucky I'm not pissed at him and I gathered his bag up, bringing it with me to The Pint.

I mean, I'm the one who got fucked over by a bomb, a shitty surgery, and a bastard brigade commander. I should be the one who's pissed.

But maybe I've spent enough time down in that pit. Maybe it doesn't have any power over me anymore.

It's strange, not being angry about it. In my mind, I'm holding the anger, cupping it in my hand. Dusting it off a little bit and putting it away, a little less powerful than it once was.

"You're quiet tonight." Eli pours a mixed drink and shakes it.

"Just thinking."

"Does it have to do with the reason Deacon's not at work tonight?"

A heavy sigh. "Got it in one."

"Are either of you going to quit on me?" he asks, sliding the glasses he's poured across the bar to a customer.

"I'm not planning on it. I rather like free drinks any time I need them." Except that tonight, I haven't had a single drink. The urge just isn't there.

Eli turns to face me, his expression serious. "Look. I love you and I love Deacon. But I fucking hate seeing you two hurting each other like this."

I press my lips into a flat line. "Turns out, he doesn't have healthy anger management techniques."

Eli grunts. "Today in No-Shit-Sherlock. Most of us don't."

"I've actually been working on mine."

"Yeah, Parker told me she's going to start going to yoga with you."

I close my eyes against the stab of hurt that lances through my chest. I'd been looking forward to doing more classes with Deacon.

"Nalini's is a really great studio. Lots of awesome classes."

The bar is quiet tonight. Eli looks around it, then sighs. "So are you guys finished or just fighting or...?"

"I don't know." I pour a drink and give Eli the quick recap of the afternoon.

"Jesus, Kelsey, why didn't you ever say anything?"

I toss back a shot of whiskey. "Really? You know how hard it is to feel like you're part of this group? I'm supposed to waltz in and be all 'yeah, had my reproductive organs blown out. Fucked with my head pretty good.'" I shake my head and pour another shot. "I handled it the best way I could. I've been handling it better since I got here and since I got all of you in my life. I've been working on it. And for Deacon to flip his shit for reasons I'm still trying to decipher...I'm not okay with that. I've got enough of my own shit to carry around. I don't need his, too."

Another shot and I close my eyes as it burns all the way down.

The next thing I know, Eli's hands are on my shoulders, pulling me close into a solid embrace. I rest there for a second, knowing he's my boss, knowing in my soul that he's the big brother I never had and better than anyone the universe probably would have given me.

"You don't have to be strong all the time, Kelsey." His voice rumbles beneath my ear and I finally push back, away from his support.

"I know. Trust me, I've had my share of weakness. I'm tired of it, to be honest. I'd like to be a little stronger, if it's all the same to you."

He grips my shoulder, over the first lotus I had inked into my skin, celebrating thirty days of not falling apart. "You're the strongest person I know."

I offer a half-grin, still to this day unable to take a simple compliment. "Thanks," I say and turn to the dude who's just walked in with a woman way too young for—"Holy shit! First Sarn't Sorren?"

I'm around the bar in a flash, pulled into a massive hug. "You look like shit," I tell him.

"Yeah, well, nice to see you, too," he says roughly. "What's with all the fucking tattoos, Ryder? Don't answer that." He turns to the young woman with him. "Jamie, this is Kelsey. I trust her with my life. But if you don't want me to have another heart attack, please for the love of God, don't get any fucking tattoos."

She reaches her hand toward me, rolling her eyes at her dad. "I'm Jamie."

"My daughter," he adds.

I share the eye roll and shake her hand then turn back to my first sergeant. "Nice to meet you. What are you doing here?"

"Campus visit with the offspring. Sarn't Major training down at Bragg the rest of the week."

I can't contain my excitement and surprise at his announcement. "They're promoting you?"

"I know; they haven't figured out their gross overestimation of my abilities. But apparently since none of you degenerates died on my watch under the rear d..." He shrugs, palm open. "Anyway, we've been touring campus all day."

"This is my first pick school," Jamie says.

"It's a really great campus," I tell her. "If you come here, definitely look me up. I'll help you get settled."

First Sarn't sighs happily. "Exactly what I was hoping you'd say. Keep my little girl safe and keep me from having to mainline nitroglycerin pills. Win-win all around." He frowns. "Where's shit-for-brains?"

On cue, my phone vibrates in my back pocket, and I pull it out to check the text the vibration signals.

All the blood rushes from my face as I look up at First Sarn't. My voice breaks as I whisper, "In the hospital."

28

Deacon

IF THERE IS A HELL, it's found in the emergency room. There's a machine that triggers the blood pressure cuff around my upper arm to randomly inflate and cut off the circulation to my fingers. The stench of disinfectant is pungent. It's eerily quiet on this side of the ER. Apparently, I was moved to the brain injury side of the house where it's supposed to be quieter.

I guess the silence and the dark is supposed to help with brain injuries and shit but it's creepy. I'm glad I'm not alone.

I'm still not really sure how First Sarn't Sorren convinced them to let him back here but damn it's nice to have company.

He's been sitting with me in this hell for the last three hours and hasn't said a word. He just walked in, as big and badass as I remember him and sat down, scaring three little kids and a meth addict.

"You know, being here really triggers my PTSD," he says after a while.

A lady in the next bed looks at him like he's lost his mind.

"Ouch, don't make me laugh. It hurts to breathe." I choke back a wet laugh as he pulls the curtain between us. "That's so fucked up."

"I wish I was kidding. I fucking hate hospitals. You'd think I'd be better at this shit by now."

I glance over at him. "Things still rough back at Hood?"

"Worse than when you were there. Nothing has slowed down. The troops have been at the breaking point for years. No one cares because it's not their kid and not their war."

I rub my hand over my mouth, trying not to wince as the movement jars my bruised ribs. "Why do you stay?"

"What else am I going to do, hand out stickers at Walmart?"

The idea strikes me as absurdly funny for some reason and I start to laugh until the tears leak out, partly because of the pain and partly because the visual of him in a blue Walmart vest is really fucking funny.

"I'm good at this Army shit. I'm good at teaching kids how to kick in doors and pull security. As long as there's a war going on, I'll stick around. At least until I piss off the right colonel or general officer."

When I can breathe again without hurting my cracked ribs, I finally start talking. "It's funny. I spent so much time running away from the Army, I never really thought about everything I gave up when I left it."

"Yeah, well, you're not missing much. Instead of sitting in a hospital in Durham, you'd be sitting in the ER at Darnall. Some things haven't changed."

"Why aren't we doing better at this shit?" I finally ask him.

He leans back into the chair and sighs hard. "Lots of reasons. Too many to unpack in an emergency room soul-baring session." He closes his eyes. "Kelsey is pretty pissed at you right now."

I press my lips into a flat line. "It's not like I put myself in the hospital on purpose. I got hit by a fucking driver who was texting. I'm lucky all I ended up with is a concussion and some cracked ribs."

"It's a fuck of a lot more serious than that, shit-for-brains. Bleeding on the brain is a really big deal."

"Ah, you're going to make me cry from all the love."

He flips me off. Goddamn it's good to see him. "Sorry you had to come here on your trip. Where's your daughter?"

"Talking to her mother about coming here. Looks like I'm staying in for thirty to pay for it."

I frown. "You can't transfer your GI Bill to her?"

"Already did. They cut the housing and book stipend for family members so I've got to keep some form of employment to help support her."

My head is throbbing like a motherfucker from laughing. "Wow, that's a hell of a sacrifice. You really going to deploy to World War III to put your kid through college? Handing out stickers at Walmart might be a better option."

"We all make sacrifices for the people we love." He makes a noise. "So what the hell happened between you and Ryder? It's only been a week; I didn't think you'd fuck things up this badly this fast."

"Clearly you underestimate my ability," I say dryly. I hold my hand over my eyes, needing to block the light. Reading my mind, he dims the overhead lights as much as he can. "Thanks. I may have gotten a little upset when I found out that not only did she get really fucked up downrange, the Army threw her out over pissing hot for expired medication. And I was too selfish to even ask if she was okay."

"Well, we all do stupid shit when we're young. It's amazing any women take chances on us."

"She tried to kill herself, First Sarn't. The surgeries she had, everything, she needs medical treatment. She's doing yoga and while I think it's really fucking cool that it's helping as much as it is, she also needs modern fucking medicine and she can't get it because she doesn't have an honorable discharge."

He says nothing for a while. "Sarn't Ryder has always been one of those people who does her best when she's deployed." He looks over at me. "She volunteered for the long runs between Mosul and Taji. Always willing to go on the roads. She's damn good at what she does." He looks up at me. "She's also stubborn as the day is long so the fact that she's willing to do anything to take care of herself is pretty fucking impressive. You should take a page or six from her book."

"I know. I was there when she started to hit rock bottom. And I fucked it up then, too."

"Well, how 'bout you stop fucking up? Tell her you love her and be a man about it. You can't protect her from the world. You can't keep her from getting hurt. You can't block out the world and stop it from taking shots at her. All you can do is love her and be strong enough to face it with her."

I narrow my eyes at him. "Why do I think we're not just talking about Kelsey?"

"Because we're not. This place is a fucking dick assembly line. Do you know how many terrible news stories there are every week about what happens to women on college campuses?"

"I guess this is what it feels like, then, loving someone and not being able to fix everything for them."

He sighs again. "It never stops. I still get calls from guys I served with a decade ago. And when they call, I answer. I always will." He looks over at me. "And so will you. Always. Because that's what we do. We take care of our own. No matter what. And when they're the women we love, we still stand with them. Nothing changes."

My eyes burn. My throat closes off and I try my damnedest to hide the tears slipping down my cheeks.

A short dark-skinned nurse with bright, calm eyes pushes the curtain aside and steps to the machine near my shoulder that's reporting on my blood pressure and a bunch of other shit. "Mr. Hunter, we've cleared Ms. Ryder if you'd like to see her?"

First Sarn't stands up. It doesn't matter that I'm a civilian now. I can't call him by his first name. He'll always be my first sarn't. "Yes, he'd like to see her." He glares down at me. "I'll see you when you get out of here. Don't fuck this one up. She's got a finite amount of patience for your dumb ass."

He stalks by the horrified nurse. "He's very loving," I tell her.

I've never seen a look call bullshit more clearly.

Kelsey

I DON'T KNOW how I feel, seeing him sitting there in a hospital gown, the needle sticking out of his arm, stark blue against his dark skin in the dim light.

I've seen all of his tattoos before but seeing the electrodes pressed to his chest, breaking up the lines of the branches and the crow's wings...it breaks something inside of me. Like a branch that snaps from too much pressure, the fear hits me in that moment.

I almost lost him again.

"Did you know First Sarn't was coming to visit?" I ask, needing a neutral topic to start with. The hurt in my chest is a tight knot, aching and still raw.

He's in a neck brace. I can see the outline of bandages beneath the hospital gown and one of his eyes is bruised and swollen. He plucks at the thin blanket covering his lap.

I don't move into the room. My throat is tight, anger a knot in my chest.

"Yeah. I may have called him last week," he admits quietly.

I tip my chin. "Oh yeah?"

"Needed some advice." He looks up at me. "On how to stop fucking everything up with you."

The knot in my chest releases, just a little. "Well, you are exceptionally good at that."

He looks down at the needle in his arm. "This is going to be really fucking expensive."

"Getting hit by a car because you're not looking where you're going tends to be."

He looks up at me, his eyes intense and wary. "It wasn't my fault the guy was texting and driving."

"He's spending the night in Durham County. Turns out the cops don't care that he was fighting with *his* girlfriend, too."

His mouth relaxes a little. "Are you?"

"What?

"My girlfriend?"

I give. I step into the room and lean my hip against the edge of his hospital bed. "Well, you got a little salty when I said we were fuck buddies so maybe we should go with a more polite term."

He laughs then and winces. "Jesus, don't make me laugh."

I tug the divider curtain closed behind me. I was going to yell at him. I was going to ask him what the fuck he was doing walking in the middle of the road during rush hour.

But instead, I stand there, unable to push the words out over the intense gratitude squeezing my chest.

"What did the docs say?"

"They're keeping me for the weekend. Guess my head isn't that hard after all because I fractured my skull when I hit the pavement. They're watching for bleeding on the brain."

Fear is a powerful thing. "That sounds terrifying."

"Mildly. If there is, they may have to drill in there to relieve the pressure. You know, outpatient surgery."

I move to the edge of his bed, sitting near his hip. He threads his fingers with mine.

"You're not allowed to die, you know. I just got you back."

He shifts, then, and tugs me down. I sink into the bed next to him, careful of his bandaged ribs. The knot in my chest breaks apart, releasing into a thousand pieces all at once, a flood of emotion slamming into me.

The tears bleed out onto his chest. "Don't cry. I'll be okay."

"I'm supposed to be the fucking train wreck here, not you," I finally say.

"I was coming to see you," he says quietly. "I was coming to say I'm sorry. I'm sorry I never asked if you were okay. After Iraq. I'm sorry I just assumed we'd pick up where we left off."

He cups my chin and I don't resist him. "I fell for you a long time ago. Train wreck and all. There aren't too many people who can make me laugh when I'm getting shot at."

"God, when you put it that way," I whisper. "You're an idiot. How the hell did you manage to get hit by a fucking car?"

He closes his eyes. "I was texting Professor Blake on my way to see you."

"The only thing you have to apologize for is nearly dying. You scared the shit out of me."

"Keep talking dirty. You're getting me hard," he whispers. "Maybe it's the universe's way of slapping me upside the head and reminding both of us that life is too short." He lifts my face to his. "I don't have much. But I want to share everything with you. The good. The bad. I'll even do yoga with you because it's important to you, and maybe if I make myself look like a fucking asshole enough, you'll forgive me for being a selfish dickhead."

"It's going to take a lot of yoga. Maybe even yoga man pants."

He laughs then, rests his cheek against the top of my head. "I'm sorry," I whisper.

"I was angry. Pissed that you were hurting. Pissed that I never once thought to see if you were okay." He presses his lips to the top of my head. "I don't like being an asshole."

"It's not your job to protect me from the world. I think we had this argument once before."

"I know."

"But I'd very much like to walk with you. Through the good. And the bad. And everything in between."

His fingers tighten in mine. "There is nothing I want more."

EPILOGUE

Deacon

KELSEY IS adorable when she's nervous. She tugs at her crisp white blouse, the blouse we went to buy especially for this occasion.

She may have sworn at me when I told her we were going to Brooks Brothers. Because she needed to be dressed for the part she's going to play today and so did I.

"Stop fidgeting," I tell her.

"I can't get my shirt to stay tucked in. It keeps coming untucked." She brushes her hair behind her ear where it's escaped the neat bun she twisted it into that morning at the hotel.

Professor Blake looks up from her laptop. "Tuck it into your Spanx," she says before going back to whatever she's working on.

I frown over at Kelsey. I don't remember this part of the shopping trip. "What the fuck are Spanx?"

"Oh, I'll show you tonight," she says with a smile. But she does as Professor Blake suggests, tucking it into something tan she's wearing beneath her pants.

She finishes adjusting her blouse then tugs her jacket into place. "You look really great," she says after a moment. "You clean up kind of nice."

"You do, too." I tug her close to me, brushing my lips against hers. "Relax. You're going to do fine. This isn't a parole board."

"I know. It's just not every day that you testify before the Senate Armed Services Committee." Her words are rushed. Breathless. Like the magnitude of what she's about to do is finally hitting her.

Professor Blake stands, tucking her laptop into her well-worn black bag. "They need to hear your story, Kelsey. They need to know the impact of their policy decisions."

She's wearing a black pin-striped suit and looks more like a retired colonel than the professor I've grown to love even more in the last few months. When I emailed her about Kelsey and asked her if there was a way to use my thesis to get decision makers to reconsider their policy about bad discharges, she didn't even blink.

She told me that was what she'd had in mind the entire time. And would Kelsey be willing to testify in front of Congress? To tell her story?

"I know," Kelsey says softly. There's no fear in her voice as she straightens her shoulders, releasing a hard breath.

"You've got this. I'll be with you the entire time." I squeeze her hand as we stand in front of the closed door Professor Blake just went through. "I'm proud of you for doing this."

She smiles over at me. "Thanks for coming with me. And suffering through suit shopping."

"Oh, that was no sacrifice at all." There may have been some dressing room shenanigans that I desperately hope were not caught on any security cameras.

She's sleeping better these days. So am I.

It's a combination of things. There's no magic bullet. No single thing that will put all the pieces back together. There are still nights I can't sleep. Nights she can't either. Those will still happen. We both know that.

But it's easier, knowing someone is there. In the darkness. Asking if you're okay.

Being there, even if you're not.

Knowing that she loves me, despite my past. Despite everything. I kiss her gently, then urge her to open the door, then follow her through.

No matter what, I'll be there with her.

It's a powerful promise.

One I intend to keep every day. For the rest of our lives.

<<<<>>>>

SNEAK PEEK AT UNTIL WE FALL

Keep reading for an uncorrected sneak peek at UNTIL WE FALL, Caleb & Nalini's book, coming early 2018.

UNTIL WE FALL

Nalini

"There isn't enough coffee for me to deal with this shit this morning."

I swear I'm not usually a violent person. I've worked a lot of my rage and trauma issues out on my yoga mat.

Except when I forget that I'm practicing nonviolence.

The smell of burning animal flesh at five in the morning is a quick way to make me regress to violence and shabbiness.

Especially since I'm running a yoga studio and it's rather disconcerting to walk in first thing in the morning to find yourself inhaling charred meat.

I breathe in deeply, needing to remind myself that I can't evict the new barbecue place next door because I don't own the damn building. And people don't take animal cruelty protests seriously any more unless it involves kittens.

Americans just love their steak too much to care about factory farming.

So my yoga studio is now conveniently located half a building away from a barbecue restaurant.

Because the universe is fucking with me.

I have the early morning class arriving in the next fifteen minutes. While I'm confident they are not going to be bothered by the smell of cooking meat, I am not going to be able to focus.

I light some incense and too many candles, then sink onto my mat, jotting down my plan for this morning's flow sequence. I breathe deeply.

And inhale the smoke from next door.

The panic wraps around my lungs, the coppery stench of burned blood filling my nose and cutting off my oxygen.

I double over, needing cool fresh air by the floor.

"Okay that's it."

I slap my notebook down and damn near rip open the door, stalking down the cool pavement to Logan's All American Barbecue.

The master key to the building works in his back door, too.

I stalk to the back and stop short.

I'm not one to admire anything when surrounded by the smell of cooking meat but standing in the middle of the kitchen is a man sporting the greatest set of shoulders I've ever seen on a man.

Broad and cut, watching him do whatever he's doing causes the smooth muscle to ripple across his back. His arms flex, glistening with sweat. The American flag logo on the back of his T-shirt clings to his frame, highlighting all the glorious details that leave nothing to the imagination.

And after two tours in Iraq, I can assure you I have one hell of an imagination.

He turns abruptly and drops the slab of meat with a shout. "Jesus fucking Christ, are you trying to give someone a heart attack?"

Okay, I might feel a teeny bit bad about scaring the shit out of him. "Are you Logan?"

He frowns, swiping the massive butcher knife on a towel. "Who the fuck is Logan?"

"The owner?" I am now thoroughly confused.

"The owner's name is Sam."

"And you're not Sam, I assume?" This is getting mildly awkward. Nothing like stalking down to someone's place of business and not finding the right person to yell at.

"Do you always walk into restaurants without shoes on?" he asks, pointing to my bare feet with the knife.

"If you're not the owner, who are you? And when will the owner be back?"

He stabs the knife into the slab of meat and wipes his hands. "Sam's out of town for a few weeks."

"And you are?"

He folds his arms over his chest and leans back against a griddle that I assume isn't on because if it was, it would have burned him on the ass. "Who wants to know?"

"The owner of the yoga studio that you're blowing the smell of cooking meat into at five in the morning."

He tips his chin and offers the kind of smirk that tempts me to reach for the knife. "What, you can't downward dog with the smell of barbecue distracting you?"

"Yeah, actually, that is the fucking problem. You need to get ahold of the building owners and make them reroute the vents or something. It's incredibly disrespectful to our practice."

"What the fuck are you talking about? And no, I'm not calling the building owner to make them rewire shit. You've lost your goddamned mind, honey."

My spine stiffens. "Don't call me fucking honey."

"Then don't come barging into someone's business being an asshole at five in the morning." He looks down at my shoeless feet again. "How did you get in here, anyway?"

"Building master key."

"Why the hell do you have one of those?"

"Don't change the subject. Are you going to at least stop cooking whatever it is you're cooking?"

He looks at me like I've got a dick growing out of my forehead. "Honey, I don't know what the hell you're smoking down at the other end of the building but I'm not calling anyone, I'm not changing up anything that Sam directed and I'm not going to stand here and entertain any more demands from some barefoot hippy psycho."

"So that's it then?"

He frowns. "Pretty sure I didn't fucking stutter."

I smile coldly. "Then this means war."

He laughs at me. The cocksucker actually laughs at me. "Don't you people practice nonviolence?"

I lift one eyebrow. "First you call me honey, then you people? Did they find you in a fucking cave?"

His jaw tightens. "You could say that. Have a nice day." He waves the knife in my direction, dismissing me.

I briefly fantasize about knocking that knife out of his hand and slapping the shit out of him.

But nonviolent, right?

"You sir, can go fuck yourself."

And that, ladies and gentlemen, was how the war started.

Caleb

If she hadn't been a raging lunatic, she would have been smoking hot. Like the kind of hot that would make a man beg for her to let him do filthy, dirty things to her in the dark.

But I don't fuck crazy.

I don't need any help in that department, thank you very much.

When Sam asked me to take over the barbecue place for a few weeks, I said yes, because, well, I didn't exactly have a lot going on. At least not anything really positive.

It was more...treading water. Kind of holding steady at the not killing myself phase of the operation.

So even though I know jack shit about running a business, I'm in business school and I figure it would give me an interesting case study to work on while I avoid doing all the grip and grin ass kissing that's known as networking these days.

Turns out people don't want to give you money when you get raging drunk on a cruise where you're supposed to laugh at the old man's money, not puke on his shoes.

There are very few ways for life to go much lower than that.

Trust me, I've tried.

So now, I'm running a barbecue joint for the next couple of weeks. I've mostly got the hang of the food prep piece. Brisket takes the longest. It has to cook slow and long to get it to fall off the bone level of done. Sam has a few tricks to speed up the process but the best way is to drag my carcass into the restaurant at five am and start the cooking for the *next* day.

I'm not sure I'd have the stamina to do this long-term.

I glance up as the door slams shut behind the crazy woman.

I wipe my hands and shoot Sam a quick text. *You have any suggestions for dealing with the yoga studio owner?*

He's on the west coast, so I'm a little surprised when he responds. *What yoga studio owner?*

The one who just declared jihad on your barbecue because she says the smell is interrupting her flow or some shit.

The little bubbles tell me he's typing. I finish loading the last of the brisket into the smoker while I'm waiting for his response.

What the fuck does her period have to do with barbecue?

I choke on my own spit and double over laughing. "Clearly you've never been around women and yoga," I mutter, still laughing.

It's too bad me and the yoga instructor got off on the wrong foot. In the thirty seconds it took me to restart my heart after she scared the shit out of me, I remember being awestruck by damn near everything about her.

Her hair was long and black, her skin a rich saffron that looked soft and warm.

In that thirty seconds before she started going off, though, I remember it was her eyes that captured me. Dark and rich, for a brief moment, I was lost, the bullshit of my life faded to black.

She was a goddess.

And then she started talking and well, my balls shriveled up and died.

I finish up the brisket and set the timers on everything else. We open every day at ten, which means I've got to get my ass to the gym if I'm going to make time for a workout today.

I'm getting better about not skipping workouts. And sleeping. That's pretty fucking important these days.

But I don't mind getting up to run the shop.

Funny how that works.

I lock up, glancing down the front of the strip mall to where a few stragglers are dragging their corpses into the yoga studio. The light falls onto the stamped pavement, illuminating the pre-dawn darkness.

Getting up that early takes some devotion, I'll give them that. I'm used to early mornings. It got ingrained in me during my plebe year at West Point and, well, I haven't been able to shake the habit.

My nemesis walks to the window. The light casts her skin in a golden glow. Her body is tight and she moves with a smooth energy that's smoking hot.

Too bad she's fucking crazy.

Continue Reading...

ABOUT THE AUTHOR

Jessica Scott is an Iraq war veteran, an active duty army officer and the USA Today bestselling author of novels set in the heart of America's Army. She is the mother of two daughters, three cats and three dogs, and wife to a retired NCO.

She's also written for the New York Times At War Blog, PBS Point of View Regarding War, and IAVA. She deployed to Iraq in 2009 as part of Operation Iraqi Freedom (OIF)/New Dawn and has had the honor of serving as a company commander at Fort Hood, Texas twice.

She holds a Ph.D. in morality in Sociology with Duke University and she's been featured as one of Esquire Magazine's Americans of the Year for 2012.

Photo: Courtesy of Buzz Covington Photography

For more information, please visit her on the web

jessicascott.net

ALSO BY JESSICA SCOTT

THE FALLING SERIES

Before I Fall

Break My Fall

After I Fall

Catch My Fall

Until We Fall (2018)

When We Fall (forthcoming)

After We Fall (forthcoming)

HOMEFRONT SERIES

Come Home to Me

Homefront

After the War

Into The Fire

NONFICTION

To Iraq & Back: On War and Writing

The Long Way Home: One Mom's Journey Home From War

COMING HOME SERIES

Because of You

I'll Be Home For Christmas: A Coming Home Novella

Anything For You: A Coming Home Short Story

Back to You

Until There Was You

All for You

It's Always Been You